Aberdeenshire
D0272160

PURIFICATION

Also by David Moody from Gollancz:

Hater
Dog Blood

Autumn
Autumn: The City

AUTUMN

PURIFICATION

DAVID MOODY

GOLLANCZ
LONDON

First published in Great Britain in 2011 by Gollancz
An imprint of the Orion Publishing Group
Orion House, 5 Upper St Martin's Lane, London WC2H 9EA
An Hachette UK Company

A CIP catalogue record for this book is available from the British Library

ISBN 978 0 575 09136 8 (Cased)
ISBN 978 0 575 09137 5 (Export Trade Paperback)

1 3 5 7 9 10 8 6 4 2

Typeset at The Spartan Press Ltd,
Lymington, Hants

Printed and bound in the UK by CPI Mackays,
Chatham, Kent

The Orion Publishing Group's policy is to use papers that are natural, renewable and recyclable products and made from wood grown in sustainable forests. The logging and manufacturing processes are expected to conform to the environmental regulations of the country of origin.

www.davidmoody.net
www.orionbooks.co.uk

Prologue

Forty-seven days ago, more than ninety-nine per cent of the population had died within an impossibly short period of time. Right across the world, without any warning or explanation, the pattern was repeated as billions of lives were inexplicably ended: snuffed out and switched off with neither dignity nor malice, unimaginable numbers of innocent people discarded and abandoned and left to rot where they'd fallen. Just a handful of terrified survivors remained, none of them able to understand or even to begin to come to terms with what had happened to their friends, family, lovers, children . . .

Within forty-eight hours, almost a third of the dead rose again. The germ (or disease, or whatever it was that was responsible) had spared a key area of these creatures' brains. Somehow unaffected, a spark of primordial instinct had survived the infection, leaving the bodies physically dead, but still compelled to move; lifeless, but incessantly animated. And as the flesh which covered these stumbling aberrations had rotted and decayed, so the unaffected region of the brain had grown in strength, and had continued to drive them forward. First their most basic senses had slowly returned, then a degree of control. The corpses didn't know what, who, or where they were. They didn't know why they existed, nor what they wanted. They had no need to eat or drink, to rest or sleep, or even to blink or breathe . . . they just *were*. This combination of increasing self-awareness and decreasing self-control gradually manifested itself as anger and hostility. Sentenced to spend every minute of every day shuffling pointlessly through the empty world, even the slightest unexpected sound or movement was enough to attract their limited but deadly attention.

With the country (and the rest of the world) now otherwise almost completely silent, the mobile dead moved randomly from their supposedly final resting places, staggering in all directions on rotting, unsteady feet, away from the towns, cities and other centres of population where they'd died, spreading aimlessly across the land like a drop of ink slowly flowing outwards over blotting paper.

Except here.

Here, in apparently nondescript fields miles from anywhere of any perceived importance, for no immediately visible reason, thousands upon thousands of inquisitive, rancid bodies had arrived, cramming themselves into the space of just a few square miles: an endless mass of empty, skeletal husks which had once had individual identities and lives and reasons to exist, but were now nothing more than emotionless collections of tattered rags, grey-green greasy flesh, withered muscle and brittle bone.

At the outermost edge of one of the vast fields, the dishevelled carcase of what had once been an affluent investment banker lifted its head and looked up, barely able to focus its clouded eyes. Surrounded on all sides by scores of similarly bedraggled cadavers, the remains of the once-powerful, dignified and well-respected man shuffled awkwardly forward, slipping and sliding through churned mud, and clawed clumsily at those bodies which stood in its way.

Survivors.

This place was different to everywhere else. It didn't know what, but it knew there was *something* near here, and it had an instinctive, insatiable desire to get even closer to whatever it was. It didn't know why – it barely even knew what it was doing – but it couldn't stop.

Buried deep underground, far below the rotting crowds, almost three hundred survivors existed in the unnatural semi-darkness of a subterranean military base. It was impossible for them to exist there without revealing their location: the world was a silent, lifeless, empty place now, and the sounds made by the people underground, no matter how slight, echoed relentlessly. The heat they produced burned like a fire, and in the otherwise cold and vacant land, the corpses were attracted to them like moths towards the last light on Earth. What had begun as a few random corpses stumbling upon the underground military base by chance had now grown into a crowd of vast, almost incalculable proportions. The movement of the loathsome creatures inevitably attracted more and more of them from the surrounding area: a slow-motion chain reaction. Now, several days since any of the soldiers had been above ground, almost one hundred thousand bodies had gathered around the bunker, every last one of them fighting to get nearer to its impassable entrance.

The dead investment banker's way forward was blocked by more bodies. It lifted its emaciated arms again and then, with unexpected force, lashed out at the figure immediately in front. Soft, putrefying flesh was ripped from bone as the decaying banker tore the unsuspecting creature ahead of it apart. The sudden outburst of violence spread rapidly through the nearest cadavers on all sides, rippling out further into the enormous crowd in every direction before petering out again as quickly as it had begun. All across this massive, decomposing gathering the same thing was happening, time and again, each of the bodies interested only in getting closer to whatever it was that was different about this godforsaken place.

Apart from the wind blowing through the swaying branches of trees and the fighting and continual shuffling movement of the dead, the world around the buried base appeared frozen. Even birds had learnt not to fly too close, because of the reaction their fleeting appearances invariably caused. In spite of the fact that the corpses were individually weak and clumsy, what remained of the rest of the world instinctively feared them, and did all they could to keep their distance. And however individually weak, in such huge numbers as this the dead were unstoppable.

Deep underground in the military base, the living fared little better. Despite being relatively strong and still able to act rationally, they were afraid to move. It was obvious to all the lost and terrified souls buried in the concrete maze below the fields and hills that the sheer number of bodies on the surface would eventually be too much for them. Their options were desperately limited, and frighteningly bleak. They could either sit and wait (although no one knew what they were waiting for, or how long it would take) or they could go above ground and fight. But what would that achieve? What use was open space and fresh air to the military? The disease still hung heavy in the contaminated air, and every one of the soldiers, NCOs and their officers alike, knew that a single breath would, in all probability, be enough to kill them. Those survivors immune to the disease who also sheltered underground knew that they would fare no better from such a confrontation.

Any attempt to clear the bodies from above the base might help in the short term, but the noise and movement such an act would inevitably cause would doubtless result in countless thousands more cadavers being drawn nearer to the shelter – and there were potentially millions more out there.

Below the surface, the survivors and the military were forced to remain apart. Designed to cope with the after-effects of chemical, nuclear or biological attack, the base was remarkably well-equipped and technologically advanced. The air being pumped through the complex was pure, and free from infection. The survivors who had taken shelter there, however, were not. Decontamination had been half-heartedly attempted at first, but the woefully under-prepared military scientists had known from the start that it would be a futile exercise. The germ could be washed away from equipment and from the soldiers' protective suits, but the survivors had been breathing contaminated air for more than a month, and they were riddled with the infection. Whilst the deadly contagion had no obvious effect on them, even the slightest exposure might be sufficient to contaminate the base and kill everyone in it.

The military occupied almost all of the complex (everything beyond the entrance to the decontamination chambers), leaving the thirty-seven survivors with the main hangar and a few adjacent storage, utility and maintenance rooms. Space, heat and light were severely limited. After fighting through the hell above ground to get here, however, the limitations of the military facility were readily accepted and hugely appreciated. The alternatives which awaited them back out on the surface were unthinkable.

1

Emma Mitchell looked at her watch and wondered whether two o'clock was two in the afternoon, or in the morning? She thought morning, but she wasn't sure. In the permanent darkness of the base it was impossible to tell the difference between day and night any more. There were always people sleeping, and always people awake. There were always people gathered in groups and huddles talking in secret whispers about nothing of any importance, and there were always people crying, moaning and arguing. There were always soldiers moving through the decontamination chambers or coming out into the hangar to check, double-check and triple-check their stockpiled equipment.

Two in the morning or two in the afternoon, Emma couldn't sleep. She lay in bed next to Michael and stared into his face. They'd made love a while back, and she felt ridiculously guilty. It had been the fourth time they'd had sex in the three weeks they'd been underground, and each time he'd fallen asleep as soon as they were finished and she'd been left alone, feeling like this. When she'd asked him, he'd said that being with her made him feel complete, that their intimacy made him feel like he used to, before the rest of the world had died. Although Emma thought she felt that way too, sex reminded her of everything she'd lost, and made her wonder what would happen if she lost Michael. She didn't know whether she slept with him because she loved him, or if it was because they just happened to be there for each other. One thing of which she was certain was that there was no room in her world for romance and other long-forgotten feelings any more. He had no trouble, but she couldn't imagine ever being relaxed or aroused enough to have another orgasm. There was no longer any seduction, or foreplay. All she wanted was to feel Michael inside her. He was the only positive thing remaining in her world. Everything was cold, apart from his touch.

In the final days before finding this bunker, Emma had grown to hate the cramped motorhome that she and Michael shared. Now she never wanted to leave it. It was a small, private space where the two of them could shut themselves away from everyone else, and she appreciated it. The others had no choice but to spend all day, every day together, and Emma didn't know how they coped. She needed this space to be able to cut herself off from what was happening elsewhere. Yesterday she'd overheard two soldiers talking about the air getting thinner on the lower levels of the base, how the sheer weight of the bodies above ground were beginning to cause problems, blocking vents and exhaust shafts. She'd spoken to Cooper about it, and he hadn't seemed surprised. The thought of what it must be like above ground now made her want to lock the motorhome doors and never open them again.

Emma heard a noise outside. She sat up and wiped the nearest window clear of condensation from the heat from hers and Michael's bodies, which contrasted with the cold air in the vast hangar. Supplies were being delivered. Two suited-up soldiers emerged from the decontamination chambers to grudgingly deliver rations to the civilian survivors. Emma was surprised they were given anything at all. She often tried to imagine what life must be like for the soldiers. Were they just going through the motions, waiting to die? How long would the contagion outside last? Was the air clear now, or would it stay contaminated for another month, or year, or decade – and in any event, how would they know? Would any of the soldiers ever be brave – or stupid – enough to risk going above ground and breathing in the air to find out? Donna Yorke had suggested that was why the military had been so accommodating towards them. She said she could see a time when they might want to use the immune survivors either to try and find a cure or, once the bodies had rotted down to nothing, just to scour the surface for food, water and supplies. That made sense.

Emma put on Michael's thick winter coat and stood up and moved to another window. It was hard to make out what was happening outside – the hangar lights were almost always turned down to their lowest setting, to conserve power. They only got brighter when the military were heading outside, and that hadn't happened for more than two weeks. Two days after the civilians had first arrived, the Army had opened the doors and made a futile attempt to clear the mess they'd made getting in. They'd been beaten back by the sheer number of bodies outside. The first few hundred corpses had been obliterated with flame-throwers, but there were thousands more behind them. Distractedly thinking about the carnage that day, she watched Cooper checking over one of the vehicles he and the others had arrived in. It was obvious from his manner that he was military (or was he now ex-military, since he was immune?). She'd often seen him exercising, or demonstrating to small groups of people how to use the military equipment which surrounded them. She knew it was important to keep themselves and their vehicles in good order; she was under no illusions. Today, tomorrow, or in six months' time – they'd have to leave the bunker eventually.

'Something wrong?'

Emma turned around and saw that Michael was sitting up in bed. His dark eyes looked tired and confused.

'Nothing. Couldn't sleep, that's all.'

He yawned and beckoned her over. She climbed back into bed and he grabbed hold of her tightly, as if they'd been apart for years.

'How you doing?' he asked quietly, his face close to hers.

'I'm okay.'

'Anything happening out there?'

'Not really, just a delivery of supplies, that's all. Does anything ever happen around here?'

'Give it time,' he mumbled sadly, kissing the side of her face. 'Give it time.'

2

'Morning, you two,' Bernard Heath said in his loud, educated voice as Michael and Emma walked together into the largest of the few rooms that the survivors were permitted access to.

'Morning, Bernard,' Emma replied. 'Bloody cold, isn't it?'

'Isn't it always? Get yourselves something to eat; they left us quite a lot last night.'

Holding onto Michael's hand, Emma followed him as he weaved through the crowded room. About six yards square, it was used by the survivors as a dormitory, a meeting place, a kitchen and a mess hall – in fact, it was used for just about everything. As bleak as its grey, featureless walls were, the fact that the room was always filled with people made it just about the best place for any of them to spend their time. At least here they weren't always looking over their shoulders, or sitting in silence, not daring to speak. At least here they could, for the time being, at least, try to relax, recuperate and heal.

A basic shift pattern had been drawn up shortly after they'd first arrived at the bunker. Although there had been the few expected protests and occasional missed shifts, most people were prepared to pull their weight and contribute by cooking or cleaning or doing whatever other menial tasks needed to be done. Rather than evade work, as some of them might have done before, almost all of the survivors now willingly worked as hard as they could – though how much was done for the good of the group was questionable; most simply craved the responsibility because it helped reduce the monotony and boredom of the long, dark days. As many of them had already found to their cost, sitting and staring at the walls of the bunker with nothing to do invariably resulted in thinking constantly about all they had lost.

Emma and Michael collected something to eat from Sheri Newton (a quiet, diminutive middle-aged woman who always seemed to be serving food) and sat down. The faces of the people around them were reassuringly familiar: Donna Yorke was at a table nearby talking to Clare Smith, Jack Baxter and Phil Croft. As the couple began to eat Croft looked around and spotted them. He nodded at Michael.

'Morning,' Michael said as he chewed on his first mouthful of the dry, tasteless rations. 'How are you doing today, Phil?'

'Good,' Croft replied, wheezing. He took a long drag on a cigarette and coughed.

'You should think about giving those things up,' Michael said sarcastically. 'They'll be the death of you, mate!'

Croft grimaced as he coughed, then managed a fleeting smile. It was a sign of the grim hopelessness of their situation that death was just about the only thing they could find to laugh about. The group's only doctor, he'd been seriously injured in a violent crash as they'd approached the military bunker. The dank conditions underground were not ideal and did nothing to aid his recovery. Although the only remaining visible signs of his injuries were a scar across his chest and an unsteady limp, as a trained medic, Croft knew that his body had sustained a huge amount of internal damage, and that he would never be fully fit again. With his private discomfort and pain continuing, and with the military on one side and thousands of decomposing corpses on the other, the potentially harmful side-effects of smoking were the very least of his concerns.

Cooper marched angrily into the room, his sudden, stormy entrance instantly silencing every conversation. Everyone looked round at him. He fetched himself a drink, yanked a chair from under the table and sat down next to Jack Baxter.

'What's the matter with you?' Jack asked.

'This place is full of fucking idiots,' the ex-soldier answered. Since returning to the base he had steadily distanced himself from his military colleagues. Perhaps symbolically, he now wore only the lower half of his uniform, and he only kept the boots and trousers on because they were the most practical clothes he possessed. In fact, they were just about the only clothes he had.

'Now who's he talking about?' Croft interrupted. 'Who're you on about now, Cooper?'

Cooper took a swig of coffee. 'The bloody jokers in charge of this place.'

'So what have they done?'

'Nothing, and that's the problem.'

'What do you mean?' Donna asked, concerned. She knew Cooper well enough to know that there had to be a reason behind his sudden foul mood. He was usually much calmer and more controlled than this.

'They won't tell me anything any more,' he explained. 'They've been *ordered* not to. I just can't understand their logic. What are they going to gain from keeping us in the dark? We've seen more of what's happened out there than they have.'

'Sounds typical of what I've seen of the military so far,' Jack said. 'So is that all that's bothering you?'

'No, it's more than that,' Cooper admitted. 'I've just been talking to an old mate of mine, Jim Franks. Jim and I go back a long way, and I know I can trust him. Anyway, he's been telling me that they think they're going to start hitting real problems soon.'

'Supplies?' Jack wondered.

'No, they've got enough stuff here to last a while longer.'

'What kind of problems then?' Emma asked, starting to feel uneasy.

'Big fucking problems,' Cooper continued. 'Nothing they weren't expecting, but big fucking problems nonetheless.'

'Such as . . . ?'

'You've got to remember that I was talking to Jim through the intercom at the front of the decontamination chamber, and he was trying to keep quiet in case anyone caught him speaking to me, so I didn't get a lot of detail, but it's the bodies. They've been taking readings around the base and the damn things still keep on coming. Jim told me that the air filtration system's still working at the moment, but it's really starting to struggle, and the problems we've heard about with ventilation are getting worse – more than half the exhaust vents are blocked, or almost blocked, which amounts to the same thing. It's just like we said they would be.'

'So what are they going to do about it?' Croft said, asking the question that everyone was thinking.

'There's no way of clearing the vents from down here,' he replied, 'so they're going to have to go above ground again.'

'But what good's that going to do?' Emma said, terrified at the prospect of the bunker doors being opened again. 'Do they think they can just clear the bodies away? As soon as they move any of them, hundreds more will take their place.'

'I know that and you know that,' Cooper said dejectedly, 'but they don't understand the scale of the problem. This is why I don't understand them not talking to us. The reality is that the people making the decisions down here don't have a fucking clue how bad things are up on the surface. Until you've seen it for yourself, until you've been out there in the middle of it, you just can't imagine what it's like out there, can you?'

'So how are they planning to keep the vents clear?' asked Donna. 'Like Emma says, as soon as they've cleared them more bodies will be lining up to block them again.'

'Jesus, I don't know. My guess is they'll try and cover them, or build something over the top. You've got to remember that this place was designed not to be noticed. You'd have to look hard just to find the bloody vents, 'cause they're really not obvious, but that doesn't matter any more, does it? I think they're planning to fight their way through to the vents, and then just do whatever they have to, to block them off. They'll try and cover the top of them, or maybe leave people out there to guard them. A trench or a wall might do it . . .'

'Pity the poor bastards who get sent out there to build bloody walls,' Jack said. 'Christ, it's hard enough just being up there, never mind having to build a bloody wall. I tell you, you wouldn't get me back outside for anything.'

'You reckon? Keep things in perspective, Jack,' Cooper said, looking directly at him. 'We've got a massive advantage over this lot at the moment because we can survive out in the open. So who says they're not going to try and use us to do whatever it is that they're planning? Argue all you like, but if you've got a gun held at the back of your head, you'll do whatever they bloody well want you to do.'

'You really think it's going to come to that?'

'Perhaps not yet, but—'

'But what?'

'But they might do eventually. Put yourself in their shoes. You'd probably do the same.'

The conversation stalled as each of the survivors stopped to take stock of Cooper's words. He knew how the military minds worked better than any of them. He'd never been anything other than straight and direct. There was no point trying to soften the blow.

'How long?' Donna asked.

'How long until what?'

'How long before they open the doors and go out there?'

'No idea. I don't expect they know either. We'll just have to sit and wait.'

'It has to happen sooner or later, doesn't it?' Michael said, his voice filled with resignation 'It's inevitable. They used to call it Chaos Theory, didn't they? If something *can* go wrong, eventually it will.'

'You're a happy bugger, Mike! Keep looking on the bright side, eh?' grinned Jack.

'He's right though,' Cooper agreed.

'We've all seen it happen,' Michael continued. 'We started off in a village hall. There were about twenty of us there. We thought we'd be okay, but we had to get away. One of us went back, and the place had been completely overrun. We found ourselves a house in the middle of the bloody countryside, miles away from anywhere, but that wasn't safe enough either. We even built a bloody fence around it, but it didn't last.'

'Same with us and the university,' Donna said. 'It really looked ideal to start with, but it didn't last. Things change, and we can't afford to just sit still and wait and hope and—'

'And you're right, the same thing's bound to happen here eventually,' Cooper interrupted. 'Something's going to give . . . more vents will become blocked, the disease will manage to get in somehow, or something else will happen. It'll take luck more than anything else to keep anybody safe down here.'

'So what do we do about it?'

'There's not a lot we can do right now,' he answered. 'We just need to be ready for it when it happens, and be prepared to get out of here fast if anything goes wrong.'

3

Three days was all it took. It was mid-morning when it began. Michael was standing in front of the motorhome talking to Cooper about the sorry state of his battered vehicle. Although it had been cleaned and overhauled to the best of their abilities with the limited resources available, the vehicle still looked desperately dilapidated. Their conversation was interrupted abruptly when the hangar lights came on fully, filling the cavernous space with unexpected glare. Having been forced to live in almost complete darkness for weeks on end, both men covered their sensitive eyes and, for a fraction of a second, found themselves thinking more about the sudden pain and discomfort than the reasons the lights had been turned on now.

Michael was the first to react. 'Shit,' he cursed as he looked around, still shielding his eyes, 'this must be it.'

Cooper saw the doors into the main decontamination chamber were opening, and from deep inside the base a steady stream of dark-suited figures began to emerge. Close on a hundred troops quickly filed out into the hangar, and although their formation and manner lacked something of the discipline and precision Cooper would have expected of his former colleagues, they were clearly well organised, and ready to fight.

'Christ, they mean business,' he said.

'What do we do?'

'Get everyone ready to get out of here.'

They sprinted across the huge room together, cutting through the soldiers' rather ragged formation. The sudden light and noise had already alerted the other survivors, and anxious faces started to appear before Michael and Cooper were even halfway across the hangar.

'What's happening?' Steve Armitage asked.

'What's it look like?' Cooper replied. 'They're about to open the fucking doors!'

Steve hadn't even had a chance to respond before a crowd of panicking survivors had shoved him out of the way and spilled out into the hangar.

'Get ready to leave,' Cooper shouted, loud enough for everyone to hear. He hoped they weren't going anywhere, but he felt duty-bound to prepare the group for the worst possible scenario. 'Get your stuff together, and get everyone into the vehicles.'

Without question or delay the frightened crowd began to rush towards the vehicles that had brought them here: a police van, a prison truck, and Michael and Emma's motorhome.

Bernard Heath looked around for Phil Croft. He grabbed the medic's arm and steadied him. Croft could walk, but not with any ease, and his injuries prevented him from getting anywhere with any speed.

'Get the kids,' Michael yelled to Donna, but she was one step ahead of him and was already ushering the four children they'd found alive towards the door of the little storeroom they used to play in. She was trying not to let them pick up on her sudden fear.

Emma, frightened and moving against the flow of most of the others, grabbed hold of Michael's arm.

'What's going on?' she demanded. 'What are they doing?'

'Get into the motorhome,' he told her. 'I'll be over in a couple of minutes.'

'But . . .' she protested. Michael pushed her away, desperate to get her to safety quickly.

'Don't ask questions,' he shouted after her, 'just get yourself over there.'

'Is that everyone?' Cooper asked as he returned to the hangar after checking the last rooms were clear.

'Think so,' Jack replied as he looked back across the immense cavern, watching the rest of the survivors trying to cram themselves and their belongings into the back of the group's three vehicles.

'You two get yourselves over there and try and get that lot sorted out,' Cooper ordered. Although no one had exactly nominated him as their leader, everyone had started looking to him for answers. His experience as a soldier, combined with his undoubted air of command, made him the obvious choice. Michael and Jack turned and ran towards the others.

As Cooper watched the soldiers, the roar of engines suddenly filled the air, echoing around the immense space, and an armoured personnel carrier took up position at the foot of the ramp which led up to the main entrance doors. Two smaller Jeeps were driven out of the shadows and parked immediately behind the first vehicle. As he started cautiously moving forward, he was already trying to work out what tactics his former colleagues were about to employ.

'Cooper,' shouted Michael as the final few survivors jostled for space in the group's battered transports, 'come on!'

Cooper ignored him, instead moving closer still to the troops. He estimated there were somewhere between eighty and a hundred soldiers in the hangar: there was no doubt this was a major operation. He knew that the officers (who, as far as he could tell, were still buried safely within the deeper confines of the base) would never risk sending such a large number of men above ground unless they had absolutely no choice.

He took a chance – after all, he had nothing to lose.

'Hey, man,' he said, reaching out and grabbing the arm of the nearest suited figure at the back of the ranks. The soldier spun around nervously to face him. The protective mask and breathing apparatus obscured so much of the trooper's face that Cooper could see only his eyes. 'What's happening?' he asked.

'Vents are blocked,' the soldier answered. Though his voice was muffled, Cooper could clearly hear his anxiety.

'So what's the plan?'

The soldier glanced around, not sure whether or not he should even be speaking to Cooper, but he figured that the preparation of the troops and equipment at the front of the hangar was sufficient distraction for him to risk a few more words.

'They reckon we can get by for now if we've got at least two of the vents clear, so we're going out there to sort 'em out, and to make sure they stay working.'

'So are you staying out there?' Cooper whispered.

The soldier shook his head vehemently. 'You've got to be fucking kidding,' he replied quickly. 'No, that's what the Jeeps are for – the vents are low on the ground, so the plan is to leave a Jeep straddling each vent to block them off and stop those bloody things out there from clogging them up again.'

The soldiers began to move forward. The trooper shrugged off Cooper's hand and retook his position in formation. Still curious, Cooper moved back towards the others, but instead of getting into one of the vehicles with them, he clambered up onto the front of one of the huge, unused military transports to try and get a better view of what was about to happen. Jack, red-faced and out of breath, appeared at his side.

'What's happening now?' he asked, panting with the effort as he hauled himself up beside the soldier.

'They're going to try and clear a couple of vents,' Cooper reported. 'They're planning to leave those Jeeps parked on top to try and keep the bodies away.'

'Got to get to the damn vents first,' Jack said. 'Do they realise what it's like out there?'

'They will in a couple of minutes. Anyway, they don't have any choice if they want to keep breathing. If there was another way I'm sure they'd have tried it by now. No matter what you might think, they're not stupid . . .'

He stopped talking abruptly as the doors began to open. At first nothing seemed to happen, then a dull scraping noise became audible over the rumbling sound of the military machines poised to drive out into the open. A second later, and the first chink of light appeared: a slender shaft of harsh grey-white brightness between the two gradually separating halves of the door, increasing as the entrance opened further.

'Christ,' Jack said under his breath, trying not to panic, '*Jesus Christ!*'

As soon as the gap was wide enough, bodies began to spill through into the hangar. Forced forward like a viscous liquid by the weight of rotting flesh pushing hard against them from behind, the first corpses stumbled down the ramp, lurching towards the soldiers with unexpected speed, even though many were tripping and falling, unable to properly coordinate their awkward movements. The soldiers responded instinctively, pushing them back and firing at them until they had managed to temporarily stem the flow of dead meat.

From somewhere deep within the ranks a muffled order was

given, and a row of four soldiers armed with flame-throwers stepped forward out of the darkness. They pushed their way further into the diseased crowd and unleashed their devastating weapons on the nearest creatures, sending controlled arcs of dripping, incandescent flame shooting out of the bunker door and up into the cold morning air. The bodies, by now virtually tinder-dry, were caught by the fire and almost immediately incinerated.

Another order was given and the personnel carrier began to creep slowly forward, emerging out into the open and pushing deeper into the burning crowd, grinding charred flesh and bone into the mud beneath its heavy wheels. To the front and on either side, the soldiers bearing the flame-throwers took up protective positions and advanced cautiously, matching the laborious pace of the massive vehicle and destroying as many corpses as their flames would reach. Beyond the mass of burning bodies, countless more of the abhorrent figures continually pushed themselves closer and closer to the centre of the disturbance, attracted by the fire, noise and sudden movements and apparently oblivious to the danger.

At the bunker entrance the two Jeeps finally emerged out into the mayhem, each of them defended by another flame-thrower-carrying soldier, and with other troops armed with more conventional but clearly less effective weapons.

As the military convoy slowly eased away from the front of the base, the remaining troops formed a heavy protective line of defence across the still-open entrance. The air was filled with billowing clouds of thick black smoke and the suffocating smell of burnt corpses. Unable to see what was happening from where he was perched, Cooper jumped down from his high viewpoint and moved up the ramp to get closer to the troops.

'Cooper,' Jack yelled at him, 'come back! Don't be stupid!'

But Cooper ignored him, and continued to edge further forward. Now he was standing behind the line of heavily-armed soldiers, he could see that the personnel carrier and its entourage had managed to carve a deep, gently curving channel through the centre of the immense crowd of corpses. The vehicles were moving painfully slowly through the bloody mayhem, still surrounded by a protective guard of soldiers who continually fired into the writhing, squirming, surging masses all around them. Hundreds of rotting figures were being obliterated by flame and gunfire, and yet hundreds more, undeterred by the annihilation in front of them, continued to stagger across the burning remains to take the place of those which had fallen.

Some three hundred yards away from the entrance to the base now, the driver of the personnel carrier turned to the officer next to him.

'Where's the vent?' he demanded. 'Where's the fucking vent?'

Those troops who hadn't been above ground before had been completely unable to anticipate the disorientating effect of so many bodies being packed so tightly together on the ground. Shaking with nerves, one overawed officer tried to trace the path they had already taken on a map. He looked up briefly to check his bearings, but the land around them was featureless, and little was visible except for the frantic, uncoordinated movements of the swarms of dead, searing arcs of flame, and dense, billowing clouds of noxious smoke.

'Should be somewhere over there,' he yelled, pointing to his right as he checked his instruments, then tried to find a more accurate visual reference. The driver steered the carrier as directed, shielding his eyes from a blast of sudden brightness as more bodies were drenched with fire and destroyed. He watched in disbelief as the creatures around them burned to a crisp – and yet continued to move, inexplicably ignorant of the flames which were consuming them. Instead, the rotting cadavers continued to stagger relentlessly forward until their last decaying sinews had been burnt away to nothing.

'Got it,' the driver said with relief as he caught a momentary glimpse of the exhaust vent amongst the seething sea of decaying figures. Originally standing just a few inches above ground level and camouflaged by mud, moss and weeds, the location of the vent was made obvious today by the mass of once-human remains which had accumulated around it. The first cadavers had originally been attracted by the faint noise and the heat coming up from the depths of the base, but after that many more bodies had become entangled with the low metal structure, and they in turn had then been trapped in place by countless more figures pushing against them, until the metal vent was partially obscured by writhing mounds of cold grey flesh and splintering bone.

'Drive straight over the top of it,' ordered the officer, his composure returning. The driver did as instructed, turning the vehicle towards the vent and accelerating through the bodies. The soldier moving just ahead of them continued to soak the apparently endless crowd with fire, burning away the nearest of the hordes of lumbering cadavers, which were scrambling ever closer to the convoy.

Other than the metal vent, this patch of land was relatively flat and featureless. The driver of the personnel carrier powered over the top of the metal covering as ordered, smashing burning bodies away to either side and managing to scrape away a thick layer of once-human remains.

Someone gestured high in the air and a group of soldiers descended upon the vent. Some took up position and started to sweep the bodies with machine-gun-fire, keeping them at bay, while two soldiers began digging out the vent, shovelling away blood, guts and gristle, and picking out bones and snagged shreds of clothing. They worked with furious speed, not looking up, but increasingly aware of bodies edging ever closer, and deeply grateful for the frequent bursts of flame and gunfire which held the advancing dead back.

Now that the way was clear, the driver of the first Jeep, following close behind, gestured for the driver of the second to position his vehicle so it was straddling the vent, as they'd planned back in the bunker. The second driver pulled forward carefully, until the metal opening was positioned directly beneath the centre of the mud- and blood-splattered vehicle. He leaned precariously out of his door to make sure he was in the right place, and saw that there were just a couple of inches' clearance between the top of the vent and the bottom of the Jeep. Perfect.

He shouted to his colleagues, then he jumped out and with the soldiers already on the ground, they raced after the troop-carrier and the other Jeep, which were now heading towards the next nearest vent to repeat the manoeuvre.

Cooper, standing behind the defensive line of soldiers standing in the entrance to the bunker, was still struggling to see what was happening. Clouds of repulsive-smelling smoke blew back into the base and stung his eyes, filling his nose and throat with a charred, nauseating aftertaste.

'What's happening now?' Jack asked. The longer the soldiers spent outside, the more Jack's curiosity had overtaken his nervousness. He'd gradually crept forward until he was standing just behind Cooper's shoulder.

'Can't see what they're doing. I've lost sight of them.'

'Do they even have the slightest idea what they're—' Jack started, but a sudden blast of flame silenced him. He could feel the heat on his face, prickling his skin. When the smoke and heat-haze cleared, he saw the remains of a small pocket of bodies which had exploited a gap in the ranks and surged forward. The fact they were burning now didn't matter; they'd got dangerously close.

'This doesn't look good,' Cooper said quietly. 'These things are relentless.'

Another arc of flame, even closer than the last, sent the two men scuttling further back into the base.

'Bloody hell,' Jack cursed, recoiling from the intense heat.

'Look at the chances they're having to take here, Jack,' Cooper said, watching the soldiers struggled to keep the dead at bay, 'and for what? This is just to keep breathing, for Christ's sake!'

Jack didn't have a chance to respond, for the soldiers protecting the entrance suddenly lowered their weapons and dropped back *en masse*. For a moment the two survivors feared the arrival of an unstoppable deluge of dead bodies, but it didn't happen. Instead the personnel carrier burst back into the bunker, followed almost immediately by the full complement of tired, shocked and battle-filthy troops.

The shooting and fire-bombing continued until the doors closed.

Jack stared at the world outside for as long as he was able. The return of the armoured vehicle and the troops had disturbed the air and, momentarily, dispersed the dirty smoke, and for just an instant, his view of the outside world was uninterrupted. He could see mounds of dead flesh, the charred and mangled remains of hundreds of bodies, lying twisted and blackened on the muddy ground. Beyond them he could see thousands more cadavers, all fighting to get closer to the base. Like a dense, grey fog, those bodies which had so far escaped destruction moved over the remains of those which had fallen, desperately trying to reach the living buried underground.

Jack missed seeing the sky and feeling the wind on his face, but the ever-present claustrophobia and the smell of dry, recycled air was a small price to pay to be kept safe from the hell outside.

4

'And that's all they're prepared to tell you?' Croft asked.

'That's about it,' Cooper said, 'although to be honest, I don't think there's much more to tell. They've cleared two of the vents and cremated a ton of corpses. That was all they went out there to do.'

'But are they going to need to clear more vents? Will they go out there again?'

'I don't know.'

'And how long do they think those vents are going to stay clear? How long's it going to be before they're clogged up with bodies again?'

'I don't know,' Cooper said again, clearly irritated by the doctor's relentless – pointless – questioning. 'Look, Phil, it doesn't matter how many times you ask me, or how many different ways you ask, I don't know anything more than what I've already told you, okay? The blokes I know have been told not to talk to me.'

It was several hours since the soldiers had returned from outside and the doors to the base had been resealed. Croft, Cooper, Jack and Donna were sitting in the relative comfort of the motorhome with Michael and Emma. That brief glimpse of outside light earlier had made the bunker's prison-like grey walls feel more confining than ever. They could still see the bunker through the windows of the motorhome, but the extra layer of separation gave the illusion of being a little further detached than usual from their nightmarish reality.

'What bothers me,' Jack said quietly, cradling a beaker of water in his hands as if it were the finest malt whiskey, 'is that they're still coming. After all this time it doesn't look like anything's changed. I looked out there today and I could see as many bodies as I saw on the day we first arrived here, maybe even more. It's been three weeks now, for God's sake. Why don't they just piss off and find somewhere else?'

'Because there *is* nowhere else,' Donna reminded him. 'You know this, Jack. Even if there are hundreds more survivors scattered round the country, they'll all have hidden themselves away like us by now. They might not be underground, but they'll be out of sight, and I'll tell you something, I bet they've all got their own bloody huge crowds hanging round them, just like we have.'

'It wouldn't make any difference whether we were underground or up a bloody mountain,' Michael added. 'Doesn't matter how quiet or careful we are; they'll keep going until they find us.'

'I know,' Jack said dejectedly.

'Did you see what kind of condition they were in today?' Donna asked.

'Didn't get much chance, sorry,' Jack replied, adding sarcastically, 'I would have got a bit closer but the soldiers and the flame-throwers and the thousands of burning bodies kind of put me off. Next time I'll try and—'

'What I mean is,' Donna snapped, annoyed by his attitude, 'were they still as mobile as they were before? When we came down here they were starting to get really aggressive. I just wondered if they've changed, got any worse?'

'I couldn't tell. Honestly, Donna, it was hard to see anything much from where I was standing.'

'It's difficult to say what kind of condition they're in,' Cooper added. 'Like Jack said, we couldn't see much more than fire and smoke out there. But what really concerns me is the fact that the guys who were left defending the entrance were kept busy all the time the doors were open.'

'So?'

'So even though there was a bloody huge engine driving right through the middle of them, and a squad of soldiers firing non-stop at them, plenty of them were still trying to get in here. We've been saying all along that these things just react to distractions. That might still be true, but to my mind a troop-carrier surrounded by blokes with flame-throwers should be a damn sight more distracting than a line of soldiers standing in an open door. I think the bodies that came towards the base must have chosen to try and get in here.'

'You are joking, aren't you?' Jack said, sounding horrified.

'I don't joke, Jack, you should know that by now. Those things outside, their flesh and bone may be getting weaker, but we've said all along that they're getting smarter too, haven't we?'

'Are you serious?' asked Croft.

'I'm just guessing here,' he replied. 'It might have just been coincidence, or a fluke that they found themselves close to the entrance. The bodies could have been heading towards the men out in the field and then been distracted by those who were left behind to protect the base.'

'How could they be getting smarter when they're rotting away?' Jack wondered, looking at Dr Croft for an answer to his obviously unanswerable question.

'How the hell am I supposed to know?' the doctor snapped angrily. 'Bloody hell, I'm sick of this – stop assuming I know what's going on! I keep telling you, I don't know any more than you do.' Annoyed and hurting, Croft swung himself around in his seat and kicked the motorhome door open with his feet. 'Mind if I smoke?'

Michael shook his head.

'How many're you down to now, Doc?' Jack asked.

'One and a half boxes,' he replied as he relit a half-smoked cigarette and slowly inhaled. 'I tell you, I'm going to go out of my bloody mind if I can't get more cigarettes.'

'So how long do you reckon that lot will last you?' asked Emma.

'I've been limiting myself to smoking half of one a day, so I've probably got a couple of weeks left – as long as you lot stop asking me stupid bloody questions and winding me up.'

'What then?'

'Not much choice really, is there?' Croft said dejectedly. 'I can either give up, or go out and get some more!'

'You should try looking closer to home,' Jack suggested. 'I bet they've got fags and drink and everything in their stores down here.'

Cooper shook his head. 'You'd be surprised, Jack. This whole operation was thrown together in minutes. They've got a lot less kit and supplies stashed away than you'd think.'

Across from Cooper, Michael sat on the edge of the uncomfortable sofa which doubled up as the bed he shared with Emma. Emma shuffled nearer to him and he wrapped his arms around her as she rested her weight against him. The others looked away, each of them feeling suddenly awkward, almost embarrassed. Emma and Michael's intimacy made them feel uncomfortable – they'd all lost everyone who'd ever mattered to them, and even the idea of such tenderness felt alien now, an uneasy reminder of a world now gone for ever.

'I always wanted a van like this,' Jack said suddenly, looking around and making a conscious effort to start a more trivial conversation. 'Me and Denise were planning on getting ourselves something like this when I retired. We were thinking about selling up and living on the road for a while.'

'I wouldn't recommend it,' Michael said. 'It's not all it's cracked up to be – we were living on the road for a couple of weeks before we found this place, weren't we, Em? Didn't enjoy it much!'

Jack smiled. 'Seriously though, I've been thinking about it a lot,' he rambled, looking out through the motorhome window and imagining he could see something other than grey concrete walls. 'Just think what it'll be like when the bodies have gone. Picture it: we'll have the whole country to ourselves. We'll be able to go where we like, when we like.'

'So where would you go?' Croft asked him.

'I think,' he began, stretching in his seat and staring up thoughtfully at the low metal ceiling above his head, 'I'd like to try and travel right round the coast. I'm going to wait until next summer, then I'll start south and work my way west. I won't plan a route; I'll just keep going, and one day I'll end up back where I started and see how much it's changed.'

'But you could have your pick of the biggest houses, or whatever you wanted,' Emma said. 'You could sit on your backside and relax, take it easy – you'd still want to travel and live rough?'

'I'm getting used to living rough now. It'd be strange to be comfortable again. I like the idea of being on the move, taking whatever I need from wherever I can find it.'

'Think you'll ever do it?' Donna asked.

Jack looked deep into his beaker of water and thought hard for a moment. 'I hope so.'

'You make it sound easy.'

'There's no reason why it shouldn't be. But there's no way of knowing other than doing it, is there?'

'It's going to get harder every day,' Donna said, sounding tired and dejected. 'As time passes there's going to be less and less for us to take out there. The last bits of food will rot. Buildings will start to crumble. Everything we used to know will gradually disappear.'

'Christ,' Jack groaned, 'here's looking on the bright side, eh?'

'I'm just trying to be realistic, that's all.'

'Anyway,' Croft interrupted, 'we've got to get out of here before you can start sightseeing, Jack.'

'I know. Frustrating, isn't it? It's us who can survive out there, but it's the bloody Army who'll decide whether we can go outside or not.'

'Think they'll try and keep us locked down here, Cooper?' Croft asked.

'Unless us being here puts them at risk, I don't think they'll be in a hurry to get rid of us,' Cooper answered. 'I still think we might be useful to them. I think they might be making plans.'

5

'What's the matter?'

Emma had woken up alone in bed. After a brief moment of blind panic she'd found Michael at the other end of the motorhome, sitting behind the wheel and staring out through the windscreen into the gloom of the hangar. The hands on the dashboard clock said it was almost four. When he heard her he glanced around momentarily and then turned back to the windscreen and looked out again.

'Nothing's the matter,' he replied. 'I was just thinking, that's all.'

'What about?'

'You know, the usual.'

'What's the usual?'

'All this bullshit,' he answered, gesturing outside the motorhome. Emma sat down next to him. He sounded uncharacteristically abrupt and distant.

'Is it me? Have I upset you or—?'

'Why do you always assume it's got anything to do with you, Em? What could you have possibly done to upset me?'

'I don't know. Maybe if you'd talk to me and tell me what's wrong, I could help . . .'

Michael turned around to face Emma and pulled her closer. She was shivering with cold.

'It's nothing you've done. Believe me, you're just about the only thing I'm not worrying about right now.'

'It's just that when I woke up and found you weren't there I started to think . . . you know what it's like . . .'

'I know.'

She paused for a moment. 'So what exactly *were* you thinking about?'

He nodded in the direction of the heavy entrance doors which separated the fortunate few inside from the vast crowds of rotting flesh outside the base. 'The bodies.'

'What about them?'

'You remember how many were outside when we first got here?'

'Thousands, why?'

'Jack said he thought there were just as many of them out there today, maybe even more.'

'I know, I heard him. So?'

'So even though we've been buried down here for weeks, they're still managing to find us out.'

'We knew this was going to happen—'

'I know that, but if they've been able to find us when we've been keeping quiet and out of sight, what the hell's going to happen now? What's going to happen now that those bloody idiots have started going out there with their guns and their flame-throwers and God knows what else? I think that every last corpse that's anywhere near here is going to end up outside those doors, trying to get in. And then more will come, then more. And the more there are out there, the more pressure this base is going to be put under just to keep functioning. Sooner or later they'll have to go above ground again, and when they do, it'll just make matters worse. It's a vicious cycle, and the dumb bastards in charge here can't even see it. They'll keep at it until this fucking place falls apart.'

'Do you really think that'll happen?'

'I think it's inevitable,' Michael answered quietly, his voice low and unemotional. 'I've said it before. It might happen tomorrow, the day after tomorrow or the day after that. It might happen in the next hour or it might not happen for weeks. The one thing I'm sure of is that it will happen eventually.'

6

'You on your own, Cooper?'

Cooper shuffled closer to the intercom fixed on the wall next to the heavy door which separated the decontamination chambers and the rest of the buried base from the hangar. He was well away from the rest of the group of survivors; he'd been sitting talking to Bernard Heath when they'd become aware of the sound of movement coming from inside the decontamination area. Through a six-inch-square observation panel he'd recognised Jim Franks, just about the last of his ex-colleagues who still dared to risk speaking to him.

'I've got Bernard Heath with me,' Cooper replied, his voice deliberately low, 'but it's okay. Bernard's all right.'

A pause.

'Okay, mate, if you trust him, I trust him,' the subdued, disembodied voice said. Franks and Cooper had known and respected each other for years. The rest of Cooper's former colleagues had either been ordered or had chosen to stop communicating with him – many of them now felt uneasy around him; they distrusted him because he was 'out there with them' instead of 'in here with us'. Perhaps they thought that being a bona-fide, natural-born 'survivor' somehow made him a different person to the Mark Cooper they had known and served alongside for some many years. Others, those few who were still committed and loyal to the military, simply feared incurring the wrath of their superiors if they dared speak to him. And a small number had become completely isolated and withdrawn. They didn't speak to *anyone* any more.

'How are things going in there?' Cooper asked, huddling closer to the intercom.

'Not so good,' Franks replied.

'Why, what's happening?'

Another brief silence, then he answered, 'The men are scared, 'cause no one knows what's happening, or why it's happening. But we know we're on our own here now, so the fucking jokers who are running this place are starting to think they're in charge of what's left of the country and that they can do what they please. The men are pretty shook-up after what happened outside. It's getting pretty fucking intense in here.'

'Did you go out?'

'Not this time,' Franks replied, 'but it'll be my turn sooner or later. You know better than I do what we're up against here.'

'It's not good,' said Bernard.

'Seems to me the phrase should be "fucking awful", never mind "not good"! Jesus Christ, we've got people walking round down here talking about fields full of thousands of dead bodies and—'

Cooper interrupted, repeating his original question. He was keener than ever to get an answer. 'So what's happening?'

'Christ, Cooper, you know what it's like when you're getting ready for a fight. You've got some blokes who can't wait for it all to kick off so they can get going, then you've got others who spend most of their time crying into their fucking pillows like little babies. Most of us just want to get out of this sodding hole, but we keep being told that what's out there is worse than what's down here and . . . and I don't know where this is all going, but something's going to give sooner or later.'

When Franks mentioned a fight, Cooper started to worry. He was pretty sure that in their present position a fight would inevitably mean the military risking absolutely everything for absolutely nothing.

'I wish I could give you some good news,' Cooper said, 'but I'd be lying if I did, because there's been no good news since this whole bloody thing started. Believe me though, mate, you're in the best place you can be. Make sure you stay down there as long as you can. I've told you before, every move you make out there will bring hundreds of thousands of bodies swarming round you like flies. You might be going crazy stuck down there, but at least you're alive, and you're not having to watch every step that you take. My advice is to keep your head down and get through this as best you can because—'

'You've got no fucking idea,' Franks snapped, raising his voice to a dangerously loud volume. 'For Christ's sake, Cooper, don't be so fucking naïve. You know the kind of people we've got down here, and there's only so much of this they're going to take. There's only so much *I* can take.'

'You don't have any choice. Go above ground again and—'

'Try telling that to this lot.'

'Seriously, Franks, I know how it seems, but you've got to—'

'Remember Carlson?' Franks interrupted.

'Keith Carlson?'

'Kevin,' Franks corrected, 'remember him?'

'The chef, right?'

'That's right.'

'What about him?'

'They found him in his bunk yesterday morning. Stupid fucker had slit his wrists.'

'Christ,' Bernard said quietly.

'He's not the first, and he won't be the last,' Cooper said quickly, blunt and unsympathetic.

'I know that,' Franks continued, 'but the problem isn't what he did, it's how to get rid of him. They can't decide what to do with the body. People are so fucking paranoid down here that they're talking about trying to burn him or cut him up into little fucking pieces, for God's sake. I've just seen blokes fighting over the corpse.'

'Fighting – why?'

'Because they want to make sure he's dead! Jeavons and Coleman are standing guard over the body, ready to hack it to fucking pieces if it starts to move.'

'It's not going to move,' Bernard said, his voice sounding unintentionally condescending. 'That would probably only happen if the body had been exposed to the outside air. I don't think—'

'I know that, and you know that,' Franks said angrily, 'but you try convincing a couple of hundred soldiers who are scared out of their fucking minds, and who feel like they've been backed into a corner. These people are trained to fight, not to sit around doing nothing. They're talking about dumping the body outside when we go above ground again.'

'Makes sense,' Cooper said, 'but that could be weeks away yet—'

'I don't think so.'

Cooper looked at Bernard. 'Something planned?'

'It's starting to look that way.'

'What?'

'Not sure, no one's saying much. Just rumours, that's all.'

'Such as—?'

The conversation faltered momentarily. Through the observation panel Cooper watched as Franks looked over his shoulder and checked he was safe to keep talking.

'I started to hear a few rumblings yesterday, and I've heard more today, from people that I trust, so it looks like there's some truth in what they're saying. Problem is, we're not getting enough air down here, and it's probably going to get worse. They cleared a couple of exhaust vents, but they need to do way more – and there's no way of unblocking them from this side, 'cause they'll risk infecting the whole fucking base, so best case scenario: we'll be heading up again soon to get a few more of the vents cleared.'

'If that's at best,' Bernard asked quietly, not sure he wanted to hear the answer, 'then what's your worst case scenario?'

Cooper glanced across at him, sharing his concern.

Another pause and then Franks spoke again.

'Some of the boys who went out last time,' he explained, 'told the chiefs that they'd managed to get rid of hundreds of those things.'

'They're not lying: they did,' agreed Cooper. 'Problem is, there're thousands – *tens* of thousands – of them left, and more coming every day.'

'Rumour has it,' Franks continued, 'that they're looking at trying to organise one massive push. Rumour has it that we're *all* going above ground, to torch the whole fucking lot of them.'

7

The lights came on, and Donna immediately jumped up from her seat as the doors to the decontamination chambers began to open.

'Oh, Christ,' she said anxiously, looking across at Emma, Clare and Bernard, who were standing nearby; they were also staring at the slowly opening door.

Alerted by the sudden brightness in the hangar, most of the other survivors had already begun to scramble across the cavern towards their vehicles, and as the first heavily-suited soldiers began to emerge from their sealed shelter, the frightened crowd of men, women and children once again sprinted towards their police van, prison truck and motorhome.

An officer standing on one side was marshalling proceedings as a steady stream of troops took up position on the ramp just short of the entrance doors. Just as they had done previously, engines were started, and an armoured personnel carrier drove out of the shadows. This time the vehicle was accompanied by four Jeeps, and was surrounded by a phalanx of eight soldiers with flame-throwers. The men moved quickly towards the front of the convoy, ready to escort the vehicles out into the open and to burn a path for them through the seething crowds of the dead.

It was three o'clock on Saturday afternoon.

'What do you reckon?' Donna asked Bernard. The two of them had stopped halfway across the hangar and were watching the troops intently. 'Think they're just going to try and do the same as they did before?'

'Looks that way,' he replied, his quiet voice trembling slightly. 'I just want them to get it over with. If they're really going to do this, I just want them to do it now and stop all this stupid, pointless—'

His words were cut short as the ominous mechanical rumbling which signalled the opening of the main doors started up. He swallowed nervously and licked his dry lips, unable to look away from the entrance to the bunker, too scared to keep watching, but even more afraid not to.

The outside world slowly began to appear. Because of the slope of the entrance ramp he saw the clouds first – a dirty, grey-black, rain-filled sky which made the day almost as dark as night. And then it began: an unexpected split-second of silence and calm was ended by a sudden deluge of bodies which began to pour into the base before being pushed back and obliterated by the soldiers with flame-throwers. From that distance Bernard couldn't make out the individual corpses; all he could see was a featureless mass of movement, constantly writhing and lurching, spilling forward into the advancing flames. For a gut-wrenching, seemingly endless moment, the weight and force of the advancing bodies looked to be forcing the furthest forward of the soldiers back into the base again, before they were able to dig in and start pushing forward. Their vastly superior strength and firepower soon allowed them to make headway into the crowd with relative ease. As the brutal, one-sided battle got started, so the familiar smell of burning again began to fill the cavernous hangar, carried along by suffocating clouds of dirty smoke.

'We need to get ready to move,' Michael said. Donna reacted instantly, but Bernard failed to respond, transfixed by the hellish sights he could now see outside. The personnel carrier began to drive forward, followed first by the Jeeps, then by other heavily armoured vehicles. The entire convoy was surrounded by a ring of soldiers who launched spitting jets of flame into the crowds.

'Cooper reckons they're really going to go for it this time,' Jack Baxter said, suddenly appearing behind Bernard. 'He says they might even be trying to get rid of the whole lot of them in one fell swoop – but what good do they think it's going to do? Get rid of this lot and more and more will come to take their place. They'll never do it.'

'You can't reason with them,' Cooper said, watching the soldiers marching out. For half a second he wondered whether he should have been fighting with them. 'Put yourselves in their shoes,' he continued. 'We don't know much about what's happened, but we know a hell of a lot more than they do. We might not have the hardware they've got, but we're better placed to deal with all of this than they are. All they know is they can't breathe

the air outside because it will probably kill them, and those bloody things out there are preventing them from getting the clean air they need to survive. They're seeing the bodies as the enemy, and the only option they think they've got left is to blow the whole fucking lot of them to kingdom come.'

'But don't they understand?' Jack asked pointlessly.

Cooper interrupted him before he could get started. 'No, Jack, that's just it: they don't, not fully. They haven't seen even half of what we've seen.'

'But the bodies won't stop, will they? They'll keep coming until there's nothing left.'

Outside the bunker, the advance troops had made steady progress. The area immediately surrounding the base already resembled a bloody First World War battlefield, and it was still swarming with movement. The bodies approached from all angles, and were beaten back by soldiers who had been kept waiting underground too long and who were desperate to take it out on those they believed responsible for their incarceration. They were there to fight. They laid into the approaching cadavers with furious anger, this sudden outburst of brutality releasing their pent-up frustrations and previously stifled emotions. Those who had not been above ground before, although shocked and terrified at what they saw all around them, were surprised by the relative ease with which the corpses could be destroyed. But from their vantage points low on the ground, they had not yet grasped the truly vast numbers of the dead, nor their relentless determination.

Heavy artillery was quickly deployed, and mortars and shells were fired into the endless crowds beyond the immediate perimeter of the base. In the near distance, explosions shook the ground constantly, each blast tearing huge numbers of bodies apart. Closer to the entrance, the personnel carrier had almost reached the first of its targeted exhaust shafts. Walking alongside one of the vents, and shielded from the battle by the protective ring of fire which surrounded the convoy, the senior officer in the field, a hard bastard called Captain Jennens, veteran of many previous conflicts in Iraq and Afghanistan, watched events unfolding around him with a degree of cautious satisfaction. His men and women were making steady progress, despite the appalling conditions. A sudden sharp shower of hissing rain had drenched everything, and now grimy pools of water puddled across the churned land until the ferocious heat from the flame-throwers turned them to steam. Jennens' boots crunched cindered flesh and charred bone into the mud.

Another vent was easily secured. Jennens peered into the distant gloom beyond the scattered remains of the hundreds of bodies which had already been destroyed. He'd seen some appalling sights in his time, but never anything like this. The size and ferocity of the apparently endless crowd was both remarkable and terrifying: as soon as one group of the dead were scythed down, more surged forward to take the place of the fallen. He watched with an uneasy fascination as endless numbers of the dark, skeletal creatures tripped and crawled through the mayhem towards his soldiers and certain destruction. Did the damn things not realise they'd be annihilated? In the midst of the confusion Sergeant Cowell, one of Jennens' most trusted men, appeared at his side.

'We can do this, sir,' he said, shouting to make himself heard through his facemask and over the squally wind and rain and the constant noise of battle. The ground rumbled momentarily as a small mortar landed short of its target and exploded nearby, sending a gruesome shower of blackened body parts flying through the air. 'If we're going to do this at all, then we should do it now.'

Captain Jennens thought for a moment. Cowell was right: the opposition, although huge in numbers, was clearly weak and apparently incapable of offering any coordinated resistance. Although wiping them out wouldn't give the soldiers any more freedom, this was, unquestionably, a perfect opportunity to take back some of what they'd lost. The defensive position they'd intended at the start had already started to shift towards going on the offensive. If they started actively attacking, and if they could destroy enough of the bodies and beat the remainder of them back far enough and keep them at a distance, they would be able to fortify the entrance to the bunker and properly clear and secure the exhaust vents. There was still no way the military personnel could survive outside the base, but Captain Jennens immediately recognised the psychological importance of ridding themselves of their perceived enemy.

'Shall I give the order, sir?' Sergeant Cowell asked, keen to take this long-overdue, decisive action.

The captain looked around the battlefield again. In the short time he'd been standing there, his troops had made even more progress through the diseased crowds. The enemy were pathetic, defenceless against the comparative might of the military. All the dead had were numbers.

Captain Jennens thought they had nothing to lose. 'Do it,' he commanded.

'Can't see,' Jack whined, edging closer to the soldiers charged with protecting the hangar entrance. 'I can't see a bloody thing.'

'Stay back, Jack,' Michael warned him.

A sudden noise from behind the small group of survivors startled them momentarily. Cooper spun around to see that the decontamination chamber doors were opening again.

'Shit,' he cursed as a second, rather ragged column of nervous soldiers appeared from the depths of the base. There were almost twice as many of them this time.

'What's all this about?' asked Bernard, feeling increasingly anxious.

'My guess,' he answered, as more than a hundred soldiers filed past them, 'is they've decided to try and clear them away completely. I think this is the showdown we were promised.'

As they emerged from the shadows into the light of the hangar, the soldiers increased their speed, breaking into a gentle jog for a few paces before accelerating and sprinting out into the semi-darkness with weapons held high, ready for battle.

'This is not good,' Jack said, feeling his stomach churning with nerves. 'This is not good at all.'

As the fighting outside increased in ferocity and volume, Cooper ushered the others towards their transports. Michael climbed into the motorhome. It was already crowded with frightened people, each of them clutching the few personal belongings they'd managed to salvage. In the front, Donna had taken up the position he usually occupied behind the wheel. Emma was sitting next to her.

'Are you two okay?' he asked, leaning into the front cabin.

Donna gripped the steering wheel tightly in readiness.

'You want your seat back?'

'It's okay,' Michael answered, 'there are enough people in here already. I'll find room somewhere else. Look, Donna, if anything happens, just put your fucking foot down and get out of here, okay?'

'Be careful, Mike,' Emma said, but he'd already gone.

Both the motorhome and prison truck were full, but there was still space in the police van.

Cooper called him over. 'Just got a couple of folks in the back of this,' he said, gesturing over his shoulder at the van. 'Do me a favour, just make sure that either you or I are behind the wheel if we need to make a move, okay?'

'Okay.'

Red-faced, Bernard Heath appeared from around the back of the van. 'I've done a quick head-count,' he wheezed, 'and I think everyone's accounted for.'

Cooper nodded, and then stood and watched as the soldiers continued to pile out through the bunker door.

Outside the base, a wide swathe of land had already been cleared. The majority of the soldiers had formed into long attacking lines, sweeping slowly out across the land from the bunker entrance, tasked with destroying as many of the bodies as they could. The main objective of the excursion had been achieved: the Jeeps had been positioned over all but one of the vents. What was happening now was largely unplanned, but so far it was still relatively well-coordinated. From just behind the advancing troops, heavy artillery was being fired over their heads, relentlessly pounding the land and the shadowy hordes, destroying scores of bodies with every shell. All around, momentary bursts of brilliant yellow, orange and white light pierced the monochrome gloom, illuminating the grotesque bodies for a fraction of a second at a time, like camera flashes. The troops moved steadily away from the base entrance, their progress quick and largely unimpeded.

The forward attacking line of infantry fanned out as the men moved away from the bunker, preventing the crowds getting any closer. A bloody but relatively constant band several yards wide remained between the advancing soldiers and the dead. Ignorant of the danger they faced, those creatures which had so far escaped the wrath of the military continued to try and move ever closer, dragging themselves over the putrefying remains of the thousands of corpses which had fallen before them.

'Aim for the head,' a sergeant yelled, trying not to think how much he sounded like a character from the horror movies he used to love to watch, as his troops unleashed another furious volley of bullets and flame at the seething mass of cadavers. Undeterred, and without a single flicker of emotion, the dead continued to surge forwards.

A short distance further down the military line, Corporal Sean Ellis, a soldier with a short but impeccable service history, stood up to his ankles in blood, mud and rancid flesh and picked out individual corpses from the constantly shifting crowd up ahead. With the skill and concentration of a highly trained marksman he managed to shut off from the rest of the mayhem unfolding all around him and aimed at individual bodies in turn, shooting them in the head and obliterating what remained of their brains. They dropped twitching to the ground and were immediately trodden down by more grotesque figures advancing from behind. Conditions were becoming steadily worse, with smoke, flame and rain combining to make it impossible to see clearly through the deteriorating light of this stormy autumn afternoon. To Ellis' left and right his colleagues continued to fight, each of them destroying as many bodies as they were able, but the crazed creatures continued to advance. For every one of them that Ellis destroyed, ten more immediately seemed to take its place. And beyond, he realised, there were thousands and thousands more. Out of view an endless number of them crawled through the darkness towards the fighting.

'Christ,' the soldier on his right cursed, 'how many of these fucking things are out there?'

They continued to shoot, and the bodies continued to advance, spilling ever forward like a thick, dark sludge. Ellis didn't have time to think or speak, concentrating instead on firing bullet after bullet into the rotting crowd. An arc of white-hot flame burnt through the air just ahead of him, illuminating the full horror of the scene for a few heart-stopping seconds. The disintegrating faces of hundreds of corpses were suddenly visible and Ellis was transfixed, staring at them in horror and revulsion, praying for the light to fade and the dark to return. The nearest corpses were less than ten yards ahead.

The line of soldiers, still advancing, reached a ditch where a meandering stream had once run diagonally across the battlefield but which had, over the course of the last few weeks, become clogged with a compacted layer of putrefying human remains. The trooper on Ellis' right, struggling to keep focused on the fighting and not lose his nerve, slipped down the slight incline, ending up on his hands and knees in the middle of the stagnant trench. A powerful wave of gut-wrenching nausea swept over him as he looked down into a mire of decayed faces, limbs and other body parts, all immediately recognisable as such. He pushed himself back up and tripped and stumbled further towards the approaching bodies on the other side of the ditch. Bile began to rise in his throat and he started to salivate – he knew he was going to vomit, but he also knew he had to stop himself at all costs. He turned back around to look for help and another searing jet of fire lit up the stormy sky above him. A fraction of a second later a shell dropped short of its intended target and landed just yards away, exploding instantly and showering the troops with mud, shrapnel and dribbles of flesh. The soldier was knocked to the ground again, and this time he panicked and started to scramble back away from the front line. He was aware of a sudden stabbing, burning pain in his back, but he ignored it and kept moving. Once steady on his feet again he reached over his shoulder and rubbed at the part of his neck which hurt the most. To his horror, he could feel a jagged shard of metal which had ripped through his suit and pierced his skin. He brought his hand back around and saw that it was glistening with blood. His suit had been compromised. Panicking, he lifted his weapon and turned back to face the dead. Just for a moment longer – no more than a few seconds – the adrenalin numbed the pain and kept him fighting.

Aware that a gap had opened up in the attacking line to his side, Ellis looked around. The wounded soldier next to him continued to fire into the swarming bodies until the infection took hold, but as he emptied another round into the crowd the inside of his throat began to swell, then it started to bleed. Knowing he was dying, but not knowing why, the soldier slowly turned on the spot, desperate for help. Frozen in position by a spontaneous nervous reaction, his finger remained on the trigger of his rifle, releasing a continuous burst of bullets. Ellis was the first of eight soldiers to drop, shot through the abdomen and neck.

The sounds of battle were muffled, down here on the ground. Though he was weighed down by his breathing apparatus and other equipment, still Ellis managed to roll over onto his back in the mud. He looked up into the dark grey sky above his head and waited. The heavy rain clattered down on his facemask, drowning out all other noise. He was aware of sudden, frantic movement all around him, and then complete and utter darkness. He felt the crowd of emaciated bodies crawling over him as they marched towards the base.

'Listen,' Cooper said as he stood by the transports next to Michael and Bernard.

'What?' Bernard nervously demanded.

'Something's happening.'

The men stood in silence, listening to the noises reverberating all around them, amplified by the vastness of the hangar.

'What?' Bernard asked again.

'Can't you hear it?'

'Hear what?' Michael demanded, feeling increasingly uneasy.

'Just listen . . .'

Michael did as Cooper said, and now it gradually became clear: there had been a subtle change to the sounds of battle drifting into the bunker from outside. Where before there had been the constant pounding of gunfire and the mortar explosions, now he could hear screams and shouts over the relentless tumult. Everything suddenly sounded desperately frantic, uncoordinated, as if all order was steadily disappearing. He looked up the ramp towards the entrance door and saw that while some of the troops who had been left behind to guard the bunker were edging forward, others were beginning to shuffle back.

'They've got no idea how many bodies are out there, have they?' Michael said anxiously. 'You tried to tell them, didn't you? Christ, there must be thousands of corpses for every soldier.'

'It'll be all right, won't it, Cooper?' Bernard asked, though he already knew the answer to his question.

Cooper ran the length of the hangar and up the entrance ramp until he was almost level with the soldiers left to guard the base. He looked out into the darkness: the frequent flashes of brilliant light from the shells provided more than enough illumination for him to work out what was happening outside. He was an experienced soldier, and he'd been involved in enough operations to know when an army's tactics were working and when they were not. He could see at least two areas ahead of him where the bodies were now between the soldiers and the base. The creatures had somehow managed to work their way through the lines of troops. The dead hordes were relentless and emotionless, and they had managed to force their way past unexpectedly isolated pockets of men and women, who were surrounded and swallowed up by the decaying masses. It was a horrific, nightmarish scene, and for a moment it transfixed Cooper, until the headlamps of the personnel carrier in the near distance caught his eye and shook him out of his daze. The vehicle was powering back towards the bunker, its headlights jerking up and down as the driver forced the massive vehicle over the uneven ground at speed. Frantic live soldiers and dead bodies occasionally crisscrossed in its path, and both were obliterated as it raced back to the safety of the base.

The corpses were close – too bloody close.

'What can you see?' Michael shouted from the bottom of the ramp. Cooper didn't answer, but continued to survey the mayhem outside. Incredibly, the balance of power on the battlefield seemed to be shifting; the longer he watched, the more chaotic and disorganised the soldiers were becoming. Three freshly opened gaps in their lines became four, then five, then more. As the troop-carrier thundered past them, the individual troopers began deviating from their orders, falling out of formation and running for cover, firing wildly at anything which moved. And then, high in the air over all of the madness, a single orange flare appeared in the sky. It hung above the carnage, lighting up the cloud base and bathing everything below in a strong, eerily beautiful light. Cooper forced himself to get back down to the others.

The flare was the signal to retreat.

'They're coming back,' Cooper yelled as he sprinted. He'd barely finished speaking when the personnel carrier crashed back into the base, careering out of the darkness and skidding down the incline, out of control. Michael and Bernard dived for cover in opposite directions as the heavy machine ploughed along the length of the hangar and then collided with the front of their police van, sending it spinning around through a quarter-turn and shunting it hard against the wall. Michael ran to help those who had been waiting inside the vehicle, completely unaware of what was happening and unable to protect themselves from the sudden violent impact. He could hear them screaming in confusion and pain as he yanked the doors open. One of them – an elderly man whose name he could never remember – was dead, his bloodied face smashed against one of the windows.

'What the hell do we do now?' he yelled to Cooper as he pulled the remaining survivors out. Cooper ran towards the personnel carrier. Most of the soldiers who had been inside had already fled towards the decontamination chamber and were hammering on the door to be let back inside.

'Get them in here.'

As Michael ushered the shell-shocked civilians towards the military vehicle, the first of the foot soldiers began to return to the base, stumbling down the ramp, still firing indiscriminately into the darkness behind them. Seconds later they were followed by the first wave of dead bodies.

There was a sudden loud crash and a flash of frantic movement, and Cooper looked up to see one of the Jeeps had crashed into the side of the entrance door. The soldier who'd been behind the wheel was now limping down the ramp, but he barely made it halfway down the slope before he was overcome by advancing bodies, their speed increased by the incline.

'We've got to get out of here now,' Cooper said to Michael. 'If they can't get that door closed, then in a couple of minutes this place will be full of those fucking things. We can't afford to wait.'

'Go!' Michael screamed at Donna and Steve Armitage, who was behind the wheel of the prison truck. The noise in the cavernous room was deafening, and at first neither of them reacted. Michael gestured frantically towards the bunker doors until Steve finally acknowledged him and turned on the engine. The prison truck began to pull forward and he started steering the clumsy vehicle around the stockpiled military equipment. Donna, who'd never driven the motorhome before, followed nervously.

As the two vehicles moved up towards the entrance, many more soldiers and bodies swarmed back down into the base. Individually, the corpses were slow and largely uncoordinated, like ants against the vast concrete vista, but together their collective movement down the steep incline gave the impression of speed and control. Gunfire continued to ring out, and as more soldiers forced their way back inside, the fighting intensified, until the hangar was filled with more deadly gunfire and the occasional flashes of barely controlled flame.

Emma searched desperately from the front of the motorhome, hoping to catch sight of Michael as they drove deeper into the confusion. Next to her, Donna tried to keep calm as she struggled to control the vehicle. She followed the prison truck, concentrating on staying close to his taillights, and matching every move Steve made. She glanced into her side-mirror, but all she could see was frantic movement at the back of the personnel carrier – and, in the midst of it all, Bernard Heath, struggling to climb inside. She watched helplessly as he was brought down by gunfire, a stray round almost cutting him in half. A torrent of bullets thudded into his right leg, his crotch, his abdomen and his shoulder. By the time he hit the ground he was dead.

'Oh God,' she said, her eyes stinging with tears, 'Bernard's gone down.'

'What?' Emma demanded, spinning around and trying to get a clear view through the back of the motorhome. She caught a glimpse of his body on the ground before another surge of corpses blocked her view. Where the hell was Michael?

Out of sight of the motorhome, Michael pulled the door at the back of the personnel carrier shut.

'Move!' he yelled. He lurched forward and then fell back into a seat as the soldier driving the transport turned it around and pulled away.

'Put your fucking foot down,' Cooper ordered. The driver didn't argue, quickly overtaking both the motorhome and the prison truck and powering up the access ramp. Countless staggering shapes – both living and dead – were dragged beneath its huge wheels.

'Which way?' the nervous trooper stammered through his cumbersome facemask. Bright electric light was replaced by comparative darkness as they drove out into the open. Intense battles were still raging on all sides as soldiers fought to get back into the bunker. The gunfights provided some illumination, but not nearly enough for Cooper to be able to make sense of what was happening around them. He knew that the main track away from the bunker was blocked by the truck the survivors had crashed when they'd first arrived there weeks earlier, so now he needed to find another route away from there. The vehicle he was in would be able to cope with any terrain, no matter how rough or uneven, but the prison truck and the motorhome following behind would both struggle with anything more than the gentlest of gradients. Resigned to the fact that conditions would probably be as bad whichever direction they chose, he made a snap decision.

'Follow the line of the valley,' he ordered, choosing what he thought would be the most level route. He had to shout to make himself heard over the noise of the engine and the relentless *thud, thud, thud* of the endless stream of bodies which launched themselves pointlessly at the metal sides of the personnel carrier. 'Just keep going straight; we're bound to pick up a road or a track at some point,' he added.

Driving slowly through the bloody mayhem and devastation which continued to unfold all around them, the three vehicles disappeared into the darkness.

The hangar was filled with bodies. Individual soldiers still managed to offer a degree of resistance, but their ammunition – and their will to fight – was almost completely gone. Terrified and exhausted, several disorientated men had ripped off their face-masks in desperation and were almost immediately killed by the infection. Others were brought down by friendly fire, but more still were ripped apart by the surging crowds of crazed corpses, huge numbers of them launching themselves at each of the troopers.

The senior officer left below ground ordered the decontamination chambers to be locked and sealed. One hundred and seventeen troops were buried underground. Almost double that number remained trapped in the hangar and out on the surface, some still fighting, the majority dead or dying.

8

Michael was thrown from side to side as he crawled the length of the personnel carrier to get to Cooper as the vehicle clattered across the uneven ground.

'So what the hell do we do now?' he demanded, knowing full well that his question was a pointless one.

Cooper had already dragged himself into the front of the vehicle and was sitting alongside two protective-suited soldiers. There were another two troopers sitting in the back with Michael, and three other survivors. Obviously the soldiers had been out fighting on the battlefield for some time, and the survivors gave them as wide a berth as was possible in the close confines of the military vehicle, because their survival suits were dripping in mud, blood and stinking gore.

Cooper didn't even bother trying to answer Michael.

Frustrated, Michael asked another question. 'Do we just keep going all fucking night?' he cursed, holding on to the back of Cooper's seat as the armoured vehicle suddenly lurched down an unexpected incline. He looked out through the blood-splattered windscreen and saw that the driver's view was frighteningly limited. 'There's less than half a tank of fuel in the motorhome,' he continued nervously, 'so we can't keep going indefinitely.'

When Cooper still didn't acknowledge him he slumped back angrily in the nearest seat, then turned to look out of the back of the vehicle. Behind them the devastating and ultimately pointless battle continued to rage. Frequent explosions and brilliant flashes filled the dead world with light for a fraction of a second at a time. The personnel carrier dipped awkwardly to one side as the ground over which they drove became increasingly rough. Following close behind was the prison truck and, further back still, Michael was able to see the lights of the motorhome as it struggled to keep up. He wished he was with Emma. How had this been allowed to happen? How had everything fallen apart so quickly? A couple of hours ago the bunker door had still been sealed and they'd been relatively safe and protected. Now people had died – and for what? And they were exposed and vulnerable once more, running without direction again. He couldn't stop thinking about Bernard. He pictured him now, lying dead on the hangar floor, surrounded by scores of bodies, and soldiers still trying to fight. Christ, he hoped Bernard had died quickly. He hoped he wasn't suffering. Imagine lying helplessly in the middle of that nightmare, unable to move and slowly bleeding to death, just waiting for it all to be over . . .

'We're bound to hit a road at some point,' Cooper finally said, snatching Michael back from his increasingly dark thoughts, bringing him back to reality. 'Then we'll stop and try and work out where we are.'

'Don't be stupid, how can we stop? If we stop then we're going to—'

'If we're sensible we can afford to stop for a little while,' Cooper interrupted, his voice slightly louder – just enough to silence Michael's outburst. 'We'll stop and regroup and decide what to do next. If we're quick there won't be time for any more than just a few bodies to find us.'

Michael grunted, to show he'd heard and understood, but in truth he'd stopped listening. All he was interested in was Emma, and nothing else mattered. He watched the constant movement all around them as bodies turned and traipsed through the night after the ragtag convoy.

In the prison truck Steve Armitage skilfully steered along the furrowed tracks the military vehicle in front of him was leaving in the mire. At his side was Phil Croft, terrified and shaking with nerves, but still alert, watching the world outside like a hawk. In the back of the truck more survivors sat huddled in the darkness together, not knowing where they were now, or where they were going, each one of them racked with an uncomfortably familiar sense of disorientation and hopelessness.

More than fifty yards behind the truck, Donna groaned with effort as she struggled to keep control of the motorhome. It was an old, unresponsive vehicle which gave a rough ride on a level road at the best of times, never mind in these treacherous conditions. Inside the vehicle no one spoke. A far more ordinary machine than the two vehicles it followed, its wide windows afforded those survivors crammed in the back a clear view of the dead world around them, a view which many of them would have preferred not to have seen. Now more than a mile from the bunker, there were still vast crowds of bodies swarming across the land all around them. Donna did what she could, but the ride was increasingly unsteady. The motorhome hadn't been built to cope with churned mud, let alone the wildly uneven terrain they were traversing. The steering was heavy and the vehicle's rear end constantly threatened to slide out of control. In the back no one dared speak for fear of distracting their already nervous driver.

Emma glanced up at the outline of a house nestled amongst the trees on the brow of a low hill. Even from a distance she could see movement, and she knew it had been overrun. It reminded her of Penn Farm, and she felt as terrified and helpless now as she had when she and Michael had lost the farmhouse. Her dark thoughts were interrupted when they stopped moving suddenly.

'What's wrong?'

Donna gestured up ahead and Emma saw that Cooper was outside the personnel carrier, untying a rope or chain that had been keeping a wide metal gate closed. The headlamps of the vehicles illuminated huge numbers of unsteady bodies which began to collide with the transports as they crisscrossed the scene randomly. Fortunately for Cooper, the light and noise of the engines were far more of a distraction than he was. They watched as he swung the gate open, kicked away the nearest corpse and then ran back to his vehicle.

'Should be easier from here,' Donna said quietly, her voice sounding tired and resigned. 'I don't think we'll—'

A foul-looking, withered cadaver slammed into the front of the motorhome. Donna jumped with surprise, and then leant forward and peered down as it began to batter the bodywork pointlessly with clumsy, barely coordinated hands. It was an appalling sight. In the time that the survivors had been underground, the condition of the bodies had continued to steadily deteriorate. This monstrosity, judging by the length of what remained of its lank, shoulder-length hair and its shredded clothing, had once been female. The lower part of its face was virtually indistinguishable. The hole where its mouth should have been was double normal size and its jawbone hung down, ripped away from one side of its head. Its skin was green-black and covered in ruptures where the flesh had been eaten away. The corpse's empty eyes stared unblinking into the headlights of the motorhome.

'They're moving,' Emma said, looking anywhere but at the body. Donna lifted her head and then gently accelerated, hoping that the initial movement might be enough to push the body away to the side. When it still didn't move, she jabbed her foot down hard instead and the repellent figure was carried forward several yards before being dragged down and crushed under the motor-home wheels.

Matching the route of the prison truck and personnel carrier, Donna carefully steered the motorhome through the gate and pulled out onto a narrow gravel track.

9

The convoy pushed on through the evening and into the night, following the twisting road through the darkness, not knowing where they were heading.

There were nine people in the personnel carrier, and for the most part none of them spoke. Cooper kept himself occupied by constantly watching the road ahead, scanning for bodies and searching for somewhere they could stop for a while and regroup. They had hardly anything with them – very little food or water, only a few weapons – and it was obvious that getting hold of some supplies was a priority. He'd known it was going to be like this if they'd needed to evacuate the base at speed. He'd intended stockpiling supplies in readiness, but the military had provided them with minimal rations, and had maintained such strict control over their equipment that it had been impossible for him to build up any reserves. They'd hardly had enough to survive on as it was, let alone any to save.

In the back of the vehicle Michael stared at one of the soldiers, who was leaning against the door, sobbing.

'What's your name?' he asked.

The suited figure turned and looked at him. 'Kelly Harcourt,' she replied.

Michael was surprised, although he knew he shouldn't have been. He'd assumed that under all the battlefield dirt and the shapeless protective suit, the trooper was male. Although it was dark and most of her face was hidden by her breathing apparatus, he could just make out her eyes and the bridge of her nose. She looked too young to be in uniform.

'First time you've been above ground?'

She nodded. 'They told us what it was like,' she said quietly, 'but I never expected this.'

'Believe me,' he said, 'whatever they told you, it's worse. You haven't seen anything yet.'

The conversation ended as quickly as it had begun. Michael regretted sounding so negative, but what else was he supposed to say? Lying to the soldier to try and make her feel better was pointless. Maybe he should have just shut up and said nothing? It seemed the harder he tried, the less he achieved. He and Emma had worked damn hard to survive since the first day, and for what? He thought about the places he'd been since then – the community centre in Northwich, Penn Farm, the bunker – and none had been as safe as they'd first seemed. He silently admitted to himself that he was as helpless, vulnerable and scared now as he'd been almost two months ago when the nightmare had first begun.

Was this how it was always going to be?

Progress along the debris-strewn roads was slow. The landscape through which they travelled was relentlessly bleak, the bodies the only things apart from them which still moved. Occasionally one would walk out in front of the personnel carrier, but for the most part they were slow to react to the noise and light produced by the little convoy, and didn't manage to stumble into the empty road until after the vehicles had gone.

They'd been driving for more than an hour when they reached the outskirts of a small town, where they changed direction, choosing not to risk driving straight through. They drove towards a collection of large, nondescript buildings sited just off the main road and the soldier at the wheel of the personnel carrier slowed down as they entered an overgrown retail park. When they looked deeper into the shadows they were able to make out a pub, a cinema, a couple of office blocks and several dilapidated factories, as well as shells of buildings in various stages of construction – it looked like the area had been in the middle of a large-scale regeneration project when the project managers, the architects, the backers, the bankers, the construction workers and everyone else involved in the project had died. Michael looked around the site hopefully. There didn't appear to be more than a handful of bodies around, although he knew they'd start coming before long.

He leant forward and grabbed Cooper's shoulder. 'Let's try here. Might as well.'

Cooper nodded and the driver cautiously led the convoy deeper into the estate, following a winding block-paved road which

connected a number of car parks the size of football pitches, largely empty, save for a scattering of vehicles, some crashed, others long abandoned by their dead owners. He slowed down outside the pub.

Cooper nudged his arm and suggested, 'Look – head for that place.' He gestured beyond the pub, past the cinema, towards a warehouse-sized store with metal shutters over the windows. The driver kept moving forward, swerving instinctively but unnecessarily around three lurching bodies which tripped out of the shadows. The building was in the furthest corner of the estate, sited at the top of a slight rise and bordered on its left side and along the back by a high chain-link fence. Beyond the fence were trees. As they approached, Cooper noticed a cordoned-off loading bay at the side of the building.

'Over there,' he said. 'Go through the gate.'

The driver did as instructed, accelerating up the hill and then carefully guiding the personnel carrier into the enclosed area. Still following close behind, the prison truck and the motorhome did the same. The personnel carrier came to a sudden, juddering halt and Michael, desperate to escape its confines, climbed out quickly and jogged across the loading area to the gate. Cooper appeared at his side and between them, they pulled it shut and secured it. A lone body had managed to squeeze through before the gap was closed and Cooper grabbed its neck and smashed its head repeatedly against the side of the prison truck until it stopped moving.

'Let's get everyone inside,' Michael said. 'If we get under cover quickly enough we shouldn't attract too many of them. We might even be able to spend the night here if we—'Another body rushed him from the side, grabbing hold of him with surprising strength—

He realised it was Emma just in time to stop him reacting violently.

She wrapped her arms around him, knocking him off-balance. 'I didn't know if you'd got out,' she said, barely able to contain her relief. 'I looked but I couldn't see you—'

'This is all very touching, but we don't have time for it,' Donna said disapprovingly as a lone body lethargically dragged itself up towards the gate. 'Get out of sight, for Christ's sake!'

The survivors and soldiers nervously climbed out of their respective vehicles and waited at a side entrance to the dark, silent building. Gavin Stonehouse, the highest-ranking of the four remaining soldiers, led the way in through a door which had been propped open for the last seven and a half weeks by the atrophied right leg of a dead member of staff. He held his rifle out in front of him, ready to fire, though not sure what good that would do. The group followed behind in a close but uncoordinated bunch.

They were completely silent until Jack Baxter spoke. 'We should make a bit of noise,' he said, 'just in case there's any of them in here. We should try and get them out of the shadows.'

'It's all shadows in here, Jack,' Michael said, looking around and trying to make sense of their dismal surroundings. 'I think we should give it a minute. Get everybody inside first.'

They had entered a huge and probably extensively stocked household store, and they were presently walking through the middle of a large electrical department. To their right was a bank of blank television screens; to their left a similarly lifeless display of stereo equipment.

Stonehouse stopped moving. 'So what now?'

'Get some bloody light in here for a start, I can't see a damn thing,' a nervous voice from the darkness replied, and Michael recognised it as belonging to Peter Guest, a quiet whisper of a man who generally kept himself to himself and to whom he had spoken only a handful of times.

'There's bound to be something in here we can use,' Donna said hopefully as she looked around through the gloom. She could hear something moving close by, but she wasn't sure whether it was living or dead. The longer she listened, the more she thought she could make out.

Standing just to Stonehouse's right, Phil Croft lifted his cigarette lighter and flicked it into life, the dancing orange flame burning an immediate, bright hole in the darkness. A body which had by chance stumbled perilously close, suddenly increased its speed and turned and scrambled through the shop debris towards the light. It lurched for Stonehouse, knocking him off-balance into a huge, useless TV screen which rocked precariously on its stand. Stonehouse calmly picked himself back up, shoved the corpse away on its already unsteady feet, and then lifted his rifle and shot it through the head. It dropped heavily to the ground, its face a caved-in mass of putrefied flesh and splintered bone. The gunshot echoed endlessly around the store.

'Nice one,' Donna said. 'Christ, make some more noise, why

don't you? We'd better get some damn light sorted out now because every dead body in this fucking place will be on its way over to us.'

'Did it cross your mind that there might be a reason why none of us bother carrying guns?' Jack added. 'A single shot might take one of them out, but there are thousands of the bloody things out there, and the noise you make getting rid of one will bring a hundred more sniffing around you.'

Donna began to search the nearby shelves for something to illuminate the dark building, gesturing at others to follow her lead. Kelly Harcourt, the soldier Michael had spoken to earlier, disappeared back outside and then returned with a handful of torches from the personnel carrier.

'Why the hell didn't you bring those in with you in the first place?' Donna yelled at her, snatching one of the torches.

'Give her a break, Donna,' Jack said as he took a torch and shone it around. Several circles of bright light tracked around the vast shop floor in different directions, occasionally illuminating corpses slowly lumbering towards them.

'Stay here and wait for them to come to us,' Cooper ordered.

The first body hauled itself into view, moving awkwardly and dragging one useless foot behind. All the torches were immediately focused on the creature. Its face (as much of its face as remained intact) was badly discoloured and had an unnatural, waxy sheen. Decay had eaten away much of its nose, right eye and cheek, and its few remaining yellowed teeth were visible through the largest hole in its flesh, grinding constantly. It still wore the tattered remnants of a store attendant's uniform – a blue shirt (with a collar that now appeared several sizes too big because of the body's emaciation) and a red tie. Donna found it bizarre that the body was still wearing a tie – it even had a name badge still pinned to its shirt pocket, though the name had been obscured by mould and dribbles of blood and other bodily discharges. Cooper disposed of it by swinging a fire extinguisher through the air and knocking its head from its shoulders. It collapsed to the ground as three more bodies stumbled into the light.

Half an hour was time enough for the survivors to rid themselves of the remaining corpses and dispose of them in a heap outdoors.

Many of the group then busied themselves around the building, collecting anything that might prove useful, happy just to be occupied for a while. The bodies outside hadn't materialised in the vast numbers the group had come to expect, so they took advantage of their non-appearance to raid all the edible food and drink they could from the kitchen of the pub nearby and the concessions stand in the foyer of the cinema opposite. It was mostly confectionery and cans of soft drinks, but it was better than nothing.

By the time those who had gone outside were safely back inside the store again, there were some twenty bodies gathered around the front of the building, and half as many again clattering against the fence surrounding the loading bay – still nothing like the massive numbers they were used to around the bunker.

'They're not a problem when they're like this and there's only a few of them,' Cooper explained, trying to educate Stonehouse. 'Problem is, if you're not careful, one of them will attract another, then another, and so on and so on until you've suddenly got hundreds to deal with. And there are thousands upon thousands of the fuckers out there, so keep the guns as a last resort. Softly softly, okay?'

Stonehouse sat opposite Cooper, slumped dejectedly in a chair in an office-like area of the store where he guessed customers would previously have sat with staff and applied for credit. Jack sat with them. Donna, Emma and Michael and several more of the survivors were also nearby. A short distance away, the three other soldiers sat in silence on a pile of large cushions and garishly coloured beanbags which looked like they had originally been designed for use in children's bedrooms and playrooms.

'So what happens now?' Stonehouse asked. Jack looked at him, trying to imagine how he must be feeling, trapped in his uncomfortable protective suit but knowing that if he took it off he'd almost certainly suffer a quick and painful death. Jack thought he might have been able to handle it himself for a few hours, maybe even a couple of days at a push, but the four soldiers now travelling with them would have to exist like this indefinitely. He didn't know how they'd be able to eat or drink, or do anything else – surely it would only be a matter of time before they were forced to take off their suits? Whether they realised it or not (and he was pretty sure they did), they were just waiting to die. They were just prolonging the inevitable.

'We should stop here for as long as it's safe,' Cooper replied, finally answering the soldier's question, 'then see what we've got and work out what we need . . .'

'Then what?'

'We move on, I guess.'

'Where to?'

'How the hell am I supposed to know?'

'Problem is,' Jack said, 'nowhere's safe any more. Christ, you lot with all your bloody guns and your tanks and everything else – you couldn't look after yourselves, could you? What hope do you think *we've* got?'

Cooper looked up and shook his head to silence him. 'Come on, Jack, we've talked about this a hundred bloody times already,' he said before turning back to face Stonehouse again. 'The bodies are rotting. They're more controlled than they were before, but the fact is they're still decaying. They'll reach a point before too long when they'll just not be able to function.'

'And how long's that going to be?'

'A few more months, I guess.'

'*Months?* Fucking hell, are we supposed to sit here like this for a few months?'

'You might have to – could you last that long?'

'I doubt it. Anyway, getting rid of the bodies won't get rid of the germ. The air's still going to be full of shit we can't breathe.'

'So what are you going to do?'

'Doesn't look like we've got any option but to try and get back to the base,' Stonehouse replied. 'Whatever happens, we're dead if we stop out here. Might as well try and get back if we can.'

'You've got nothing to lose,' Jack said quietly.

'Seems to me everything's lost already.'

10

Clare's watch said it was a quarter to three. The cavernous store was echoey and cold. She was lying restlessly on the floor next to Donna on a dusty mattress they'd dragged over from the furniture department hours earlier. She was physically exhausted but unable to sleep. She raised herself up onto her elbows and looked around. Perhaps as many as half of the others were awake too.

Clare needed to relax, but she couldn't get comfortable. Her guts were twisting with sudden waves of cramp – it was probably just nerves, she told herself, either that or the overdose of sugary food she'd had earlier. Whatever the reason, even the thought of eating now made her want to vomit. She'd had diarrhoea an hour ago – Christ, that had been humiliating. She'd sat on a dried-out toilet pan in the furthest corner of the building and had cried with the discomfort and degradation. She was sure that everyone had heard her. Even now after living rough for weeks and going without even the most basic of human necessities, sometimes it was still too much for her. She was a teenage girl, and despite what had happened to the rest of the world, her body had continued to develop as it would normally have been expected to – she'd started her first period just a few days ago. Donna had helped her and had reassured her as much as she could, but it hadn't been easy. Donna was struggling too. Everyone was struggling.

Clare lay back down again and looked up at the high ceiling, studying the metal girders supporting the roof and the lights. She wished they could switch them on. They'd been living in almost constant darkness for weeks now.

Her eyes were heavy, but she still couldn't sleep. She knew that as soon as day broke they'd be up and out again, and she didn't know when they'd next be able to stop. She didn't know if she'd have enough strength to be able to make it if she didn't get some rest. It was hard enough just keeping going when they didn't know where they were or what they were going to do or . . .

She could hear something.

She sat up and listened. In the distance she could definitely hear a noise: a faint, mechanical sound. More soldiers escaped from the bunker, perhaps? The world was otherwise so completely silent that this new and unexpected noise seemed eerily directionless. Was she imagining it? Was it just her tired mind playing cruel tricks, or maybe it was something else hiding inside this unfamiliar building?

It was getting louder.

She realised she wasn't the only one who'd heard it. Other people were sitting up now. She leant across and shook Donna.

'What?' Donna grumbled lethargically before suddenly remembering where she was and jumping up fast, worried that something was wrong. 'What's the matter?'

'Listen.'

The noise was definitely moving closer now. It sounded like an engine, but not anything she could recognise. It continued to steadily increase in volume and then gradually become clear: a constant chopping, thumping sound over the engine groan.

Donna thought she knew what she was hearing, but she refused to believe it . . .

It was getting louder and louder now, until the whole building felt like it was shaking with the deafening sound.

Michael got up and ran to the front of the warehouse, pressing his face against the glass, trying to look through the holes in the security grille. High above the store, from out of nowhere it seemed, a brilliant shaft of bright white light suddenly shone down. It swooped along the length of the industrial estate several times and then stopped, illuminating the loading bay at the side of the store. It took a few seconds for the reality of the situation to sink in.

There was a helicopter hovering directly overhead.

'Is this one of yours?' Jack asked Stonehouse.

'Nothing to do with us,' he answered.

Cooper grabbed one of the soldiers' rifles and disappeared out through the side door they'd originally used to enter the building. Stonehouse and Jack followed him out into the loading bay and ducked down next to him beside the prison truck, all of them shielding their eyes from the bright light and whipping wind. The pilot of the helicopter skilfully lowered the machine and set it down in the space between the three vehicles. Cooper anxiously watched every foot of its slow descent.

The helicopter's engine and its lights were extinguished. The swirling rotor blades began to slow and as the noise faded away, the all-too-familiar sound of bodies clattering against the wire mesh fence immediately filled the silence.

'Who the hell is this?' Jack asked, but before anyone could answer, the doors on either side of the helicopter cabin opened and two people jumped down onto the tarmac, both of them crouching down to miss the still-spinning blades. A well-built man and a smaller, more rotund woman moved until they stood together in front of the aircraft. They looked around for signs of life.

'Hello,' the man called out, 'anyone here?'

His calls provoked a sudden, intense reaction from the crowd of corpses on the other side of the fence, but nothing else. After a few seconds spent silently weighing up the options, Cooper slowly stood up and stepped out of the shadows. He still held the soldier's rifle tightly in his hands, and made sure it was clearly visible, but he kept the barrel very obviously pointed down towards the ground.

'Over here,' he shouted, and the strange man and woman turned and walked towards him. To his relief they looked relatively normal: scruffily dressed, unarmed civilians. 'Where the hell did you pair come from?' he asked.

'Just outside Bigginford,' the man replied. 'I'm Richard Lawrence. This is Karen Chase.'

'Everything all right, Cooper?' Michael asked, suddenly appearing outside, flanked by a soldier and two others. A further crowd of people were stood in the doorway just behind them, watching intently. Cooper ignored them all and moved closer to the new arrivals.

'How the hell did you find us? We've only been here for a few hours—'

'Not hard from up there,' Richard answered, nodding back towards the helicopter. He brushed his long, windswept grey hair out of his face so that he could clearly see Cooper. 'We saw the crowds earlier, so we knew something was happening around here,' he continued, referring to the battle at the bunker. 'So we've been on the lookout for anyone trying to get away. And you lot stick out like a sore thumb.'

'Why?'

'I've been flying helicopters for years,' he explained. 'You get used to how things should look from up there. It's easy to spot things that are out of the ordinary, especially when everything else is so fucked-up. You don't often get vehicles like the ones you've got here parked around the back of places like this. Not exactly delivery trucks, are they?'

He had a point, Cooper silently admitted.

'How many people have you got here?' Karen asked, looking at the crowd by the door.

'Don't know exactly yet,' Cooper replied. 'Between thirty and forty.'

'We should talk inside,' Michael suggested, already walking back towards the door, acutely aware of the effect the helicopter's arrival had had on the steadily increasing mass of bodies nearby. The strangers followed him inside and by the time they reached the main area where the rest of the group had been camped, just about everyone was up and awake and aware of what had happened. Nervous, subdued conversations were immediately silenced as the two unfamiliar figures entered the store. Suddenly the centre of attention, Richard and Karen found themselves standing in the middle of the group, nodding acknowledgments to the few faces they were able to make out in the half light.

'This is Richard Lawrence and Karen Chase,' Cooper announced to the others. 'They've come from Bigginford.'

'That's miles away,' Jack said quietly.

'They've got a bloody helicopter, you idiot,' Croft sighed, frustrated by his stupid comment.

The room was suddenly silent in hushed expectation. No one spoke, and yet each person had countless questions to ask.

Donna cleared her throat. 'So do you spend all your time flying around in the middle of the night looking for survivors?' The tone of her voice was unexpectedly abrasive, clearly lacking in trust.

'Not usually,' Karen replied, matching her mistrust.

'So how did you know where to find us?'

'We've known for some time that there was something going on around here.'

'But we didn't know what,' Richard continued, playing with his short white-tinged beard as he spoke. 'All we could see from up there was a few thousand bodies. We knew something had to be attracting them, but we didn't know what it was.'

'So where were you?' Karen asked.

'Underground,' Jack said.

'I flew over this area a couple of days ago and it was pretty bloody obvious that something was going on. There was a hell of a lot of smoke around, but I couldn't see what was happening. We came back again and saw the fighting. We thought that some of you might have got away so we've spent the last couple of hours flying around trying to find you.'

For a moment no one spoke, everyone considering the explanation they'd just heard. It sounded feasible. They didn't have any reason not to believe what they'd been told.

'So how did you end up with a helicopter?' Emma asked.

'I used to fly for a living,' Richard told her. 'I used to work for local radio, those "eye in the sky" traffic broadcasts they used to do – I was up there when this all kicked off. We were in the middle of a broadcast and it got the reporter. Beautiful girl, she was. Died in the seat next to me . . .'

'So are there many of you?'

'Not as many as you, by the look of things,' Karen replied. 'There are just over twenty of us, but we're split at the moment.'

'Split?'

'We've been based at Monkton Airfield since this all started, but we're getting ready to move on.'

'So where are you going?'

'You probably know what it's like from your own experiences,' Richard said, taking up the story, 'you make a damn sound out in the open these days and you'll find yourselves surrounded by those bloody things out there before you know what's happening. What with the helicopter and the plane—'

'You've got a *plane* too?' Jack interrupted, amazed.

'Only a small one. Anyway, with the noise we've been making

we've been surrounded by thousands of them since we first got to the airfield.'

'So where are you planning to go?' Michael asked, repeating the question. 'Surely it's going to be just as bad wherever you end up?'

'We've found an island,' Karen said.

'An island?' Emma gasped, her mind immediately filled with images of sun-drenched beaches and endless yellow-gold sand.

'It's just off the northeast coast,' Karen explained. 'It's cold, grey and miserable, and there's hardly anything there, but it's a hell of a lot safer than anywhere on the mainland.'

'How big is it?' Michael asked quickly. 'What kind of facilities have you got there? Are there many buildings or do you—?'

'It's early days yet,' Karen said, holding up her hand to stop his barrage of questions. 'We spent a lot of time looking for the right location, but we do finally think we've found it. It's a little place called Cormansey. It's about a mile and a half long and a mile wide. There were about five hundred people living there originally. There's one small village – that's where most of them lived – and a few houses and cottages dotted all around the place. There's an airstrip on the far side of the island and—'

'What about bodies?' Michael wondered, desperately trying to keep his sudden excitement under control.

Richard continued. 'We're planning on culling what's left of the local population. We're trying to fly a few people over each day to gradually get the place sorted out. We've only known about it for a few days. I flew three people over yesterday morning and three more today. That's how I came to be flying over this place. We've sent some of our strongest people over there, and they're going to work their way down the length of the island, getting rid of the dead. Like Karen says, we think there were only a few hundred people there originally and from what we've seen it looks like a lot of them are still lying face-down on the ground. As far as we can tell there aren't any indigenous survivors, so that just leaves us with a couple of hundred corpses to get rid of and a bloody big clean-up operation.'

Jack stared at the pilot in awe. Like everyone else around him, he was slowly beginning to come to terms with the implications of what he was hearing. Imagine being somewhere where they were free to move, and where there were no bodies anywhere. Imagine being somewhere where they could make as much noise as they damn well pleased without fear of the repercussions. It sounded too good to be true. Perhaps it was.

'Once we've got enough people over there we'll start moving into the village,' Richard continued. 'We're planning to clear it, building by building, until we've got rid of every last trace of the dead.'

'What about power and water?' Croft asked, his mind racing.

'Come on, Phil,' Donna said pessimistically, 'don't get ahead of yourself. How do we know any of this is true?'

'They turned up here in a bloody helicopter, Donna,' Cooper said, annoyed by her attitude. 'Why should they lie? It might not all be as easy as it sounds, though.'

'We never said it was going to be easy,' Richard said. 'It's still early days, and we've got a lot to do, but there's no reason why we can't make this work. And who knows, in the future we might be able to get fuel and power supplies working again.'

The future, Michael thought to himself. Bloody hell, these two survivors who had suddenly appeared from the sky were in a strong enough position that they could actually allow themselves the luxury of stopping to think about the future. Okay, so they clearly still had a huge amount of work ahead of them, and the danger they faced was far from over, but at least they could sense an end to it. They could see the direction that the rest of their lives might possibly take. In comparison, he didn't know which way he was going to run or what he was going to have to face in the morning.

The conversation was repeated over and again as more previously silent survivors suddenly found their voices and started asking more and more questions of the new arrivals. As those questions were patiently answered the clear, rational details of the plan being presented became increasingly apparent. Individually, people started to understand the potential importance of what they were hearing.

In a brief pause, a single unexpected question came.

'Do you know what happened?' a woman asked, her voice sounding quiet, almost unsure whether she should have asked that.

Every other conversation stopped.

'Do you?' Richard asked the group rhetorically. The room had become deathly silent. 'What about you?' he asked again, this time looking directly at Stonehouse and the other three suited soldiers grouped around him. 'You must have known something.'

'We weren't told anything,' Cooper replied for him.

'You're military too?'

'I was.'

Richard looked into space, and thought carefully before he spoke again. 'Look, I can tell you what I've been told, but I can't tell you if it's right or wrong.'

'How can he possibly know anything?' Donna demanded angrily. 'There's no one left who could have told him.'

'How can you know that for sure?' Croft said, trying to placate her.

'There's just no way,' Donna said, looking at the helicopter pilot and pointing her finger at him accusingly. 'You can't know . . . you just *can't*.'

'Like I said,' Richard continued, unfazed, 'I can tell you what I've seen and heard and you can choose whether or not to believe me or forget it. It makes no difference to me what you think. My gut feeling is that what I've heard is right, but that doesn't necessarily mean it is.'

'Just stop all this bullshit and tell us!' Peter Guest shouted. His angry outburst was completely out of character for such a normally withdrawn man.

As Michael waited to hear more, he asked himself whether he really wanted to listen to what Richard was about to say. What possible difference would it make? How would knowing what had happened change anything now? It might make him angrier. It might make the situation worse. It might even affect his relationship with Emma, although he couldn't quite see how. No, regardless of what might or might not happen, he knew that he had no choice but to listen to Richard Lawrence. He wanted to know why his world had been turned upside down so quickly and so cruelly, why everyone he'd known had been killed in a single day, and why his life had become nothing but a relentless, exhausting struggle.

Richard cleared his throat, sensing the group's collective unease.

He looked around the dark room, staring in turn at each of the faces he could see.

'You really want to know what did this?' he asked. Silence. 'Then I'll tell you what I've been told.'

11

Richard Lawrence sat down on the edge of a counter and started to talk. 'I was hiding about a week after it started. I was with another bloke, Carver, and we'd shut ourselves away in the ruins of a castle – sounds impressive, but it wasn't, trust me: it was just a gatehouse, a couple of towers and a few sections of crumbling wall in a grassy field, but it had a moat that was still half-full of water and we reckoned that would be enough to keep pretty much everything out. We blocked the drawbridge and used the helicopter to get in and out, landing it in what was left of the main courtyard and living, sleeping and eating in a little wooden gift shop – well, it was more like a shed than anything else.

'We were still flying the old helicopter I'd used for work, but we were getting low on fuel, so we either needed to find somewhere to fill it up, or we had to get ourselves another aircraft. On the tenth day we ended up flying low over a couple of army bases and government buildings, trying to spot any decent equipment we could take. We didn't see anyone at the first base, and there were just a handful of soldiers in suits and breathing masks at the second. There were plenty of bodies around, though. I guessed that some of the military knew what had happened, but it looked like hardly any of them had managed to get to shelter in time.

'You'd have thought we'd have picked up a load of survivors while we were out there because of the noise we made, but we hardly found anyone – I still don't know whether that was because there just wasn't anyone left, or because they were too afraid to let us know where they were when they heard us.

'Anyway, this one afternoon we were flying over the motorway, going south towards Tyneham, when Carver spotted a car moving in the distance. We followed it, and when the driver clocked us he pulled over and stopped in a service station car park. As we got out of the helicopter, the driver started calling us over – he's a real awkward, gangly-looking lad in his late teens. He told us his name was Martin Smith – he was really nervous and anxious. I reckoned we were probably the first people he'd seen since it happened. He kept bursting into tears, and there were bodies starting to appear all around us, but he wasn't even looking at them. It was like he was thinking about something else entirely.

'So Carver kept the bodies at bay while I tried and calm him down. "She knows what happened," he was saying as I walked up to him, "she might be able to help. She might be able to do something!" He was really emotional.

'By this point I was thinking that the kid'd lost his mind, and that's perfectly understandable given the circumstances because we've all come close to losing it recently, haven't we? So now he was pointing into his car, and when I looked inside, lying across the back seat was a woman in a protective suit, not like yours' – and he pointed at Kelly Harcourt – 'though it had a facemask and everything, but it wasn't military-issue. It looked cleaner, less practical and more scientific than anything the British Army would have. I opened the car door and leaned inside, but the woman didn't move. When I touched her shoulder she opened her eyes for a second, and then let them flicker shut again. I could see that she was in a really bad way. Her face was thin and white, and it was obvious that she hadn't eaten or had anything to drink since it all kicked off. She smelled just about as bad as the bodies, and the back of her suit was all soiled. I tried to talk to her, but I didn't get any response; I couldn't even get her to open her eyes again and look at me.

'Then Carver shouted over to me, because there were more bodies around than he felt comfortable with, and so, being as careful as I could, I picked her up and took her into the service station. Carver and the boy, Martin, followed me inside. We took a chance and left the helicopter, knowing that we'd fight our way back out to it if we had to.

'I put the woman down on a plastic bench in this little burger bar.' He winced, and with a grimace said, 'The place absolutely stank of rotting food and rotting bodies. Carver had a quick look around for supplies while we were there, but there was nothing worth having.

'So I sat down with the kid next to the woman, making sure we're out of sight of the windows, and I asked him who she is and he told me her name is Sylvia Plant. I asked him how he came to be with her, and at last he started to calm down a little as he told me his story. She was a friend of his parents, and she worked in the monitoring centre at this place called Camber, which was about thirty miles away from where we were sitting. She used to work with his dad a few years back, but he hadn't seen her for a long time, not since his dad retired. I know the place he was talking about: it's one of those huge, featureless buildings where lots of people used to work but no one ever talked about what they did.

'So I started thinking maybe he was going to tell me this woman was responsible for everything that's happened, but he didn't; he told me that she found him about three or four days earlier – she'd been driving around since it started looking for survivors – but he said she was sick then, because she hadn't eaten, and she'd been getting progressively worse ever since. I started to press him, getting hard with him, because I really wanted to know what was going on, and I still thought he might know.

'So the boy told me he'd asked the woman that – if she knew what was going on – and she told him that she did – she told him that she'd been cleaning a lab when it happened, and that was why she was wearing the suit, and why she was still alive. Everyone else around her had been caught and killed. She'd told him she'd walked around the building for hours looking for help, but she hadn't found anyone, though she'd used security passes belonging to dead colleagues to get into the parts of the building where she'd never been able to go before, to check if anyone was still alive. That was how she had been able to piece together what had happened, from what she'd seen. She told Martin that this was all caused by something she'd first heard rumours about years ago – there'd been stories doing the rounds for almost as long as she'd worked at Camber.

'So: do you remember the Star Wars project?'

Most people looked blank at this apparent non-sequitur, but a couple nodded, and he continued, 'Back in the eighties, before the end of the Cold War, there was a lot of noise made about this plan to build a shield to protect countries from nuclear attack. I don't know if it ever got off the ground, but according to this woman, when terrorists really started hitting their targets with force, those same countries started working on ways to protect themselves from the threat of attack by other less conventional means. She said that they wanted to create an artificial germ which would latch onto chemicals or poisons in the air and neutralise them; that was the plan, at any rate. She found out that the development had been going on for some time, and she also found out that a version of this "super-germ" had been created, and that it was thought to be stable. It was intelligent and self-replicating and, because of increased terrorist threats, it had already been released. Apparently that had happened a couple of years ago, and we've all been breathing the germ in every day since then.

'Anyway, the woman – Sylvia Plant – told Martin that finally there had been a chemical attack, and that rang true because I remembered hearing something on the news just before this all started; there was a gas attack on an airport terminal in Canada. Sylvia told Martin the reports were of huge numbers of deaths in the surrounding areas, way out of line for the amount of poison that was supposed to have been released, so it seemed like the germ had tried to do its job and neutralise the attack, but it mutated as it did it; whatever happened, it set off a chain reaction that spread. It was the mutated germ that did all of this. It changed to try and protect us, and instead it became something that killed just about everyone. Bloody ironic, isn't it?

'Martin told me that the woman pieced all this together from information she found – she saw the records confirming that communications had been lost with most of Canada, and then with other countries too. The information stopped coming altogether pretty soon after that.

'You can call it bullshit if you like and dismiss everything I've just told you, but it's the only explanation I've heard so far that makes any kind of sense. We can all probably come up with a hundred other reasons why all of this might have happened, but this is the only version that has any evidence to support it. Martin wasn't lying to me – he had no reason to – and Sylvia Plant had no reason to lie to him either. And if she really was from the monitoring centre at Camber, then she would have had access to all kinds of confidential information. I believe what I heard: that everything kicked off so quickly because the germ was already there, and as the mutation spread, so everyone died around us. As for why the corpses got up and started to move – the germ was designed to prevent death, so maybe it did its job after all? Maybe it destroyed the bodies, but spared the brain. But whatever actually happened, it doesn't matter now.

'We sat there with the pair of them for a few hours, until it was dark, then we pushed our way through the bodies back to the helicopter and flew back to base. Sylvia Plant was dead by the following afternoon. Martin Smith is still with us.'

'Rubbish,' Phil Croft said, disturbing the heavy silence which had descended upon the already quiet room. 'Utter bollocks.'

'Might be,' Richard said. 'Doesn't really matter, does it?' He'd been speaking for a long time now, and sounded exhausted.

'And is that it?' Donna said. 'Is that all you've got to tell us?'

'What else do you want me to say? I've told you everything I know. What you do with the information is up to you.'

He stood up, stretched, and walked back towards the helicopter to fetch himself some food.

12

'Do you believe him?' Emma asked, looking straight into Michael's eyes.

'I believe he's telling us the truth about what happened with this guy Martin Smith,' he answered, 'but whether I believe the rest of the story or not is a different matter.'

'There's no reason he'd make it up.'

'True.'

'I think I remember hearing about something happening in Canada. I think it was probably the last thing I saw on the television.'

'Me too, but that doesn't mean—'

'And I'm sure I've heard about that place at Camber too – and there had to be a good reason for the woman to be wearing a protective suit.'

'Also true,' Michael said, struggling to sound interested.

'Bit of a coincidence that they managed to find Martin Smith though, and that he found the woman, or the woman found him.'

'Suppose so, but it's as much a coincidence that we were all in here together tonight, isn't it? It's only because of coincidence that Richard Lawrence found us – and even that you and I came across each other.'

Emma yawned and stretched her arms up into the cold early morning air.

'Ironic, isn't it?' she said. 'If it is all true, I mean. Something originally put there to try and protect us ends up doing all this damage.'

'Sounds about right for this fucked-up planet. Anyway, there's no point going on about it. We can't prove or disprove it, and even if we could, it doesn't make any difference. What's happened has happened, and that's all there is to it. There's nothing any of us can do about it now.'

'I know.'

'It reminds me of something my dad used to say,' Michael said, smiling wryly and allowing himself to reminisce for the briefest of moments. 'When things weren't going his way at work he'd get really wound up, and sometimes we'd go for a pint together and try to put the world to rights. Dad worked for a steel manufacturing company until they went bust. Every day he'd come home and tell us that they'd lost orders, first to other local firms, then to companies overseas. Mum used to get worked up about the work going out of the country, but Dad didn't. He said it didn't matter where the work was going, the fact was that his firm had lost it. He used to say to her that if you got knocked down, did it matter what colour the car that did it was? That's how I feel today. Like I said, what's happened has happened, and finding out why or what did it just isn't important. I can't get excited about any of this bullshit. We are where we are.'

He stopped talking, and in the sudden quiet he thought about his dad again. He hadn't thought about his parents for days now, maybe even weeks. He had subconsciously built a wall around the past to stop painful memories from getting in the way.

Emma stood up and walked to the front of the building. She looked out of the front of the store, shielding her eyes from the brilliant orange sunrise which was shining through the grille and beginning to fill the building with bright, warm daylight. The long tripping shadows of occasional stumbling corpses stretched across the grey car park towards them.

'What are you thinking?' she asked, concerned by his sudden silence.

'Nothing,' he lied. 'What about you?'

'I've got all kinds of stuff going through my head,' she admitted. 'I don't want to get carried away here, but . . .'

'But what?'

'But I can't help thinking that we might have found a way out of all of this, Mike. This time yesterday we were buried underground just sitting and waiting. Today we're—'

'This time yesterday we were relatively safe,' he interrupted, correcting her. 'Today we're exposed and vulnerable and on the run and we've got nothing.'

'Christ, you can be such a negative, miserable bastard at times,' she said angrily. 'Why can't you be positive for once?'

'I am positive,' Michael protested, 'but I'm a realist too. Until I've seen this actual island and I've stood on the beach and shouted at the top of my voice and no bodies have come crawling out after me, then I'm going to stay sceptical. We need to be careful here and not rush into anything that's going to cost us.'

'So what are you saying? That we should just say our goodbyes and wave these people off into the sunset?'

'No, that's not what I'm saying at all, but you know what I think. If something can go wrong—'

'It will go wrong. I *know* that – change the bloody record, will you? It doesn't mean we have to sit around and wait for crap to happen, for God's sake. It doesn't mean things *can't* work out right for us, does it?'

Michael chewed his lip and thought about what she'd said. Perhaps she was right and he was being too negative. Truth was, he felt like he'd already lost too much to risk being positive. He couldn't stand the thought of them building themselves up, only to be knocked down again.

'Sorry,' he mumbled apologetically. 'You're right, I'll shut up.'

'I don't want you to shut up,' she said, moving back towards him, 'I just want you to give this a chance. Have an open mind. Come on, Mike, think about what might happen if this works out – if this island is everything they say it is, then before long you and I could have a house together. We could have our own bedroom, with a proper bed. We could have a kitchen, a garden, a living room . . . We could have privacy and space.'

'We thought we'd got all of that at Penn Farm.'

'I know, but this is different, I can feel it. If it hadn't been for the bodies then we'd probably still be at Penn Farm, maybe even somewhere better. Bloody hell, if it hadn't been for the bodies then we could be anywhere we damn well please. And now we're talking about going someplace where there aren't any bodies.'

'No, we're not,' Michael said, quickly slipping back into his negative mindset again, 'not yet, anyway. At the moment we're talking about going to an island and clearing a couple of hundred bodies from it. There's a big difference.'

Emma shook her head. It wasn't worth talking to him when he was in this kind of mood. She turned and walked away, fed up with arguing pointlessly. Michael watched her go. He hadn't wanted to upset her, but he couldn't bear to see her getting carried away with half an idea that might eventually end up costing them everything.

For a while he sat alone and watched the bodies outside.

13

Trying to get to the airfield and join the other survivors there was the only sensible option available to the group. Any other logical alternatives were nonexistent: they had nowhere else to go.

In their weeks of incarceration underground, the structure of the group had barely changed: some people had held back, trying to blend into the background, watching everyone else doing the work around them and never actively contributing themselves. Other, more confident people had, by default, begun to take control and organise the group. Now, in the cold light of day this morning, there had been a subtle shift in people's attitudes. The introduction to the equation of both the soldiers (who until yesterday had maintained an enforced distance from the group) and the arrival of the helicopter had dramatically altered the make-up of the frightened little community. Individuals who had previously been content to hide away in the shadows were now keen to push themselves to the fore, desperate not to get overlooked and left behind.

'I'll do it,' Peter Guest said anxiously, stepping around Jack and grabbing a map from Richard Lawrence's hands, 'I'll navigate. Show me where we are and where we're going.'

Richard took the map back from him and folded it down to a more manageable size. He pointed to the general area where they were presently hiding. He had spent the last half hour writing down basic directions to Monkton Airfield for them to follow; then he'd asked for a volunteer to navigate.

Showing more enthusiasm than he had done at any time during the previous month, Peter anxiously began re-reading the directions and cross-referencing them with the map, plotting the route to Bigginford and the airfield beyond.

'You travel with Cooper in the personnel carrier,' Michael suggested. 'Steve can follow behind in the truck and I'll follow him.'

'Not in that motorhome of yours, you won't,' Steve Armitage said from across the room. He'd been outside checking over the three vehicles and had just returned, breathless and cold. He wiped his greasy hands on a dirty rag. 'It's knackered, mate. Axle's broken. I'm not surprised, after the journey we had here last night – I'm not even sure how it made it this far.'

'Shit,' Michael said under his breath.

'What are we going to do now then?' Emma asked, feeling strangely saddened by the loss of the vehicle. She'd started off hating it, until recently, when it had provided the illusion of being a safe haven.

'We'll have to go out and find something else,' said Donna who had been sitting nearby and listening silently. 'We won't all fit in otherwise. There's bound to be something around here we can use.'

'There aren't too many bodies out there,' Steve said. 'I reckon we'll be all right to go and look around as long as we're sensible and quick.'

'Can't we try and manage with just two trucks?' Emma wondered.

Michael was about to respond when Stonehouse said, 'You're going to have to get yourselves two vehicles.' The soldier had been standing at the back of the group; now he stood up and walked to the front. His sudden movement was unexpected, and he made an imposing figure in his heavy protective gear, carrying his rifle and flanked by one of his men.

'Why's that?' Cooper asked, genuinely confused.

'Because we're going back to the base,' he replied. 'It's our only option.'

'Don't be stupid,' Croft said, 'the place was overrun yesterday. You can't go back there.'

'We can and we will. We can't stay out here.'

'But we need your vehicle, and—'

'We need to get back underground. We're completely fucked if we stay up here.'

'Doesn't look like you've got much choice,' Michael said. 'You're dead whatever you do. Might as well come with us and—'

'And what exactly? Sit and watch you lot run? Sit in these bloody suits and wait to die?'

'At least you'd be giving *us* a chance,' Croft yelled at him, his face suddenly flushed red with anger. 'Do things your way and *everyone* loses.'

'Tough shit.'

'Bastard,' he said as he moved towards the soldier, wincing as he landed heavily, aggravating his still painful injuries.

Stonehouse shoved him out of the way, and the doctor, already off-balance, crumbled to the ground at his booted feet. Stonehouse lifted the butt of his rifle and held it inches away from Croft's face.

'Leave it, Doc,' Cooper said. He turned to face Stonehouse. 'Just fuck off and go.'

'What the hell are you doing?' Croft yelled from the floor, looking up at Cooper in disbelief. 'Have you gone completely mad? We need that vehicle!'

Cooper looked down at him and glared. He grabbed his arm and pulled him to his feet.

'No,' he replied abruptly.

Stonehouse watched, surprised by his ex-colleague's reaction. He had anticipated some kind of resistance from Cooper at least.

'Christ, Cooper,' the incensed doctor cursed as he brushed himself down, 'there are only four of them. We'll end up driving to Bigginford in a convoy of twenty bloody cars if we're not careful.'

'No, we won't,' Cooper calmly replied. All eyes were suddenly on him as he began to walk towards the exit, away from the confrontation. Then, without warning, he suddenly stopped, turned around and ran back in the opposite direction, then dived through the air and smashed into Stonehouse and the soldier standing next to him. In the confusion the two troopers were knocked to the ground. Stonehouse was quickly up on all fours, but Cooper had already grabbed hold of his facemask and he yanked it up and off his face before Stonehouse had a chance to react.

The second soldier immediately began to scramble away, but Cooper was too fast for him. He jumped onto his back and pulled and tugged at his mask and his breathing apparatus until they came free and he could see the soldier's bare flesh underneath. He was aware of the other two soldiers running away, fleeing deeper into the vast store, and he readied himself in case the troopers on the ground got back up and attacked him.

Stonehouse was the first to drag himself onto his feet. He

grabbed his rifle and started to run angrily towards Cooper – but he'd barely made it a couple of feet before the infection caught him. With a look of pained surprise on his face, he fell back on top of the other soldier, who was still on the ground and already suffocating. Fighting for breath, Stonehouse shook and convulsed, still grasping his rifle tightly. Eyes bulging, he stared at Cooper until he lost consciousness.

'You killed them,' Donna gasped, appalled. 'You bastard, you killed them!'

'They were dead already,' Cooper responded, disdain in his voice, 'and they were about to kill us.'

14

Michael, Jack and Cooper ran together through the silent car parks of the industrial estate, desperately searching for a suitable vehicle to get them to the airfield. There were more bodies around than there had been last night, but they knew they had no choice but to risk it.

'Van,' Michael said breathlessly as he pushed his way past another lurching corpse, 'over there.'

He pointed to the far right corner of the football pitch-sized car park they had just entered. Standing on its own next to an office building was a red Post Office van, and lying in the road in front of it was the gnarled body of a postman. The man's motionless corpse was twisted, and looked like a piece of washed-up driftwood eaten away by decay. The strap of an empty mail bag was still wrapped around his neck.

Cooper ran around and yanked the driver's door open while Michael frantically fished around in the wizened corpse's pockets for the keys. He threw them to Cooper, then had to jump to his feet to fight off two bodies which had stumbled uncomfortably close. He had Stonehouse's rifle slung across his back. Feeling unexpectedly nervous, he swung it around and primed it. Cooper had taught him to shoot while they'd been underground, but until now he'd never actually needed to fire a weapon. They usually had to deal with many, many more corpses than this, and guns were only good for getting rid of them one at a time. Holding his breath he brutally shoved the barrel of the rifle into a dark hole on one side of the nearest body's broken nose, aimed up into its skull and pulled the trigger. A deafening crack rang around the car park, echoing off the walls of every building in the immediate vicinity, and Michael was knocked back by the unexpected force of the weapon. He tripped over his own feet and fell as a shower of dark crimson gore and splintered bone erupted from the back of the creature's head, splattering the wall behind it.

'Push the damn thing!' Cooper shouted from the front of the van. He couldn't get it started – the engine wouldn't turn over.

Michael picked himself up off the ground again and shot the second corpse in the side of the head before swinging the rifle onto his back and running around to the rear of the vehicle to help Jack, who was already pushing. He shoulder-charged the van, and the sudden impact started it rolling forward slightly. Cooper jumped out of his seat and began to shove against the driver's door, leaning in through the open window to steer.

'Christ, Cooper, have you still got the bloody handbrake on?' Jack half-joked, red-faced and wheezing as he strained against the back of the van. He threw his full weight forward again, screwing his eyes shut with effort. When he opened them again he saw that more decomposing bodies were creeping dangerously close.

With all three of the men pushing, the van finally began to gain momentum and started to roll across the car park with relative ease. Cooper jumped back behind the wheel, slammed his foot down on the clutch and tried again to start the engine. After a few seconds of ugly mechanical groaning and straining, it finally spluttered into life and he accelerated away, revving the engine hard and leaving Michael and Jack running after him through belching clouds of dirty exhaust fumes. He turned the van around and went back to collect them, making only the briefest of diversions to wipe out another couple of meandering cadavers which had dragged themselves into the car park.

Inside the store, Emma had managed to find the two remaining soldiers, who had disappeared when Cooper had attacked the others. They were hiding together in a large stockroom.

'Just leave us alone,' one of the soldiers sobbed as he heard Emma approaching. His strained voice was high-pitched, full of desperation and fear. 'That bloke Cooper's a fucking psychopath. He's always been the same. He'll fucking kill us!'

The frightened trooper cowered away in the shadows, and a couple of yards away from him, Kelly Harcourt, her heart thumping in her chest, pressed herself back against a storage rack, hoping she would melt away into the shadows.

'He's no psychopath,' Emma said as she took a few cautious steps further into the room, trying to pinpoint their exact location, 'he's a survivor, that's all.' She peered across the room, sure she'd just seen a flicker of movement out of the corner of her eye. 'You'd probably have done the same if you were in his position.'

She didn't find it easy defending Cooper's actions, no matter how relieved she was that he had reacted so quickly. She'd forgotten that, until recently, these two soldiers had served alongside him. They probably knew more about him than she did. Was he a psychopath?

'He'll do it again,' the male soldier whimpered. 'All he's got to do is open our suits and we've fucking had it. That's all that any of you have to do.'

'But no one's going to do that to you, are they?' Emma sighed. 'Why the hell would we?'

'You'll do it if you have to,' Kelly shouted, the sudden volume and direction of her voice immediately giving her location away. 'You'd kill us just as quickly as you get rid of those bloody things outside.'

'You're wrong. Cooper didn't have any choice. Stonehouse forced him to do it.'

Kelly slumped against the racking and slid down to the ground. Emma could see one of her feet sticking out into the aisle. She walked towards her and crouched down at the side of the terrified soldier.

Kelly lifted her head and looked up at Emma. 'I just don't know what to do,' she admitted. She had tears running down her face, but no way of wiping them away. 'I can't handle this any more—'

'It's all right,' Emma said quietly, putting a gentle hand on her shoulder. 'We're all struggling.' She paused, not sure if Kelly was listening, or whether it was even worth continuing. 'Listen, I'll be straight with you: you two have got the worst deal of all here. You're stuck between a rock and a hard place. You're trapped in those bloody suits and it must be hell, but you don't have much of a choice, do you? You can try and find some transport and get back to your base, or you can stay here, or you can come with us. Like I said, as long as you don't put anyone at risk then—'

'Then what?' Kelly demanded. 'Then Cooper won't kill us?'

Emma sighed with frustration. She got up and walked back towards the door. 'Look, we're all too busy trying to keep ourselves alive here. No one's interested in killing you.'

15

Under the unfocused gaze of a crowd of fence-rattling corpses, the group piled into their vehicles. As many of them as possible crammed into the back of the personnel carrier, the strongest vehicle in the convoy. Cooper took the wheel with Peter Guest at his side, ready to navigate. Steve Armitage took up his usual seat behind the wheel of the prison truck – he had begun to fiercely guard his position, not just because there were few other people amongst the survivors who could have driven the truck as well as him, but also because the responsibility which he attached to the role made him feel worthwhile, gave him a reason to be alive. Strange, he thought, that what had previously always felt like such an ordinary, menial job should now give him such sense of purpose.

There were fewer survivors travelling in the back of the prison truck than on earlier journeys, and the spare space was taken up with useful supplies and equipment which they'd stripped from the store. There were just a handful of people in the final vehicle in the convoy, the bright red, ridiculously conspicuous post van. Donna sat in the driver's seat, with Jack Baxter on the passenger side and Clare wedged between them. Behind them were the two surviving soldiers, with yet more supplies packed around them. Donna looked at them in her rear-view mirror. Kelly Harcourt seemed genuinely afraid; she wasn't a concern. Her male colleague, however, was far more unpredictable. His name, she'd just discovered, was Kilgore. He was a short, wiry-framed man, and he was far too jittery and agitated for her liking.

A few minutes earlier, Richard Lawrence and Karen Chase had left in the helicopter, taking with them the four remaining children – eight year old Dean, two younger boys, and a small girl called Alex. The remaining people had crowded around and watched in awe as the powerful machine had lifted up into the clear blue early-morning sky. Having spent weeks underground, cowering away in the shadows, witnessing the aircraft rising up into the sun with such strength and sheer bloody noise had been strangely emotional: a two-fingered salute to the rest of the dead world. As the helicopter disappeared, however, the sounds being made by the horde of rabid bodies smashing themselves furiously against the metal fence had suddenly seemed louder than ever. The closeness and anger of the corpses was a reminder to each of them of the relentless danger they faced.

Before leaving, Cooper and Peter had gathered the other drivers around them, to run through the proposed route in detail one last time. It was crucial that they all knew the way, and the potential problems they might face along the road. Using road atlases he had found in a corner of the store, Peter had highlighted the directions they needed to take, and had produced a handwritten set of notes for each vehicle. He was desperately keen to share with the others the information which Richard Lawrence had earlier given him.

'You see,' he explained, talking with unprecedented energy, 'they've obviously not needed to spend much time on the ground, and so this was the most direct route they were able to come up with. Now I've not personally spent a lot of time in this part of the country, so I'm not completely sure where we're—'

'Do me a favour,' Steve Armitage interrupted, 'and just shut up and let me have my bloody map, will you?'

Undeterred, Peter continued, 'Richard told me they've not seen any particularly large gatherings of bodies between here and Bigginford.'

'What's "large" supposed to mean, then?' asked Cooper. 'Twenty-five of them? Two thousand? Half a million?'

'Not sure,' he quickly admitted, and continued, 'Anyway, it looks like we'll be able to stick to the motorways for a good part of the journey – they're probably not going to be completely clear, but from what they've seen from the air they think we should be able to work our way through without too much bother.'

'What about cities?' Jack Baxter asked anxiously. 'We're going to stay away from the cities as best we can, aren't we?'

'We'd like to,' Cooper answered, deliberately denying Peter the opportunity to respond, 'but we've got to try and balance out safety and risk. To get to Bigginford we're going to have to get pretty close to the centre of Rowley for a start.'

'What does "pretty close" mean?'

'Like I said, it's going to be about balancing safety with risk. If we bypass Rowley then you're right, we'll probably avoid a whole load of potential trouble spots. The problem is, we'll also end up adding a hell of a lot of distance and time onto the length of the journey. Obviously we'll be in a better position to make a final decision when we get nearer, but my feeling is we'll be better off following this route. I'd rather take a chance and go for the quicker option than risk running out of fuel because we've driven further than we needed to. We could end up stuck out in the middle of nowhere.'

'I don't like it,' Jack complained.

'No one likes any of this,' Cooper sighed, 'but that's how it is. Let's just see how the land lies when we get there, okay? Chances are no one's been anywhere near Rowley for weeks. Most of the bodies will probably have drifted away.'

'Suppose.'

Peter seized on a momentary lull in the conversation to start talking again. 'Cooper's right, Rowley might be a problem, but once we're through it should pretty much be plain sailing until we get to the airfield.'

'Plain sailing?' Steve grunted. 'Bloody hell, when was the last time anything was plain sailing?'

'Did Richard tell you much about the airfield?' Jack asked.

'He said it used to be a private commercial site,' Cooper answered. 'He said it's pretty small, with just the one runway and a few buildings. There's supposed to be a fence running all the way around, to keep trespassers and plane-spotters out.'

'But does it keep bodies out?'

'At the moment.'

'And what do you mean by that?'

'Sounds like they've got the same kind of problems we had at the base and back in the city.'

'Such as?'

'Hundreds of bodies – probably thousands.'

The positivity and excitement of the helicopter's arrival had all but disappeared. Now they were crammed into their respective vehicles, facing the prospect of lurching headlong into the unknown once more, every last person – military and civilian alike – felt sick to the stomach with nerves.

Cooper, Donna and Steve started their engines and slowly moved towards the exit. Michael undid the latch and let the gate swing open. No longer restrained, noxious cadavers immediately began to spill towards him on unsteady feet, reaching out with flailing arms. He sprinted around to the back of the personnel carrier, climbed inside and slammed the door shut and Cooper began to edge forward, buffeting bodies out of the way and leading the convoy back out into the dead world.

16

Good fortune and sensible planning combined to their advantage and the three-vehicle convoy reached the first section of motorway less than half an hour after leaving the industrial estate. It was mid-morning when they joined the main road, and, in the hours they'd subsequently been travelling, the earlier bright sun had steadily been swallowed up and hidden by impenetrable dark cloud. A light autumn mist had begun to fall, barely noticeable but soaking everything.

Peter Guest, navigating for Cooper, had again become withdrawn and quiet, reverting to his more familiar demeanour and losing the sudden confidence and interest he had temporarily found. No one was surprised. Cooper had anticipated having problems with him, as had Michael.

'Junction twenty-three,' Cooper said. Peter looked up, then anxiously checked his map again, frantically trying to confirm they were still on the right road. The fact that they hadn't taken any turnings since he'd last checked didn't seem to matter: the further they moved away from the warehouse, the more nervous he became.

'Everything all right, Cooper?' Michael asked, pushing his way closer to the driver and leaning over his seat.

'I'm okay,' he replied, concentrating on the road ahead. Michael struggled to peer out through the front of the personnel carrier. In the gloom it wasn't easy to see the direction the road took. The sudden mist obscured much of the landscape around them, and the ground ahead was carpeted with a tangled layer of dead bodies and crumpled machinery. Luckily, the vehicle Cooper controlled was powerful enough to push a path through the debris, allowing the others to follow in its wake. Rowley, the second largest town in the county, was now less than ten miles away.

'Bloody grim, isn't it?' Michael grumbled unhelpfully from just behind Cooper's shoulder.

'This place was grim at the best of times.'

Even allowing for traffic and other delays, this journey would probably have taken two hours at the most a few months ago. Today it had taken double that time just to reach the outskirts of the town. Although they had been relatively fortunate – they had not come across many serious obstacles along the way – progress through the ruined landscape had been painfully slow. Cooper's head was thumping with the effort of having to concentrate so hard for so long. He wanted to stop, to rest and stretch his legs, but he knew that wasn't possible. The personnel carrier's headlights were constantly illuminating random, fleeting movement on all sides as lumbering shadows continually emerged from the mist and then disappeared back into the darkness again as the personnel carrier, prison truck and van thundered past them.

'Which way, Peter?' Cooper asked again, getting annoyed that he had to keep pressing for directions. Peter was staring out of the window, transfixed, and hadn't noticed they were rapidly approaching a fork in the road. Until a few seconds ago it had been hidden by the mist.

'Um . . . I'm not sure,' Peter stammered unhelpfully. In sudden pointless panic his eyes darted around the map on his lap, which he'd been trying to follow by torchlight.

'Come on, you should be onto this,' the ex-soldier snapped angrily at him, allowing his exhaustion and unease to show. 'For Christ's sake, you're the one with the damn map in front of you!'

'Think I've got it,' he said, squinting into the darkness to try and read the dirty, unlit road sign. 'Take the 302.'

Peter's indecision meant that Cooper had to yank the personnel carrier hard over to the left to change direction before they passed the junction, and his unsuspecting passengers were thrown about in the back.

'Are you sure about this?' he asked as he drove down a dark roadway which curved round and down to the right and then snaked back under an elevated section of the carriageway which they'd just been following.

'This is right,' Peter said quietly, trying his best to appease Cooper. 'I'm sure it is. We need to follow this road for another couple of miles, cross the river and then find the road to Huntridge – that way we'll have bypassed the city centre.'

Cooper swerved the personnel carrier around a crashed double-decker bus which had toppled over onto its side; it straddled virtually the full width of the road. The prison truck followed close behind, then the post van.

'Bloody hell,' Donna cursed as she forced the two off-side wheels of the van up the kerb and over a grass verge to squeeze past the wreck of the bus. Although much smaller than the other vehicles, she didn't have the power to smash the remains of cars, bikes, trucks and other obstacles out of the way like they did, and rather than clearing a way through for her, the debris left by one driver as he battered his way forward through the wreckage was frequently dragged back out into the middle of the road by the second vehicle and left directly in her path.

Like Peter in the front of the first vehicle, Jack was also studying the maps.

'Not far now,' he said, keeping his head down, preferring to look at the map rather than outside. Whenever he did lift his eyes he could see the grey, constantly shifting silhouettes of bodies converging on the convoy. Jack knew they'd probably be okay as long as they kept moving, but the fact that they were so close to the dead again scared the hell out of him.

The road they were now following was a wide and recently built expressway, a bypass which skirted around the main part of the city centre. Like everywhere else it was covered with scattered remains of the people of Rowley and the surrounding districts. As their proximity to the lifeless heart of the city increased, so too did the amount of buckled metal and rotting flesh around them, threatening to block their way forward. Many, many people had fallen and died here on the city's outskirts when the rush-hour crawl had been devastated by disease almost eight weeks ago. No one travelling through the decay today was surprised. It was nothing they hadn't seen before.

The bright rear brake lights of the two vehicles she followed were Donna's guide through the grey gloom outside. She was finding it easier to simply match their twists and turns, rather than trying to find the route for herself. Suddenly, without any warning, the brightness of the red lights increased as both the personnel carrier and the prison truck stopped suddenly. Her heart began to beat more quickly. Clare, who had managed to snatch a few precious minutes' sleep, sat up with a start when the van stopped too.

'What's wrong?' she demanded anxiously, frantically looking from side to side. 'Why have we stopped?'

Neither Donna nor Jack said anything. As Donna glanced into her wing mirror, a random corpse tripped out of the darkness and collided heavily with the side of the van. The two soldiers sitting in the back jumped up as the creature began to hammer its rotting fists lethargically against the metal side of the vehicle. A few seconds later and another four of them had appeared and were doing the same. Donna saw more figures crowding and jostling around the back of the prison truck up ahead.

'What's happening?' Kilgore asked anxiously from behind her. He pressed his facemask against the window in the back door of the van and saw more corpses were emerging from the heavy mist all around them.

'What the hell are they doing, Donna?' Jack asked. Donna was about to tell him that his guess was as good as hers when Michael suddenly appeared out of the back of the personnel carrier and ran around to the front, out of sight. Donna pulled the van further forward so that they could get a better view of what was happening, dislodging the battering cadavers, and stopped when they were level with the prison truck.

'Christ,' she said when she saw what had happened, 'what are we supposed to do now?'

A short distance in front of them was a narrow, one-lane bridge, with traffic lights at both ends, now as useless and dead as the rest of the world. Just over halfway across a medium-sized truck had crashed and had somehow spun around through almost ninety degrees, leaving it wedged awkwardly between the concrete balustrades on either side. Twenty feet or so below the bridge was a wide river, its once-clear water now a stagnant green-brown sludge, poisoned by the seeping decay it carried away from the nearby city.

'What now?' Clare asked. Jack looked down at the map on his lap again.

'There are another two bridges,' he said. 'One's about three miles further north, the other four or five miles back the way we came.'

'Either way we'll add hours to the journey. Fuck, this isn't good.'

Michael was hidden from most of the nearby bodies by virtue of the mist and the various vehicles abandoned by the bridge. He surveyed the obstruction ahead, but as he ran back to the personnel carrier a single corpse, managing by chance to somehow find a way to squirm through, threw itself at him from nowhere, exploding furiously out of the shadows without warning. Caught by surprise, he took the full force of the impact head-on and was slammed back against the side of the transport by the creature. The inescapable stench of rotting flesh filled his lungs, making him gag and spit. He instinctively lifted his arms to protect his face, and recoiled in disgust as he grabbed hold of the decaying cadaver. Most of its ragged clothing had long since been ripped off or torn away, and instead of grabbing cloth, his fingers squelched through the decaying flesh which covered its bones. Michael closed the fingers of his right hand, wincing as dead skin flapped and as the remains of putrefied organs began to dribble down his arms, and grabbed its partially exposed ribcage then pushed back against the corpse, ran forward and forced it over the side of the bridge. The body fell out of sight for several seconds before landing in the murky water below.

Pausing only to wipe his hands on a patch of wet grass at his feet, Michael scrambled back into the personnel carrier.

'You okay?' Emma asked.

'Fine,' he told her brusquely as he made his way forward back towards Cooper. 'It looks like it's just the truck blocking the road, but it's pretty well wedged in. We won't be able to shift it by hand. You'll have to try and push it off the side of the bridge.'

Cooper didn't waste any time discussing options but accelerated slowly towards the blockage. The prison truck, now surrounded by between forty and fifty uncontrollable cadavers, all scrambling and fighting constantly to get at the people inside, also began to move. In the post van, Donna, surrounded by a slightly smaller but no less animated or violent crowd, followed close behind.

'See where the corner of the bonnet's sticking out?' Michael said, still breathless, leaning over into the front of the personnel carrier and pointing at the crashed truck just ahead of them. 'If you hit it there and give it a decent shove you should be able to push it through the wall.'

Cooper didn't respond, concentrating instead on trying to work out the physics of the situation in the few seconds remaining before they made contact. Michael seemed to be right; the truck looked like it was positioned in such a way that if he did manage to catch it properly, its back-end would be forced through the concrete balustrade and out over the edge. Its own weight should then do the rest of the job for him.

'What's that?' Sheri Newton asked. She was sitting next to Michael, peering over Cooper's shoulder through the front of the vehicle and across the bridge.

'What?' Cooper grunted, struggling to concentrate. Sheri lifted her finger and pointed ahead.

'Over there.'

Michael looked up: there was definitely movement on the other side of the crashed truck. The mist was slightly thinner on the far side of the bridge and as he stared into the dull greyness, he realised he could see bodies, at least ten or twenty of them . . . No, wait, there were many more than that. With perfect timing, the wind gently blew away more of the drifting fog and for a moment revealed a densely packed crowd of figures filling the narrow carriageway across the river, all trying to move in the direction of the light and noise coming towards them. As Michael watched the constantly shifting mass of decaying shapes, several of the creatures at the front of the gathering began to rip and tear at those surrounding them, whipped into a frenzy by the approaching vehicles.

'Why are there so many of them?' Sheri asked nervously, her voice little more than a whisper. The answer to her question, although no one bothered to respond, was simple: the sound of the convoy had attracted the attention of just about every wandering corpse in the local area. The creatures on both sides of the river were gravitating towards the source of the noise, and the narrow bridge was the only means of getting across the river for those on the other side. The growing crowd was channelled forward by the sides of the bridge, and just as the wreck of the truck was preventing Cooper and the others from making progress, so it had also stopped the bodies from getting any closer. Oblivious to the obstruction, and as before, more and more of them had continued to head relentlessly towards the noise until they'd packed themselves into a swollen bottleneck of diseased flesh.

Cooper was vaguely aware of the bodies, but he was concentrating on shifting the truck: did he ram it, or just push against it with slow and steady force? The machine he was driving was powerful and responsive, and rather than risk injuring his passengers by crashing into the blockage and trying to smash it out of the way, he instead elected to take the more cautious option. He increased his speed just slightly to give himself enough momentum, and steered towards the truck's protruding front bumper. The people in the back of the personnel carrier lurched forward and then dropped back in their seats as the two vehicles made contact. Metal began to grind and strain against metal.

'Come on,' Michael said under his breath as Cooper accelerated, willing the wreck in front of them to move. It shifted back a couple of inches, but then stopped when the rear off-side wheel wedged up against the kerb. Cooper accelerated again and pushed harder. Still no movement. He pushed harder again, and then, after what felt like an interminable wait, and with his engine straining, the truck finally gave way to the force being exerted upon it and the back wheels jumped up into the air under the pressure and the twisted chassis shot back a further few inches. Another push; Cooper could feel the truck scrape against the wall. Peter Guest leant out of his window and watched as showers of dust and huge lumps of broken masonry tumbled down into the polluted waters below.

'You've almost done it,' he said, keeping one eye on the bodies up ahead. 'Give it another push and it'll be—'

Cooper was tired of waiting; he accelerated again with force, shunting into the front of the truck again and this time it went flying back through the hole in the wall. For a split-second it remained balanced precariously, teetering on the edge, before finally tipping back, flipping over and crashing down into the river below. The moment his path was clear Cooper drove forward at speed, powering into the crowd of advancing bodies with massive force, mowing them down in a torrent of blood, bone, disease and decay, obliterating a mass of them almost instantly.

Now free to move again, the convoy powered across the rest of the narrow bridge with ease and continued their journey skirting around the remains of the dead city.

17

The route on the other side of the river was clear and relatively trouble-free. Within a mile, the road they had been following opened up again into a dual carriageway, the city-bound lanes clogged with the depressingly familiar sight of hundreds upon hundreds of ruined vehicles crashed nose-to-tail, some with the emaciated remains of their drivers and passengers still trapped inside, fighting to get out as the convoy neared. By comparison, the two lanes running in the opposite direction were almost completely empty; far fewer vehicles had been travelling away from Rowley when the infection had first struck.

After a few minutes Cooper led the convoy across the central reservation, smashing a hole through an already damaged section of metal barrier. Driving on the wrong side of the road felt annoyingly unnatural, but it was undoubtedly quicker and easier.

A brief respite in the mist and rain increased the afternoon light levels for a short while as the road followed a long, gentle arc with woodland on one side and the shadows of the city of Rowley on the other. No matter how much time had elapsed since the germ had struck and destroyed so much – if that really was what had done all the damage – the sight of a once-busy city drenched in total darkness was still unsettling. It was a stark reminder of the magnitude of what had happened to the world.

Peter Guest now seemed a little more composed again. 'In about half a mile we should reach a series of roundabouts on this road,' he explained, carefully following every inch of their progress on his map and cross-referencing with his handwritten notes. 'Keep going straight until we hit the fifth one, then it's left. Another twenty miles or so after that and we should just about be there.'

Michael crouched on his knees on the floor in the back of the personnel carrier and washed his hands with the strong disinfectant they'd taken from the store earlier, trying to get rid of the obnoxious smell of dead flesh. Emma sat at his side, watching him intently. Occasionally she'd glance out of the window as every couple of seconds the light from one of their vehicles would catch in a window or on the windscreen of a motionless car, reflecting back for an instant, making her look twice and wonder whether there was anyone there. She knew there was no one, but still she kept looking . . . just in case.

His hands stinging and his eyes watering, Michael finished what he was doing and collapsed heavily into his seat beside her as the personnel carrier swerved around the first roundabout.

'You okay?' Emma asked.

'Fine.'

'You stink.'

'Thanks a lot.'

She didn't know what was worse, the smell of dead flesh or the acrid stench of the disinfectant Michael had doused his hands with.

'I was thinking,' he said, leaning against her and whispering quietly, 'if this works out, then I want to try and get over to that island as soon as I can. I think we both should.'

'Why?' she asked, her voice equally quiet.

'Because if you believe everything we've heard, it could well be the place where we end up spending the rest of our lives. I want to make sure we've got everything we need out there.'

'That's a bit selfish, isn't it? What about—?'

'I'm not suggesting doing anything at the expense of any of the others,' he explained quickly, wanting to make it clear that he wasn't being completely self-centred, 'I just want to be sure we get what we need. And I'm not just talking about you and me either; I'm talking about all of this lot too.'

He looked around the personnel carrier at the other people travelling with them. It was a little disheartening that even now, after having spent so much time together, the group remained fragmented: the survivors generally fell into one of two very distinct categories, those who talked about the future and did something about it, and those who didn't. Interesting, Michael thought, that he could name all those who had at least tried to look forward and make something of the little they had left. The others – those who still spent each day silently wallowing in self-pity and despair – remained nameless and faceless.

'All I'm saying,' he said to Emma, keen to make his point, 'is that we need to make sure we stay in control here, not roll over and take second best just because they've got a bloody helicopter. This little control is all we've got left.'

Two vehicles behind, tempers were beginning to fray.

'Will you two just quit your fucking moaning,' Donna shouted, looking over her shoulder at the two soldiers slumped in the back of the van. 'All you've done for the last hour is bloody complain. If you haven't got anything positive to say, don't say anything at all.'

'I've got plenty to say,' Kilgore shouted back. 'Problem is, you won't listen.'

'Just take your bloody mask off then so we can hear you properly.'

'Come on, Donna, that's a bit harsh isn't it?' Jack whispered across the front of the van. 'Just let it go, he's not worth it. He's just a bloody idiot who's scared to death. They both are; you can see it in their eyes.'

Donna watched in the mirror as Kilgore angrily slumped back in his seat like a chastised child, crossing his arms and turning his back on her and looking out of the window.

'We should kick them both out now,' Donna said out of the corner of her mouth. 'I don't know why we're even bothering to bring them with us. We should do what Cooper did to the other two and—'

'Come on,' he sighed, sounding disappointed, 'you know as well as I do why Cooper did what he did. This is different. At the end of the day they're just people, like you and me.'

'Whatever.'

Jack shook his head sadly. He knew – he hoped – that she didn't mean what she was saying. Maybe it was just the tension of the day getting to her, just like it was getting to them all . . . Not wanting to prolong the conversation any further, he returned his attention to his maps.

The convoy rapidly approached the third of the five roundabouts they were expecting to pass along the road to the airfield. Donna was tired now, but she sat up straight in her seat and allowed the post van to drop back a little way so she could get a better view of the road ahead. In the centre of the island in the middle of the carriageway a needle-like stone war memorial was outlined against the darkening sky. At its base it had been hit by a juggernaut that had lost control when its driver had died. The huge lorry was twisted around the obelisk awkwardly, its cab leaning over to one side and half its wheel-base lifted off the ground.

'Take it easy round here,' Jack warned as the two vehicles ahead of them slowed down to navigate their way around the crash scene.

A body hurled itself out of the darkness and into the path of the personnel carrier, distracting Cooper and causing him to swerve. Steve Armitage, following too close behind and not paying enough attention, clipped the rear end of the beached juggernaut, shunting it further forward into the base of the memorial. He glanced up in time to see that the tall stone monument had been disturbed. He increased his speed and drove quickly towards the exit that Cooper had just taken.

'Shit,' Donna yelled as she watched the truck and personnel carrier disentangle themselves and move on. From where she was she could see that the monument, already unsteady, had been seriously weakened by the new impact and subsequent vibrations, and as the prison truck powered away, the pointed top of the memorial began to sway. Its collapse was inevitable, and rather than take any unnecessary risks, Donna slowed the van and they watched from a distance as the tall stone needle fell crashing to the ground, splitting into three large pieces. Even before the dust had settled it was obvious that the road ahead was completely blocked.

'Bloody typical,' Donna said, banging her fist against the steering wheel in frustration.

'Doesn't matter, just go around the other way,' Jack suggested, looking around anxiously at the bodies suddenly converging on them from the shadows. 'Do anything, but for Christ's sake just keep moving.'

Donna pulled forward again and began to steer anti-clockwise around the island, doing her best to concentrate on following the road and ignoring the swarming corpses.

'Which exit?' She was confused now they were travelling around the roundabout in the opposite direction.

'Third,' Jack told her, sounding less than sure, 'no, wait, fourth.'

His indecision, coupled with the sudden intense pressure, the random movement of corpses all around her and the various obstructions which littered the road, caused Donna to take the wrong exit. Their mistake was immediately obvious.

'Damn,' she cursed, slamming on the brake and stopping. In her rear-view mirror she could see that the road behind was filling with bodies; it would be impossible to reverse back. Ahead, moving rapidly away to the left, she could see the taillights of the personnel carrier and prison truck, following the route they should have taken. 'I can't turn around here,' she said, desperately looking around for another way out.

'Keep going forward,' Jack said as the first bodies began to slam against the sides of the van. 'Just keep moving. I know where we are on the map. I'll get us back on track in a few minutes.'

'They'll find us,' Cooper said firmly, hoping to silence Peter Guest, who was babbling nervously about the missing van.

'But they could be anywhere—'

'Listen, they've taken a wrong turn, that's all. They've got maps. They know where we're going and they're not stupid. They'll find us.'

'But what if—?'

'They'll find us,' he repeated. 'And if they don't, then they'll just have to make their way to the airfield by themselves, just like we agreed. They're going to expect us to keep following the route we've planned and not waste time looking for them. Stopping and turning around, leaving this road now, that will make things harder for everyone.'

18

The situation in the van was deteriorating rapidly as recriminations and arguments became heated. More bad decisions had been made.

'You told me to go right,' Donna yelled at Jack.

'I said left! Tell her, Clare, I said left, didn't I?'

'I'm not getting involved,' Clare answered, sinking down nervously into her seat. She was literally in the middle of the argument. 'Anyway, it doesn't matter who said what, just get us out of here, will you?'

Whatever the instruction from Jack had or hadn't been, the fact remained they were now hopelessly lost. The light had almost completely gone, and each dull, shadowy street looked virtually the same as the next and as the last. It had taken only a couple of wrong turns for them to become completely disorientated.

'Haven't we been down here before?' Clare said.

'How could we have been here before?' Donna yelled angrily at her. 'For God's sake, we've been driving in a straight line for the last ten minutes. We haven't turned around, so how the hell could we have been here before?'

'Sorry, I just thought—'

'Well, don't. We took two left turns and one right, remember? Since then I haven't done anything except drive straight. Now shut up and let me concentrate.'

'Leave her alone,' Jack said angrily, 'she's only trying to help.'

'If it wasn't for you and your bloody useless directions we wouldn't need help.'

'Come on, Donna, we both screwed up. I got it wrong and you got it wrong and now we're—'

'Now we're in a real bloody mess because—'

'We should try and find somewhere to stop so we can work out where we've gone wrong,' Kelly Harcourt suggested from the back, doing her best to end the pointless bickering. 'All we need is—'

'We can't stop,' Donna snapped, cutting across her. 'Don't you understand? This place is crawling with bodies. We can't risk not moving.'

'You think?' the soldier said, her voice calm in comparison to the others. 'Seems to me we can either stop now and take a chance to sort ourselves out, or just keep driving round in circles all bloody night until we run out of fuel and end up stopping anyway.'

Donna didn't say anything.

'Maybe she's right,' Jack cautiously suggested, wary of how Donna might react. 'We should find somewhere to park the van until we're sure of where we are and where we're going. We don't have to get out or anything. Even if a hundred bodies manage to find us, if we keep quiet, then they'll disappear off before long.'

'Bloody hell, Jack,' Donna said as she steered around the rubble of a shop frontage decimated by a crashed ambulance, 'just how naïve are you? All it takes is for a couple of those things to start banging and hammering on the van and we'll have bloody hundreds of them around us in no time. They don't just lose interest and turn round and disappear any more, remember?'

Jack didn't respond. He sat silently in his seat and looked out into the darkness around them feeling frightened, frustrated and slightly humiliated. He returned his attention to the map and tried again to work out where they were.

'Find a landmark,' Kelly suggested.

'What?' said Jack.

'I said we should find a landmark,' she repeated, clinging onto the side of the van as Donna swerved and weaved her way down another road filled with wrecks. 'We need to try and find something recognisable so that we can orientate ourselves to the map. Come on, this is basic stuff.'

'It's pitch black,' Donna yelled back at her. 'How the hell are we supposed to find a fucking landmark when we can't fucking see anything?'

Desperate for inspiration, she turned left and drove down another narrow street. It was more residential than those they had driven along so far, and more cars looked to be parked rather than crashed, perhaps indicating that it had not been a particularly busy throughway. On either side of the road were houses; very dark, unremarkable Victorian terraced houses. The relative normality of the scene momentarily silenced the raised voices. It had been a long time since any of the survivors had found themselves anywhere so inoffensive and reassuringly familiar. Jack's fear and nervousness gave way to a stinging pain, and a desperate sadness as the normality of the things which surrounded him made him remember all that he had lost.

'What about a church?' Kelly suggested, pointing out the silhouette of an imposing building nestled behind the row of houses on their right.

Donna took two turnings in quick succession and found the building surprisingly quickly. She steered the van down a narrow service road which bent around to the left then opened out into a small rectangular car park. In front of them, was the church, on the other side a school.

'We going to stop out here, or take a chance inside?' Kilgore asked from the back. He looked out through the rear window and watched as a single corpse tripped awkwardly down the service road after them.

'Inside?' Jack suggested, looking at Donna. 'In for a penny, in for a pound? Come on, this place looks pretty quiet, and we've been driving for hours.'

'Everywhere is quiet, you idiot,' Donna said. She didn't want to move, but she didn't want to sit outside, exposed and vulnerable, either. She had to admit that it made sense to make the most of this unexpected break in the journey.

'We don't have much to lose,' Jack said. 'Our necks are on the line whatever we do, so let's do it.'

'Okay,' she agreed reluctantly as the solitary body approached the van. She was exhausted. She pushed herself up out of her seat and clambered out, her legs stiff and aching. The three survivors and two soldiers ran over to the dark school building and disappeared inside through an open door, leaving the corpse to clatter clumsily into the side of the van, then turn and start to stumble after them.

19

The airfield was close now. Cooper knew that, not just because Peter Guest had been talking constantly and with renewed nervousness for the last ten minutes, but also because there were suddenly many more bodies around than there had been before. The city was behind them and the road they now followed ran between open fields. He could see figures moving on either side of them. Some were distracted briefly by the noise of the trucks, but most continued to shuffle steadily forward in the same general direction. It was logical to assume that the living and the dead were all heading towards the same destination.

'How far?' Michael asked from the back of the personnel carrier.

'Just a couple of miles now, I think,' Peter replied.

'And how are we going to get in when we get there?'

Michael's question was sensible but unanswerable. Peter and Cooper exchanged momentary glances before returning their attention to the maps and the road respectively. Michael slumped back in his seat next to Emma. He hadn't really expected any response. As foolish as it sounded, getting access to the airfield hadn't been something they had discussed at any great length with Richard Lawrence and Karen Chase – they'd been a little vague about this end of the journey, assuring Cooper and the others that they'd know when they arrived and that they'd make sure they had a clear passage to safety. From the distance and relative comfort of the warehouse hours earlier that had sounded reasonable to everyone, but now, as they rapidly approached the airfield and the huge crowds of cadavers which would inevitably be waiting there for them, nerves and doubt were beginning to take hold.

Michael's concern increased tenfold as they came round a sharp bend in the road and saw the airfield, for the first time, there in the distance. Located in the middle of a wide plain, it was instantly recognisable, first, and most obviously, because of the light which shone out from what he presumed was an operations room or control tower, the only artificial light the survivors had seen since they'd left the military base. It burned brightly in the low gloom of the night. He could see that the lit building stood just off-centre in the middle of a vast fenced enclosure. The land around was clear for several hundred yards in all directions, and the entire estate was ringed by a tall chain-link fence. On the other side of the fence was the second, far more ominous indicator that the survivors were close. Around the perimeter of the site, for as far as they could see in every direction, a heaving crowd of thousands upon thousands of verminous bodies had gathered. From where he was sitting it was difficult to estimate with any degree of accuracy, but it seemed to Michael that in most places the crowd ahead of them was at least a hundred bodies deep. Maybe deeper.

Cooper slowed the personnel carrier down, toying with the idea of stopping short of the base and trying somehow to attract the attention of the other survivors from a distance.

'Something wrong?' Peter asked anxiously.

Cooper shook his head. 'No,' he replied quickly, his voice quiet as he gazed out into the distance, looking hopefully for some movement on the airfield.

'Are they really going to see us? Do you really think they're going to—?'

The ex-soldier was tired of his incessant chatter. He looked across at Peter, silencing his increasingly irritating babbling with his stare. Although conditioned by years in the forces, and too professional to let his feelings show readily, Cooper was also beginning to feel nervous. If he could see the airfield, he reassured himself, then the people there could probably see him – if they were looking, that was. As bright as the light from their control tower was to him so, surely, the light from their vehicles would be also. As they got closer to the airfield, however, his doubts began to increase. He couldn't risk going much further forward until he was sure they'd been seen. Driving too close to such an enormous crowd without an escape route would be tantamount to suicide.

'There!' Sheri Newton shouted from close behind him. 'Look!'

Michael sat up and leant forward to try and get a better view of what was happening. It was difficult to make out much from this distance, but their slightly elevated position on the approach road helped a little. He thought he could see definite movement on the airfield: Several small lights – torches and lamps, perhaps – were moving away from the control tower towards a dark shape at one end of an equally dark runway. After a delay of a few seconds the helicopter began to climb and then hovered some thirty or forty feet above the ground.

'This is it,' said Cooper as he began to increase his speed again. The road continued its gentle descent towards the airfield, and as they approached, the helicopter began to move powerfully through the sky to meet them, switching on its bright searchlight as it hung over the road, illuminating the route they needed to follow. The brilliant burning light also illuminated a sizeable section of the seething, volatile crowd which surrounded the airfield, and the sudden incandescence caused their ferocity to increase massively.

'How the hell are we supposed to get through that lot?' Peter asked sensibly as the personnel carrier made contact with the first few corpses, knocking them away to the side.

'Just drive straight through, I guess,' Cooper answered, 'same as always.'

'But there are *hundreds* of them.'

'There are always hundreds of them,' he said, struggling to see the dark line of the road through the increasing crowds.

As they neared the airfield it became apparent that the helicopter was beginning to drop down again. When a gap of no more than a few yards remained between its landing skids and the heads of the corpses, it stopped moving. Hundreds of grabbing hands reached up towards the machine, but the bodies, weakened by decay, were like drunks, barely able to hold their ground; they were thrown about and buffeted by the violent, swirling downwind from the helicopter's rotor blades.

'What the hell are they doing now?' Michael asked, craning his neck to get a clear view. He watched in confusion as someone in the back of the helicopter hung out over the side of the aircraft. Held by a safety harness of some sort, two figures, one on either side, emptied large cans of liquid over the crowd directly below. Cooper hung back as the pilot gently swung the helicopter from side to side, ensuring that as many bodies as possible were drenched with the liquid. When the canisters were empty they were dropped into the enraged mass below, knocking down several of them at a time. The speed of the operation suddenly began to increase as the helicopter quickly flew higher.

One of the figures in the back of the helicopter lit something – a torch or a flare or a bottle of something flammable – and casually let it drop into the crowd. The bright flame seemed to be falling for ever, spinning over and over, until it reached the cadavers below, and in an instant the substance which had soaked many of them combusted, exploding in the night air and destroying scores of the rotten bodies with remarkable speed.

'Here we go,' Cooper announced as he slammed his foot back down and sent his vehicle careering at speed towards the airfield. The bodies which had been incinerated left a relatively clear area at the point where the road entered the enclosure, and as the personnel carrier and the prison truck hurtled towards the fence, a group of six men and women pulled open a solid-looking gate that had previously been hidden by the mass of corpses swarming nearby.

More bodies were approaching now, stumbling over the burning remains of those that had already fallen, and the helicopter swooped and dived through the air above them like a giant bird of prey, distracting them from the two vehicles which disappeared quickly into the compound.

A scant few minutes after opening, the gate was closed.

20

'I'm not sure,' Jack said. 'I don't see why we can't just wait here for a few hours longer and then try and get to the airfield. What difference is a couple of hours going to make, for God's sake?'

Donna was already beginning to regret their unscheduled stop. She wished they'd taken their chances and just kept driving until they'd got back on course. The others didn't seem that concerned. Clare, Jack and the two soldiers were content to sit and wait for a while before making their move.

'Let's forget it until morning,' Clare suggested. 'We might as well. We're pretty safe here, and it's pitch-black out there now.'

'She's got a point,' Kelly agreed. 'It'll be easier to see where we're going in the morning.'

'And it'll be easier for the bodies to find us,' Donna argued. 'We're vulnerable here. I think we should leave now.'

'Seems to me we're vulnerable everywhere,' Kelly said dejectedly, her voice distorted by her facemask. While Jack, Donna and Clare stood and shivered in the cold, she and Kilgore were sweating under their heavy layers of protective clothing. What she'd have given to feel the cold wind and rain on her face again . . .

'We've been here over an hour now,' Jack continued, 'and there are still hardly any bodies around out there.'

He gestured for Donna and the others to look through the window he'd been staring out of. The group had hidden themselves away in a first-floor classroom in the small school, overlooking the imposing church where they'd originally planned to wait. Donna peered down into the car park below and saw that he was right: there were only a handful of bodies nearby. Most of them seemed to be wandering around as aimlessly as ever, either oblivious to the presence of the survivors in the school, or unable to find a way through. A few of them had crowded around the van and were pressing their diseased faces against the glass. She could see several more around the edges of the car park. Strange how they seemed almost to be keeping their distance.

'It doesn't matter *when* we get to the airfield, as long as we get there,' Jack continued, trying to convince himself as much as anyone else. 'They're not going to be in a position to pack up and leave right away, are they? Richard said they've only just started flying people out.'

Clare sat on a desk, tired of this conversation. She leant down and picked up a book from where it had fallen on the wood-tiled floor. The name on the front was Abigail Peters who, she worked out from the school year she was in, had been nine or ten when she'd died. Jack had stopped talking, but she hadn't noticed. He stood watching her flick through the pages of the book. Poor kid, he thought to himself. As hard as what had happened had been for any of them to deal with, it must have been infinitely harder for Clare. Everywhere Jack looked he could see evidence of young lives ended without justification or reason, the innocence of childhood shattered brutally and without explanation. Fortunately the school day here had obviously not quite started when the nightmare had begun: the building was virtually deserted. In the playground, there were thirty to fifty dead children, around them the bodies of their parents and teachers. They'd all died waiting for the school day to begin.

'Where's Kilgore?' Donna asked, immediately concerned.

'What?' Jack mumbled, looking around. He could see Clare and Kelly, but not Kilgore.

'Did anyone see where he went?'

No one answered. Donna, followed closely behind by Jack, left the classroom and ran down the long, straight staircase which led to the ground floor. The slamming of another door at the far end of a corridor to their right gave away Kilgore's location. Picking their way cautiously through the shadows, they ran down towards him.

'What the hell are you doing?' Jack demanded as they entered the classroom and confronted the missing soldier. He was crouching down in front of a glass tank. The remains of several decomposing goldfish were floating on the top of six inches of stagnant water.

'All the animals are dead,' he said. 'Look.' He gestured towards two more tanks adjacent to the first. At the bottom of one was the dehydrated husk of a lizard, and in the other were three mounds of mouldy fur which had once been rodents of some sort – gerbils, mice or hamsters.

'Kilgore,' Donna said angrily, incensed by the soldier's stupidity, 'get back upstairs, you bloody idiot.'

'What's the problem? There's no one here to see me, is there? I'm just looking at—'

'We can't afford to take risks just because you fancy having a wander around. You're putting us all in danger by—'

'I'm not putting anyone in danger,' he protested. 'I'm not doing anything.'

'Just get back upstairs, you stupid bastard.'

Donna marched out of the room and back up to the classroom. Kilgore followed, not agreeing with her, but knowing he was outnumbered and remembering what had happened to his fellow soldiers earlier. He couldn't understand why she had such a problem with what he'd been doing – he hadn't done anything wrong. He'd kept quiet and he wasn't putting anyone in danger. He was a skilled professional, for Christ's sake. He knew how to keep out of sight and under cover. He was damn sure Donna hadn't had the training he had. Vile bloody woman.

Jack watched the soldier as he traipsed out of the room. He was about to follow when something caught his eye – a sudden, quick scuttling movement on the ground over in the far corner of the classroom. It was gone in less than a second. He walked back into the room, peering into the darkness, and crouched down next to a shelf full of reading books. He could tell from the smell and the debris on the floor around him that animals had been foraging in the building. A fox? Dogs? Rats, perhaps? That must have been what he'd seen. Whatever it was, it was nothing worth worrying about.

He looked up, and found himself face to face with the horrifically disfigured remains of what must once have been the class teacher. The corpse (which was so badly decayed that he couldn't tell whether it had been male or female) had lain sprawled across its desk for more than eight weeks, and whatever it was that had been scavenging in the classroom seemed to have been taking much of its nourishment from the corpse. The face had been eaten away, both by disease and by the sharp teeth and claws of vermin.

A half-moon of yellow-white skull was exposed. In shock and surprise he tripped and fell backwards, knocking over a cupboard full of percussion instruments, and as triangles, drums, cymbals, maracas and other assorted instruments crashed to the floor the school was filled with ugly noise. With cold sweat prickling his brow and his legs suddenly weak with nerves, Jack froze. As the God-awful din finally faded away (it seemed to take for ever), a body slammed angrily against the large window at the other end of the class and began beating and hammering on the glass. It seemed to be looking straight at him, and he could see at least two more, coming up through the shadows behind it.

'You fucking idiot!' Donna cursed as he dragged himself back upstairs, his heart still pounding. 'Have you seen what you've done?'

Jack looked out through the first-floor window. There were corpses approaching the school from all directions.

21

Richard Lawrence flew back towards the dead city of Rowley in search of the missing van and its occupants. Bloody idiots, he thought to himself. How difficult was it for them to stay together and get to the airfield? This didn't bode well for the future. These were people who, inevitably, he was going to have to rely on in time – and just how was he going to be able to do that when they couldn't even get to the airfield in one piece? If it hadn't been for the fact that he'd already been airborne he wouldn't have entertained the idea of going out again tonight for a moment. Dumb fuckers could have waited until morning.

Richard's journey – already unnecessary in his opinion – was further complicated by the number of people involved. The helicopter was designed to carry a maximum of five: the pilot, and four passengers. As if the risks he was taking searching at night weren't enough, he now also faced the potential problem of trying to get back to the airfield with six on board – and he was having to travel alone. He felt isolated and exposed, much more vulnerable than usual. No one else could fly the helicopter but, for safety's sake, he always flew with at least one passenger, to navigate, or to help with the controls, or to do whatever else he needed them to do so that he could concentrate on keeping the machine safely up in the air. If anything went wrong tonight, he was on his own; if he crashed and survived, the bodies would get him. And thanks to the lack of power back at the airfield, he didn't even have the comfort of radio communication. Once again Richard cursed the handful of idiots lost in the city beneath him.

From the air, Rowley looked like a slightly darker stain on an already dark landscape, little more than a featureless scar. Richard had trouble seeing where the city ended and where it began. Christ, he wished he'd gone with his instincts and waited until morning. The relentless blackness of the night made him feel like he was flying with his eyes closed and one hand tied behind his back. He planned to fly directly across the city and then retrace the route he'd given the survivors earlier in the day, concentrating his search around the area where the missing five had become separated from the others. If they were still on the move he'd probably be able to spot them. His fuel supplies were sufficient, not endless, and he decided he'd search for no more than an hour before turning around and heading back to the airfield. If these people had any sense (and he was seriously beginning to wonder whether they did) then he hoped they'd get their heads down and keep themselves out of sight until they heard him.

Jack was looking out into the car park again. 'There are only about twenty of them out there,' he said, trying to make the best of a bad situation for which the others seemed to be holding him completely responsible. 'We can deal with that many, can't we? We've done it before. We can get back to the van and get out of here.'

'We don't have much choice,' Donna said, still seething with anger. 'I knew we should have kept moving. Bloody hell, we could have been there by now.'

'Or we could still have been driving round in circles, using up our fuel,' Kelly reminded her.

'Okay,' she said, struggling to stay focused and calm, 'let's check the map again. We'll plot a route out of here and then make a break for it.'

Jack spread out the map on one of the low desks and illuminated Rowley with his torch. 'This is where we are,' he explained, circling the general area on the map with his finger, 'and that's where we need to be. And around here,' he continued, moving his finger back down the page towards the southern side of the city again, 'is where I think we went wrong.'

The map they were studying was too large a scale to be of any real use in helping them plot a route from their present location back to the road that would take them to the airfield. Jack took a book of town centre street maps from the rucksack he'd been carrying and flicked through until he found the right page.

'What's the name of this place?' he asked.

'Bleakdale,' Kilgore said, holding up a child's exercise book which had the words 'Bleakdale Primary C. of E. School' printed across the front cover.

'Bleakdale . . . got it,' Jack mumbled. He began to run the torch over the page again as he looked for a school and church in close proximity to each other.

'There,' Donna said, peering over his shoulder and pointing at the map. 'There's the school and there's the service road leading up to it. That's the turning we took to get in here.'

'Right, so if we work our way back . . .' His words trailed away as he concentrated on finding his way back to the traffic island where they'd made their original mistake.

'Don't want to pressure you, but we really need to get a move on,' Kelly warned. She was standing next to the window with Clare, looking down into the car park. Although it was slow, a constant trickle of bodies dragged themselves towards the school building, many of them spilling out from around the corner, near the classroom where Jack had first unwittingly attracted their attention. Some of them had become a small but animated crowd around the front of the van.

'More bodies?' Donna asked.

'Plenty more.'

From their first-floor viewpoint Kelly could see along several of the streets surrounding the school. The longer she stared into the night, the more scrambling, stumbling creatures she saw. In the deep-blue darkness, the figures looked like insects scuttling across the landscape as they staggered through the streets and alleyways to converge on the source of the noise which had filled the air just minutes earlier. For the first time she witnessed the effect she'd previously been warned about: the nearest of the dead were themselves now causing enough of a disturbance to summon more and more of them to the scene. Some stood still with their arms hanging heavily at their sides. Others tirelessly pummelled on the sides of the van and on the ground-floor windows and doors of the school building. The few of them gathered in the car park didn't bother her unduly; it was the mass approaching the school from all angles which posed the biggest threat.

Jack forced himself to concentrate. 'I reckon we should just turn around and go back the way we came, sticking to the main roads,' he suggested. 'We turn left out of the car park and keep following the road until it loops back around onto the first road we drove up by mistake. Follow that back and—'

'—and we should be on track again,' Donna said, finishing his sentence for him.

'Why go backwards?' Kelly asked, moving away from the window and looking down at the maps with the others. 'Why not just keep going forward?'

'We could,' Jack replied, obviously unsure, 'but that means going deeper into the city.'

'So? Do you really think that matters now? According to this map we're close to the city centre anyway. I don't think another couple of miles is going to make that much difference, do you?'

'I don't know,' Jack mumbled, not sure if he wanted to admit she had a point.

'Look,' she explained, grabbing Donna's torch so she could show them what she was thinking. 'We could go left as you suggested, Jack, but then turn left again at the next roundabout instead of going straight over. By the time that gets us onto the right road we'll only be a few miles short of the airfield.'

The soldier's plan made sense – the risks they were facing were great whichever direction they chose, so surely it would be more sensible to leave the school and go forwards, not back?

'I'm still not sure,' Jack said.

'Well you'd better make your minds up quickly,' Clare said from by the window.

'Why?'

'Helicopter,' she said, pointing up into the sky at the flashing lights on the tail of the aircraft high above them.

For a second no one moved. Then Kelly grabbed her stuff and started to run, followed quickly by the rest of the small group.

'How will they know where we are?' Clare asked as they thundered downstairs.

'We need to get moving,' Donna said. 'They'll have more chance of seeing us if we're in the van.'

'You reckon?' Kilgore asked, pausing by the exit door.

'Hope so,' she said as she pushed her way out and ran over to the van. It was surrounded by corpses and she ripped the first few of them away, then forced her hand through a gap between them and yanked open the van door. They were all immediately aware of huge movement around them as bodies turned from all directions and were now moving quickly towards them, lurching desperately at them with ominous speed and purpose. The evening gloom was disorientating; it made the perception of distance surprisingly difficult. One of the nearest cadavers reached out for Kilgore and caught hold of him before he even knew it was there.

'Get it off me!' he screamed in panic, 'Get this fucking thing off me!'

He spun around, trying desperately to dislodge the emaciated creature, to somehow grab hold of it and drag it around in front of him. The corpse's slimy skin and constant writhing movements made it impossible for him to get a grip.

'I've got it,' Kelly said calmly as she wrapped her arm around its neck and yanked the loathsome figure off him. She threw it angrily to the ground and stamped on its head with her standard-issue British Army boots until it was still. There were many more of the dead around them now, too many to try and deal with. Kilgore, shocked by the sudden attack and not thinking straight, immediately began to check his suit for damage as the others bundled themselves into the van, until Jack shoved him and he scrambled inside. Donna started the engine and pulled away, turning around in a tight circle, her wheels skidding on the gore of downed bodies as more corpses thumped against the bodywork. They roared out of the car park and along the service road, wiping out another oncoming group as they swerved out onto the road.

'There!' Clare shouted as Donna threw the van around the second sharp turn. She pointed up at the helicopter, which was moving quickly through the sky ahead of them. 'There it is!'

'Left here,' Kelly ordered from the back, not about to let Donna screw up again. Donna did as she was told, guiding the van between the parallel wrecks of a car and a burned-out milk float. The van's headlights lit up swarms of movement ahead of them as bodies emerged from all sides and stumbled towards the light and noise.

'He'll never see us,' Kilgore moaned from the back.

'Of course he will,' Jack said, really sick of the soldier's pathetic, defeatist attitude, 'there's nothing else to see out here, is there?'

High above the streets, Richard Lawrence had completed his first sweep of the city centre and was trying to find an excuse for giving up for the night when he caught sight of a momentary flash of light below. It was the only illumination in the whole of the dead city, making the van easy to pick out and follow. He took the helicopter down as much as he dared: low enough to keep track of the vehicle below, but still at a sufficient height to avoid any tall blacked-out buildings, electricity pylons or similar. He knew he probably wouldn't see such obstacles tonight until he hit them.

On the ground, the van had reached a blockage in the road – nothing too serious, but the tangled wreckage of a three-car crash had covered enough of the carriageway to force Donna to slow down to little more than walking pace and drive on the pavement to negotiate the obstruction. Richard switched on the helicopter's searchlight, both to let them know he'd seen them and to provide extra illumination. Bodies stumbled into the light, drawn like moths.

To the right of the van was a row of buildings, but on the other side of the road, another half-mile ahead, Richard could see an expanse of open land – a park, or playing fields perhaps? He eased the helicopter forward to hover above the grassland and saw that directly beneath him were two sets of football posts. Even if the pitch wasn't full size, he knew he had room to land. He started to move the searchlight to point down at the pitch in a rudimentary attempt to signal to the people on the ground.

'What's the hell's he doing now?' Donna asked, concentrating on driving and relying on the others to tell her what was happening above them.

'He's moved over to our left,' Jack replied, 'and now he's hovering.' He stared up at the helicopter.

Once clear of the remains of the pile-up, the van sped up again, slamming into a random body and almost cutting it in two. Its head and shoulders thumped against the glass, leaving a bloody smear.

Donna flicked on the wipers.

'He's definitely stopped moving now,' he continued, struggling to see clearly through the dirty glass. 'Try and get closer.'

'I can only follow the bloody road,' Donna said anxiously. 'What do you want me to do?'

'Wait . . . He's dropping down.'

'What?'

'I think he's landing.'

Donna allowed herself to look up from the road. Jack was right.

'Stop the van,' Kelly ordered from the back. 'Quick! Stop the van and we'll find him on foot.'

'Are you bloody stupid?' Kilgore protested.

'It's a park,' Jack said as they passed a momentary gap in the tree-lined metal fence that lined the road they'd been following. 'Kelly's right – Donna, stop the van and let's make a run for it.'

Donna didn't argue. She was cold and tired and frightened and she wanted this wild and pointless chase through nowhere to be over. She forced the van up onto the pavement and as she climbed out a body threw itself at her, almost knocking her to the ground. She quickly regained her balance and shoved the corpse against the fence, then sprinted after Jack, Clare and the two soldiers, who were already up ahead, trying to find a way into the park.

Now that they were out of the van, the sound of the helicopter filled the air. With his legs already burning with effort, Jack forced himself to keep moving forward, trying to keep up with the others, who were all much younger and in far better physical condition than him. Being at the back of the pack terrified him, but he couldn't move any faster. He allowed himself a momentary glance over his shoulder and saw bodies shuffling after them. There seemed to be hundreds of them, dragging themselves out of the shadows from every direction, all gravitating towards him. He looked forward again and concentrated on following Donna, who had just overtaken him. He didn't dare look back a second time, but he was sure the bodies were gaining. How close were they now? Was one about to grab hold of him?

'Through here,' Clare shouted as she reached an open wrought-iron gate and ducked through under the overgrown branches of a bush. She ran into the park and was immediately able to see the helicopter in all its magnificent glory. It was the most incredible thing she'd ever seen, hovering imperiously some ten feet above the ground and waiting for them.

'Has he seen us?' Donna yelled as she tripped through the overlong grass which had been left to grow wild for weeks. She began to wave her arms furiously, hoping that the pilot would see her and respond. At first nothing happened. The brilliant white searchlight lit up almost all of the park, illuminating the crowds of cadavers swarming towards the helicopter from all sides. The relative speed and control of the survivors made them easy for Richard to pick out through the crowds, but he didn't dare risk setting down until they were almost directly underneath him. At the last possible moment he dropped the final few feet down to the ground.

'One in the front with me and the rest of you in the back,' Richard yelled over the deafening engine and rotor blade roar as Kelly yanked the helicopter door open. 'Strap yourselves in if you can; just hold on if you can't.'

The pilot's voice was barely audible over the noise. Clare and the two soldiers climbed in, finally followed by Jack. Donna had waited for him at the side of the helicopter; she had to push him up into his seat. Dizzy with exhaustion, he slumped back and sucked in long, cool mouthfuls of damp evening air as she slammed the door shut in his face.

'Come on,' Richard urged. The bodies were damn close now. He could see the decayed faces of the nearest of the dead staring back at him. Donna scrambled into the front and pulled the door shut, and by the time she'd buckled up they were airborne. Directly below, where the wind whipped the wild grass furiously, the bodies converged and tried pointlessly to reach up for the rapidly disappearing machine.

22

The flight to Monkton Airfield took less than fifteen minutes, and the stillness which greeted them when they finally landed and the helicopter shut down was in stark contrast to the chaos they'd left behind. Oblivious to the thousands upon thousands of cold, dead eyes which stared at them from beyond the other side of the distant fence, Jack, Clare, Donna, Kelly and Kilgore stumbled out of the helicopter, exhausted but relieved, and followed Richard Lawrence across the tarmac. He led them towards a collection of dark buildings – a large, half-empty hangar, a control tower, and several smaller buildings which had once been offices, rudimentary canteen facilities, waiting rooms and a public lounge. Jack was impressed. Even though it was dark, the place looked better equipped and more substantial than he'd dared imagine it might. It looked like it had been an unusual cross between a small commercial airport and a flying club; he guessed it had probably been used for private planes, chartered flights and pilot training. He noticed the prison van and personnel carrier parked a short distance away, and their presence was an enormous relief. The rest of the group had made it safely to the airfield.

A dull light was shining out from the very top of the control tower, illuminating the way as they followed Richard into the building, across a small open area and up two flights of echoing metal stairs. The events of the last few hours had been physically and mentally exhausting, and Jack in particular was struggling to keep moving forward. They finally reached the top of the building and entered a large room through a pair of heavy swinging double-doors. Inside, the room was light and warm, and was buzzing with noise and relaxed conversation. It couldn't have been more different to the cold silence of the outside world. The sight of familiar faces dotted around filled the new arrivals with a sudden surge of energy again.

'You finally made it then,' Cooper shouted sarcastically from across the room. 'Where the hell have you lot been?'

'Piss off!' Jack replied, managing a tired grin. 'We took a couple of wrong turns, that was all!'

'Just a couple? Bloody hell, we'd almost given up on you. We've been here for hours!'

Donna stood in the doorway and soaked up the atmosphere. The mass of people around her – both those she knew and the twenty or so faces she didn't recognise – looked at ease. She too suddenly felt much calmer, as if the stresses and problems that had continually plagued her for almost eight weeks had finally begun to be stripped away. Was it because she'd reached the airfield that she felt that way, or was she just relieved that Cooper and the others were safe? Whatever the reason, she hadn't been in such a comfortable and welcoming environment for a long, long time. In fact, now she stopped to think about it, she hadn't felt free like this since – well, before this nightmare had begun. For a few precious moments the relief was such that she couldn't move. The hell outside suddenly seemed a thousand miles away.

'You okay?' someone beside her asked. It was Emma.

'I'm fine,' she answered quickly, suddenly self-conscious. 'I'm sorry, I was just—'

Donna stopped mid-sentence, but Emma knew what she was trying to say. She'd experienced the same bewildering range of emotions herself when she'd first arrived at the airfield.

'This is great, Donna,' she continued. 'These people have really got themselves sorted out here.'

'Looks that way . . .'

'You won't believe some of the things they've been telling us. You know, when we first saw the helicopter this morning I knew it was going to be important, but I didn't realise just how important. None of us had time to stop and think about it, did we? Christ, these people have been up and down the length of the whole bloody country. They've seen other bases like the one Cooper came from, and—'

'I know, I heard Richard talking earlier. So how come there's so few of them?'

'I suppose they've just been taking the same approach to all this as we have,' Emma answered. 'Mike and I decided right from the start that we couldn't afford to spend all our time looking around for other survivors. We knew we had to forget about everyone else and concentrate on getting through this ourselves. Looks like these people have spent their time doing that too.'

'So how many of them are there?'

'Not sure exactly. I think someone said there are about twenty or so of them here, with another six already on Cormansey.'

'Cormansey?'

'The island, remember?'

Donna nodded. She was tired and her brain wasn't functioning properly.

Tonight she looked drained and weak, a shadow of her normal self, Emma thought, and she passed her a drink. It was a small bottle of lemonade. The sweet liquid was warm and gassy, but it was very welcome.

'Much happened since you've been here then?' Donna asked, wiping her mouth dry on the back of her sleeve.

'Not really,' Emma answered, 'we've just been waiting for you lot to turn up. What happened? Did you run into trouble?'

'Stupid cock-up,' she admitted. 'We took the wrong exit on the roundabout where that bloody memorial came down, and then made more mistakes trying to get back on track and catch up with you.'

'You're here now. That's all that matters.'

A sudden loud burst of laughter came from the far side of the room. It was an unexpected and strangely startling noise. Donna looked up and saw that Michael, Cooper and several others were talking to people she didn't recognise. At first she didn't question who these people might be, or what they might have found amusing. Instead her mind was preoccupied with the fact that she'd just heard laughter for the first time in weeks. Whatever it was they were finding funny, it unexpectedly touched a nerve. Normally strong and determined, to the point of sometimes seeming cold and uncaring, Donna now felt ready to crumble and burst into tears. She dismissed her feelings as just a passing moment of weakness, probably brought on by exhaustion. She turned and looked out of a window behind her before Emma could see she was upset.

'See that woman sitting next to Mike?' Emma asked.

Donna turned back around and nonchalantly wiped her eyes.

The woman sitting between Michael and Phil Croft was rotund, red-faced and very loud. In a world where silence was now the key to staying alive, Donna wondered how the hell she'd managed to survive for so long.

'The big lady?' she replied, choosing her words carefully.

'That's right.'

'Who is she?'

'Her name's Jackie Soames. It doesn't look like anyone's officially in charge here, but she seems to be involved with most of the decision-making.'

'She doesn't look . . .' Donna began.

'She doesn't look like the kind of person who'd be sitting in a place like this dishing out advice,' Emma interrupted, successfully anticipating what Donna had been about to try and say. 'She's got a lot of respect here, though. I've spoken to a few people, and they've got only good things to say about her. Apparently she used to run a pub. Story is she slept through everything that happened on the first day, went to bed with a hangover and woke up at midday and found her husband dead behind the bar.'

'Nice. Who else is there?'

'See the young lad on his own with his back to us?'

'Yes.'

'That's Martin Smith. He's the one who—'

'—who reckons he found out how all this happened?'

'That's him. And the bloke standing looking out of the window over there,' she continued, nodding across to the diagonally opposite corner of the square room.

'The one with the jacket and the hair?'

'That's the one,' she replied, 'I think his name's Gary Keele. He calls himself Tuggie.'

Donna looked at the man and felt a strange combination of emotions. Whilst just about every other survivor she'd seen was wearing whatever clothes they'd been able to salvage, this man's appearance seemed to suggest that, for some inexplicable reason, he still considered it important to be well-dressed and presentable. His hair – in contrast to just about everyone else – was surprisingly well-groomed. He looked conspicuously out of place, somehow separate from the others. But was it because he'd chosen not to mix with them, or did the rest of the group not want to associate with him? Whatever the reason, in a room full of people he was very much alone.

'So what does he do around here?' she asked, guessing that the man must have had some relevance to the group for Emma to have pointed him out.

'Apparently he's the one who's going to fly the plane and get everyone to the island.'

'Why do you say it like that? What do you mean, "apparently"?'

'That girl over there – she's called Jo – told me that he used to fly little tug planes at a gliding club.'

'Hence the nickname?'

'That's right. Anyway, she says he's not flown anything as big as the plane they've got here yet.'

'Does he need to? They've got the helicopter, haven't they?'

'The plan is to keep sending people over to the island in threes and fours to make it safe. When it's all clear they'll load up the plane and take everyone and everything else over.'

Donna finished her drink. 'So what's the problem?'

'Richard Lawrence told me he found him hiding under a table in an office at another airfield when he stopped to refuel the helicopter. The guy's a bloody nervous wreck. I'm not convinced he's going to be able to fly anyone anywhere.'

'Great,' Donna mumbled.

Jack Baxter crossed her line of vision and began to walk towards her. The tension and fear so evident in his face earlier had now disappeared and had been replaced with a relaxed, almost disbelieving grin.

'You two all right?'

'Fine,' Donna answered. 'You?'

'Bloody fantastic!'

'That good, eh?' she mumbled, unable to match his enthusiasm.

'Yep, that good.'

'And what are you so happy about?'

'Can't you feel it?'

'Feel what? We've only been here a few minutes, Jack. I haven't had a chance to feel anything yet.'

'This is going to work out.' He grinned. 'I can feel it in my bones. I tell you, it won't be long now before we're out of this mess.'

23

The control tower had become the focal point of Monkton Airfield. It was the strongest-built building, and the safest, so that was where the survivors ate, talked, slept, planned, argued, cried and did pretty much everything else. The first people to arrive at the airfield had chosen it because of its height and its distance from the perimeter fence and the decaying hordes, which gave at least the illusion of security. With the unexpected arrival of the group from the military base, however – nearly forty extra people – space was suddenly at a premium. Michael and Emma found a small, dark room at the foot of the stairs, opposite the main entrance, where they sat together, draped in blankets to ward off the bitter cold. Winter was still a couple of months away officially, but the temperature felt like it was dropping daily. Maybe it just seemed that way.

Michael had something on his mind. He'd wanted to talk to Emma since an earlier conversation he'd had with Cooper and Jackie Soames, but she seemed more relaxed today than he'd ever seen her and he found it difficult to talk when he knew that what he was going to say would inevitably upset her.

After skirting round the subject for what felt like the hundredth time, Michael took a deep breath. It was time.

'Em,' he began slowly, trying to choose his words with care, 'I was talking to Cooper earlier—'

'I know,' she replied, 'I saw you. The pair of you looked as thick as thieves.'

'Remember the conversation we had on the way here?' he continued, 'when we talked about the island? And I said I wanted to try and get over there pretty quickly so we could make sure we get everything we needed?'

'I remember,' Emma said, already anticipating what he was about to say next.

'Well, I'm going to go over on the next flight,' he told her, wanting to get the words out as quickly as he could.

Emma nodded, but she didn't say anything, and in the dark it was difficult for him to gauge her reaction.

As the uncomfortablc, prolonged silence dragged on, Michael felt compelled to explain himself. 'There are a couple of damn good reasons why I should go. Most important is that I really do want to get over there to try and make sure that this island is everything we need it to be. And second—'

'What happens if it's not?' Emma interrupted. 'What are you going to do? Ask them if they wouldn't mind just dropping you back so you can start looking for somewhere else?'

'And second,' he continued, ignoring her anger, 'have you looked at the people left around here, Em?'

'What about them?'

'Just go upstairs and have a look around. Most of the people here are empty. There's more life in half the bodies outside than in some of them up there. It's not their fault; they just can't handle what's happened.'

'What point are you trying to make?'

'Jackie Soames says they've already sent their strongest people over there, but they're planning to clear out the village in the next couple of days, and they're going to need as much manpower as they can get.'

'I know that, but why you – why not send Cooper, or—?'

He took her hand in his and squeezed gently. 'Cooper's a hard bastard; he'll be more use here keeping this lot moving in the right direction. And if I'm honest, I *want* to do this, Emma. I want to go. I need it.'

'So when do you think you'll be leaving?' she asked, not sure she really wanted to hear his answer.

'They're planning the next flight for sometime tomorrow. Probably early afternoon.'

She didn't say anything, and her silence bothered Michael. He knew he was doing the right thing – hell, he was sure they *both* knew that – but that didn't make it any easier.

'It'll be okay,' he said, his voice soft and quiet. 'This place seems secure, and—'

'You say that every time we find somewhere new to shelter and yet within days we're on the run again,' she snapped at him. 'You and your bloody chaos theory.'

'This place *seems* secure,' he repeated, 'but we both know it probably won't last. The bodies will keep coming . . .'

'So you thought you'd leave now, before we're overrun?'

'Come on, Em, that's not fair. I want to go over to the island to make sure things are moving, that's all. The place could be cleared of bodies in a couple of days, and by this time next week we could all be over there, standing out in the open without a hundred thousand bloody corpses watching our every move.'

Emma was starting to regret what she'd said. Michael was right; it had been unfair, and unnecessary. 'Sorry,' she said quietly.

'It's okay—'

'It's just that I don't want you to go,' she continued. 'I don't want to be here on my own.'

'But you're not going to be on your own, are you? There are more people here now than we've seen since this whole thing kicked off.'

'No, that's not what I meant. You and I have been together since this started, and I don't want that to change. I've been okay as long as I've been with you. We've had some pretty bloody awful times, but we've got through them all . . . I guess I'm just frightened that you'll leave here and things will go wrong – something will happen to you, or you won't come back, or—'

'Shh,' he soothed. 'Come on, now you're just being silly.'

'Am I?'

'Yes, you are. Look, Em, this is nothing: I'll go over there in the helicopter tomorrow and the job'll be done and you'll be over there with me before you know it.'

'You make it sound easy.'

'It is easy.'

'Is it? Is it really? Wake up, Mike! In case you hadn't noticed, nothing's easy any more. Finding the next meal isn't easy. Keeping warm and dry and out of sight isn't easy. Keeping quiet isn't easy. Driving around the country running from place to place isn't easy, so please don't patronise me by telling me that getting into a frigging helicopter with a man we barely know and flying God knows how many bloody miles to wipe out this island's already dead population is going to be easy either.'

Now Michael was becoming irritated by her negativity and defeatist attitude. 'Look,' he said, 'I've got a chance to do something tomorrow that might mean an actual future for us – the two of us, together. And if I'm honest, I think I have to do it because I don't trust any of those other fuckers upstairs to do it properly. This is really important, and we can't afford to take any chances with this.'

'I *know* all that,' Emma replied, sounding equally emotional, 'I *know* why you're going and I *know* what has to be done – but none of that makes it any easier to deal with. I just don't want you to go, that's all. You're all I've got left.'

24

'You okay?' Jack Baxter asked, sounding concerned.

Kelly looked up and nodded. She was slumped in a seat in the furthest, quietest corner of the room at the top of the control tower. Kilgore was asleep, curled up in a ball on the ground at her feet like a faithful dog. Unlike him, Kelly couldn't switch off. Her head was spinning, filled with frequently painful thoughts. The hard, bloody fight outside the bunker and the subsequent journey to this place had been a long and difficult distraction, but now, sitting here in the calm silence, there was nothing to think about except the grim inevitability of her future.

'No, I'm not okay,' she said to Jack with what he thought was admirable honesty. 'Are you?' She didn't look at him, but stared impassively out of the window, into the darkness.

'I'm all right,' he replied, pulling up a chair and sitting down next to her. For the first time since leaving the base Jack thought the young soldier looked odd, out of place even, in her heavy protective suit. In the chaos of the last couple of days he had become used to seeing soldiers, guns and helicopters, but Kelly and Kilgore suddenly didn't fit in with their surroundings. He could see her dark, melancholy eyes behind her visor. The poor kid! She could only be in her early twenties. Jack felt desperately sorry for her, but he was already regretting sitting down next to her. There was absolutely nothing that he – or anyone else – could do to help her, not even to soften the blow of what was almost certainly going to happen to her in the near future. He'd sat down originally with the intention of trying to start a conversation, but now he found he didn't know what to say.

Jack was about to get up and walk away again when she spoke. She'd realised she didn't want to be alone. 'My dad,' she said, her voice flat and empty, 'he would have liked it here. He loved planes. He was turning into a proper old-fashioned Grandad. He used to take my nephews, my sister's boys, to the airport and they'd spend the whole day watching the planes taking off and landing.'

'Never really appealed to me,' Jack admitted.

'Me neither. Dad loved it, though – you should have seen him at my passing-out parade! Mum told me she had to keep reminding him to watch me. He spent the whole time looking around the base and admiring the kit instead of looking at me.' She faltered.

Jack, feeling slightly more comfortable now there was a topic of conversation he could follow, asked, 'So tell me, how did you end up in uniform?'

'I had two older brothers in the Forces – like I said, Dad was always interested in the military, so I guess I just grew up surrounded by it. I didn't really know what I wanted to do when I left school, so I just sort of stumbled into it. I figured what was good enough for my brothers was good enough for me too.'

'Glad you did it?'

'I had some good times, knew some good people.'

'You talk about it as if it's over.'

'Come on, Jack,' she sighed, 'cut the bullshit. You know it is.'

'But doesn't this feel like it did every time you went out to fight? What I mean is—' He groped for the right words to express himself. 'Well, you knew that you were putting your life on the line every time you picked up your weapon, didn't you?'

'This is different,' she explained. 'At least on the battlefield you had a chance. Here I'm just sitting and waiting for it to happen, and that's what makes it so bloody hard to deal with. There's nothing I can do about it – there's nothing anyone can do.'

'I'm sorry, I shouldn't have—'

'Forget it. It's not your fault.'

Jack wondered whether it would be better for both of them if he just got up and walked away now . . . or perhaps he owed it to her to stay and try to repair some of the damage he was sure he was doing? The pity he suddenly felt for this young woman was both overpowering and humbling. He couldn't even begin to imagine how she must have been feeling.

'If I could have my time again,' she said quietly, 'then I never would have signed up.' Her voice, although muffled by her breathing apparatus, suddenly sounded tearful and full of regret. 'I probably would have left school and got myself a normal job like all my friends did.'

'Why do you say that?'

'Because if I hadn't signed up, then I wouldn't be sitting here now, talking to you and waiting to die. If I hadn't signed up then I'd probably have died on the first day, like I should have. I'd have died next to my mum or my dad or my boyfriend, not on my own out here.'

'You're not on your own.'

'I don't know anyone, other than Cooper and this idiot,' she sighed, gently nudging the soldier on the ground with the toe of her boot. 'Honestly, Jack, it would have been so much easier that way.'

'But you don't know. You might—'

'Please don't try to make me feel better with bullshit. There's no point.'

'You might be able to breathe,' he continued. 'There are almost fifty of us here who can.'

'And there are millions of dead people out there who couldn't. I think there's a pretty good chance I'm not immune, don't you?'

'But you've made it this far – why stop and give up now?'

'Because now that I have stopped I can see that there's no point. I'm just prolonging the inevitable. It's going to happen sooner or later.'

'So why not later?'

'There's nothing to hang on for. You'll all be gone soon anyway.'

'So come with us.'

'Why? It might as well happen here as anywhere. If you've got any sense you won't bother taking me and Kilgore over to your island, we'd just be taking up precious cargo space. You might as well use the space to take something that's going to be useful.'

'There might be somewhere on the island that we can adapt so that—'

'Shut up, Jack! It's not working – I appreciate the thought, really I do, but you're just digging a bigger hole for yourself now. Honestly, what are you going to do? There's only one village on the island, for Christ's sake. I don't even know if there's a hospital. There won't be anywhere for me and Kilgore – or were you planning to bubble-wrap a house so that we can live in a fucking oxygen tent? Thanks for your concern, but it's just not going to happen.'

Jack finally realised that it really was time to stop talking. He'd meant well, but she was right. He wasn't helping. 'So what are you going to do?' he asked after a while.

Silence.

'Nothing,' she eventually replied. 'I'll just sit here in this bloody suit until I can't take it any more. Then I'll end it.'

25

Michael woke up in agony next morning. He and Emma had spent the night together, sleeping on the floor of the little room they'd found. He'd been lying on the hard concrete, and Emma had been lying on him; now every bone in his body ached. He opened his eyes and looked around. Their difficult conversation was still echoing around his head, and his heart sank when he remembered that he would be leaving her today.

Emma was still asleep, so he carefully eased himself out from underneath her and made sure that she was warm and comfortable before leaving the room. He tiptoed across to the main entrance, pushed the door open and stepped out into a bright, cool morning. The sun was high in a clear blue sky, and a gusting wind blew across the airfield and wakened him fully. A short distance ahead of him was the helicopter, and the sun glinted on its curved surfaces and reflected back at him. He stood and stared at it for a moment before remembering what he'd actually come outside for. He found a less exposed corner of the building, leant against the wall and began to empty his aching bladder.

'Morning, Mike,' a voice suddenly said, making him jump and quickly look around.

Donna was sitting on a fold-up garden chair at the edge of the runway, not looking at him but staring out across the airfield at the bodies on the other side of the distant fence.

A couple of months ago Michael would have been mortified at being caught urinating publicly like this. Today he didn't care. 'Morning,' he said nonchalantly as he shook himself dry, then did up his fly and wiped his hands on the dew-wet grass. 'You all right?'

'Fine,' she replied, shielding her eyes from the sun as he walked towards her.

'What you doing out here?'

'Originally the same as you,' she answered factually. 'Other than that, not a lot! I just wanted to get some air – I still can't get used to being able to be outside like this.'

'Bloody cold, though, isn't it?'

Donna looked up at him. He sounded distracted. 'You okay?'

He crouched down next to her, but didn't answer immediately. From here the bodies on the other side of the fence looked miles away, and he couldn't make out individual figures any more; there was just a constantly shifting mass of grey-green decay. Phil Croft had mentioned that he thought the corpses might not be able to see the survivors for much longer because of the steady deterioration of their faces and eyes. Their limited eyesight might be getting worse day by day, but that didn't seem to be making much difference to their behaviour: there were still vast numbers of them on the other side of the fence.

'So Cooper tells me you're leaving us,' Donna said.

'You make it sound like I'm going for good. I think we're planning to leave later today. All depends on Richard being able to fly in this wind, I suppose.'

'And how does Emma feel about it?'

'She's ecstatic,' he answered sarcastically. 'Yes, she's really pleased.'

'I bet.'

'She understands.'

'What happens on Cormansey is important.'

'I know.'

'Do you realise *how* important? This could be the difference between living and just existing, Mike. This is the best chance we've had, and it's probably the best chance we're going to get.'

'I know,' he said again. 'That's exactly why I'm going with them.' He stood up, brushed himself down and walked out onto the runway. He thought about what Donna had just said, the gravity in her voice, and the sudden importance of the day was humbling. Until now he hadn't stopped to think about what he was going to do in any great detail – he'd considered the practicalities of getting over to the island, and he'd paid lip service to helping slaughter the dead for the good of all, and to starting to build a future for the whole group. Standing outside, however, with the biting wind blowing into his face and the smell of death still hanging in the air, he suddenly began to fully appreciate the enormity of the task ahead.

Behind him Richard Lawrence emerged from the door at the base of the control tower and walked over to where Donna was sitting. 'You two all right out here?' he asked.

'Just taking in the air,' she replied, giving him the same answer she'd given Michael minutes earlier. 'It's been a long time since we've been able to do this.'

Michael turned around when he heard the pilot's voice.

'We'll be looking to leave around midday, okay?' said Richard.

'Will we be all right with this wind?'

'Believe me, this is nothing,' he answered, laughing. 'I've been up in far worse than this recently. Trust me, mate, this is a good day for flying. A little breezy perhaps, but nothing I can't handle.'

Michael realised he'd been quietly hoping for a delay. Events were suddenly unfolding at an uncomfortable speed, and now he wanted to spend some time with Emma before he left. They'd spent just about every minute of the last eight weeks together, but that they were going to be apart soon, and every last second suddenly felt more precious. He turned and jogged back to the control tower to find her.

26

The morning disappeared in minutes. For the first time in recent memory Michael prayed that time would slow down. Take-off had been delayed by an hour, but that wasn't enough. He'd wanted longer.

The helicopter's powerful rotor blades sliced through the air above their heads as Richard flew Michael, Peter Guest and Danny Talbot, one of the few teenagers, across the dead land. The spare seat between Michael and Peter was piled high with their belongings and supplies, with every scrap of space filled.

What was quickly becoming a regular, almost run-of-the-mill journey for Richard was far more of an unsettling experience for his passengers. As well as being used to flying, Richard had also grown accustomed to the view of the scarred landscape from the air. For Michael, Peter and Danny, the turbulent journey was a harsh education: a painful reminder of the almost incomprehensible scale of the devastation down at ground level.

For the first half of the journey Michael had been preoccupied with thoughts of Emma. He hadn't been able to get her tearful face out of his mind, and now that he'd left her he felt hollow and alone. He'd looked down from the air and watched her grow smaller and smaller, until she'd disappeared from view. He tried to comfort himself with the thought that if everything went according to plan they would be back together in less than a week, but there was a lot of work to do before then . . . and these days, things rarely seemed to go according to plan. Michael was already bitterly regretting having left her. It was as she'd said in the early hours of the morning just passed: so far they'd struggled through almost every second of the nightmare together. Being away from her now just didn't feel right.

Forcing himself to clear his mind and focus on what was ahead, he looked across the interior of the helicopter at Peter Guest. Peter was sitting with his head resting against the glass, and he was staring down, transfixed, watching the ground rush by beneath them at a furious speed. Michael turned and looked out of his side. The bright sun of the morning had long gone; now the late-autumn afternoon sky was dull, and filled with rain. He peered down as they flew over a small town. It might have been the speed, or even his imagination, but everything below looked blurred and undefined. It was almost as if the buildings and roads were being swallowed up and melting back into the land.

Danny Talbot, a stocky, acne-ridden teenager who had ridden in the back of Steve Armitage's prison truck, found himself instinctively looking out for survivors amongst the ruination. But almost everything was still, and he saw nothing. If I was down there on my own, he thought, when I heard the helicopter I'd go outside and I'd made damn sure they saw me. So why couldn't he see anyone down there now? Why could he see only rotting bodies shuffling painfully across the silent landscape? Was it because any survivors who heard the helicopter were too scared, or too slow or too vulnerable to react? Or was it just because there were no more survivors? He was beginning to think that was the most probable explanation.

'Cormansey,' Richard Lawrence announced a little over twenty minutes later, and pointed to the island on the misty horizon. The mainland was behind them now, and the helicopter raced out over the ocean. Michael had closed his eyes and had been on the brink of falling asleep when the pilot's words had made him quickly sit up again. He felt nervous as he stared out of the rain-streaked window. The longer the journey had gone on, the more he had become used to the feeling of protection the helicopter gave him. The thought that they would soon be back down at ground level and in the midst of the mayhem again was disconcerting.

The helicopter soared over the deceptively smooth ocean, dropping closer to the waves. The frothing surf was just a few feet below them and, for the first time, the passengers were able to fully appreciate the speed at which they were travelling. The dark blur on the horizon quickly grew in size and definition and in a few minutes more they were over the island.

'This is it then,' mumbled Peter as he looked down at the rough, unwelcoming landscape beneath them. It looked just as Michael had imagined: cold and bleak, grey rock giving way to lush green grassland, with the occasional patches of russet-red and orange-brown vegetation. The sea was relentlessly battering the island's coastline, huge waves crashing against the rocks and sending plumes of froth high into the air. And here below them was the village Richard had talked about. It was little more than the intersection of several short roads lined with buildings, and they could see bodies, lying motionless where they had fallen months earlier. Although they were only over the place for a matter of seconds, it was time enough for them to spot several corpses, shuffling ominously between the buildings. Strange, Michael thought, that they gravitated to the buildings, even with no one living there.

Richard flew further along the length of the island, and Michael continued to stare at the land they passed over, the rich colours below a stark contrast with the grey sky. He could see narrow roads, and gravel tracks leading up to the doors of isolated houses. Virtually every home on the island, although in sight of other buildings, stood a distance apart from even its nearest neighbour. Some looked even more remote than Penn Farm.

'Almost there,' Richard shouted as the helicopter climbed quickly to clear a sudden elevation in the otherwise flat landscape. They passed over a rocky scar which ran across almost the entire width of Cormansey, and once over the rocks they had a clear view of the rest of the island. Just ahead, Michael could make out a short landing strip cut into the relatively flat grassland, and a little further on he could see more buildings, including a small, white-washed cottage. From behind the cottage a plume of smoke rose up into the squally air. Unperturbed by the swirling winds, Richard skilfully brought the helicopter down in the middle of the runway. None of them moved at first, not even to unbuckle their safety belts.

'They'll be here in a couple of minutes,' Richard said, lowering his voice as the powerful engine slowed and died.

'Who will?' asked Peter, panicking. Did he mean the bodies?

'The others,' he explained. 'Brigid, Harry, and the rest of them. There're only half a dozen here at the moment, but they've been working hard.'

Michael wiped a section of window clear of condensation. Now that the helicopter had landed they could both hear and feel the full strength of the fierce wind, which whistled through the rotor blades and buffeted the aircraft so forcefully it almost felt as if it was being shunted back along the runway. Michael had felt safer up in the air.

'So where are these people coming from?' Peter asked. 'Not that it really matters, I suppose. Can't take long to get from one place to the other here.'

'Takes fifteen minutes to drive from one end of the island to the other,' Richard said. 'We drove round the whole island when we first got here, to get our bearings. We based ourselves at this end because of the airstrip and the hill – the bodies will really struggle to get over the rocks, so we figured they'd mostly stay around the village at the other end. Hang on, here they are.' He opened his door and climbed down onto the runway, then helped the others out.

As he stepped down onto the tarmac Michael saw a pair of bright headlights moving along the airstrip towards them. As the vehicle approached he could see that it was a new-looking Jeep. It stopped a short distance from them and a large woman climbed out of the driver's seat.

'You okay, Richard? Good flight over?'

'Not bad,' he replied. 'How've things been here?'

'Quiet,' she answered. 'Quieter than I'd expected, actually.'

The woman looked at the three new arrivals.

'Brigid Culthorpe, this is Michael Collins, Peter Guest and Danny Talbot,' Richard said, introducing them, and as each of them acknowledged her, he continued, 'They were with a group that joined us yesterday. Remember I told you about the crowd of bodies we saw on our way over here last time? That was these guys. They'd been holed up for a while in some military installation or other. Had some trouble and ended up having to make a break for it. Karen and I managed to track them down and get them back to the airfield.'

Michael stood next to the helicopter with his arms folded across his chest, looking around anxiously, only half-listening to the conversation. It still didn't feel right to be standing out in the open like this, exposed and defenceless. Were there really so few bodies around here that it didn't matter?

'Come on,' said Brigid, 'let's get into the warm.'

She helped the men unload the supplies from the helicopter and throw them into the Jeep. Michael, Peter and Danny crammed themselves into the back of the vehicle. Though all three had dozens of questions, they sat in silence as Brigid turned around and drove back down the runway.

'Been keeping yourself busy then, Brig?' Richard asked.

'You know me, Rich, I always do,' she replied. 'What about you? Everything all right back on the mainland?'

'The same as when you left really. There are a few more of us now, that's all.'

'And are you going to be able to get Keele to fly that plane over here soon?'

'I bloody well hope so. I'm sick of doing all the donkey work. Christ, the number of times I've flown backwards and forwards between the airfield and this bloody island . . .'

'Don't make it sound like such an ordeal,' she laughed, leaning forward and wiping condensation from the windscreen with the back of her hand. 'You love it when you're here.'

'I do,' he agreed. 'It's going back to that dead place that I can't stand.'

A narrow dirt track curved away from the end of the airstrip and disappeared between two low, dune-like hills. Brigid drove onto the rough track and followed it around to the right. Sandwiched uncomfortably between Peter and Danny, Michael looked out through the windscreen and saw that they were approaching the billowing cloud of smoke he'd seen from the air. They rounded another corner and pulled up behind the whitewashed cottage, where a short, athletic-looking man was standing, pumping up the tyres of a car. He stopped what he was doing as the Jeep approached.

'Here we go: home,' Brigid announced as she turned off the engine. 'What're you doing, Richard? Coming in or going straight back?'

'I'm knackered. I've told the others I'm stopping here tonight,' he answered. 'There's not a lot of point trying to get back until morning. I'd rather stay here anyway.'

Once Peter was out, Michael clambered out himself and stretched his arms and legs.

The man who had been working on the other car walked over to him and held out his hand. 'Harry Stayt,' the man said brightly. 'How're you doing?'

Michael found Harry's grip was unexpectedly strong. 'Good, I think,' he replied, feeling slightly overwhelmed. 'I'm Michael. This looks like quite a place you've found here. I didn't think that I'd get to see anywhere like this again.' To his embarrassment Michael found that talking coherently had suddenly become stupidly difficult. This was such a quiet, unremarkable place, and yet he was struggling to take everything in. It wasn't the location that had affected him, or the physical appearance of the island, which was at once very different to the decayed land he'd left behind and at the same time not at all what he'd expected. It was the atmosphere, and the attitude of these people – that had taken him by surprise. They seemed to be amazingly relaxed and at ease. Here they were, standing outside and talking freely, unconcerned by the level of their voices, and not looking constantly over their shoulders.

'I'll tell you something,' Harry said, 'this place is the business. As soon as we got here I knew it. Once we get it cleared up and get everyone else out here we'll be set for life.'

Michael didn't respond. He just stood still and listened to the wind and breathed in the air. Apart from the occasional waft of smoke from the fire nearby, everything smelled pure, fresh.

'Is there much left to do?' he asked after a moment.

'Not really,' he replied, 'not here, at any rate. All that's left now is the big one.'

'The big one?'

'Danvers Lye.'

'What the hell's that?'

'The village. They have told you about the village, haven't they? We're going to start clearing it.'

'Yes, of course, Richard told us about it. So when do we start?'

'Next couple of days, probably – we might even make a start tomorrow, now there's a few more of us here.'

Michael heard another engine approaching and moved sideways to look around the side of the cottage, where another road stretched out away from the front of the building. A pickup truck was moving towards them, but it drove past the cottage and carried on towards the plume of smoke rising a short distance away.

'Who's that?' he asked.

'Bruce Fry and Jim Harper,' Harry answered. 'They've been cleaning up.'

'Cleaning up?'

Harry walked after the truck and towards the smoke and Michael followed him to the top of another low hill. They looked down into a natural hollow. There was a bonfire burning at the bottom of the dip, and the truck was parked on the other side.

'It's the only sensible way of doing this really,' Harry explained as they watched the two men climb out of the truck. Both of them were dressed in protective overalls, fishing waders and rubber gloves.

'Doing what?'

One of the two men acknowledged Michael and Harry, then went around to the rear of the truck and dropped the back down. Between them they began to drag bodies out of the vehicle and dumped them unceremoniously into the flames.

'These are just the ones we've found lying around. We've got rid of about thirty so far,' Harry explained as he turned around and began to walk back towards the cottage. 'Only another few hundred to go!'

Michael stood and watched the fire for a while longer. If he looked carefully he could definitely make out charred bones (skulls, hands and feet were particularly distinct), and there were scraps of partially burned clothing around the edges of the pyre. Eventually he turned away and jogged after Harry.

'There are six of you here, aren't there?' he asked, as he caught up with him.

'That's right.'

'So where are the other two, in the cottage?'

'No, they're out. They'll be back in a while. They're scouting around somewhere.'

'Doing what?'

'Just checking the place over. Don't forget we've not been here that long,' he said as he reached the back door. 'We've managed to get quite a bit done already, but we wanted a little more muscle with us before we tried anything too risky.'

'Risky?' Michael repeated as he followed him into the dark, low-ceilinged kitchen. Through an open door he could see Danny and Peter, sitting in an equally gloomy living room. They were talking to Richard and Brigid.

'We've been taking things steady,' Harry continued. 'We need to be completely sure of what we're doing before we do anything we might regret.'

'Such as?'

'Such as walking into Danvers Lye and getting our arses kicked by a hundred corpses.' He grimaced.

'Point taken,' Michael said as they walked into the living room. Although it was as poorly lit as the kitchen, the room was warm and dry, and considerably more inviting than pretty much anywhere else he'd been in the last two months. It still didn't feel right, though, standing here in full view of the rest of the world like this and talking without a care, as if nothing was going to come at the sound of their voices and try to tear them apart. He felt nervous and on edge. What if there were bodies nearby?

'You okay, Mike?' Richard asked, noticing him standing in the corner.

'Fine,' he replied. 'I'm just a little—'

'Tired?'

Michael shook his head and struggled to think of the right words to properly convey how he was suddenly feeling. 'Disorientated, I guess.'

'You'll get used to it,' Brigid smiled. 'It won't take long.'

Michael sat down on a comfortable armchair next to an unlit fire. Christ, it felt good to be able to sit down like this, he thought. He leant back and stretched his legs out in front of him as he looked around at the others, who were chatting away. At first he was content to sit and listen, without taking an active part in the discussion. He'd been too active for too long now.

After a couple of minutes another car pulled up outside and the final two island inhabitants entered the cottage and introduced themselves to the new arrivals as Tony Hyde and Gayle Spencer. They'd been out on reconnaissance all afternoon; they'd driven to the outskirts of Danvers Lye to check out the situation there in readiness for the cull of corpses which would have to start at some point, and sooner rather than later. When Tony said they had been able to get closer to the village than they'd expected, Michael was confused.

'I don't understand,' he said, looking up at Tony and Gayle, who were sitting opposite him. 'How did you manage to get anywhere near the village, and why were you risking your necks out there anyway? Surely the bodies would have reacted to you just being that close to them?'

Gayle shook her head. 'We think the behaviour of some of the bodies here is changing.'

'Changing?'

'We noticed it yesterday,' she said. 'When we first arrived here, everything was pretty much as we expected: we only had to cough and every body within earshot started swarming around us.'

'So what's different now?'

'When we got up yesterday, we were expecting the bodies to have surrounded us, because of the noise we'd made – and the fire, of course – and we'd pretty much decided to play it that way so we could try and get rid of a few of them. We figured we might as well start drawing them out gradually, you know, bringing them to us rather than us running around after them? Anyway, when we got outside there were only a handful of them, and we got rid of them pretty quickly. We assumed that the rest just hadn't made it over to this side of the island yet.'

She looked at Tony, who took over the story. 'So mid-morning, three of us drove over to the village. We just wanted to see what we were up against, get an idea of the lie of the land. We stopped the car at the end of the main street and waited.'

'What happened?'

'Now this is the weird part,' Gayle continued. 'The bloody things weren't reacting to us – at least, they weren't all reacting how we expected them to. Some of them did, they came straight for us, but most of the others stayed out of the way. We managed to get a little closer until we could see them, but this is the weird part: it was like they were waiting for us – *hiding* from us, almost.'

'Bullshit!'

'I swear, we could see them waiting in the shadows, and inside buildings that had been left open, but keeping out of our way.'

'So what did you do?'

'Nothing,' Tony said. 'Christ, we didn't want to get too close. The last thing we wanted to do was antagonise them.'

'*Antagonise* them?' Michael scoffed. 'You don't think these things are about to roll over and give up, do you?'

Brigid shook her head. 'Oh no, I think there's plenty of fight left in them.'

'So what's changed?' Peter Guest asked.

'I've been thinking about this a lot,' she replied. 'I don't know what the rest of you have seen, but I've watched these things changing since the day they first got up and started walking around again. In the beginning they were just able to move, then they could hear and see, then they became more aggressive, and now it looks like they've started to . . .'

'To think?' Michael suggested when she paused.

'I suppose so. They've gained another level of control. It's a logical progression, if you can call any of this madness logical.'

Michael looked around the room. 'I've seen something similar happening, but not to the extent you have. We've got a doctor with us, and he told me that he thinks part of their brains survived the infection. It's like they're gradually coming around again, despite the fact that their bodies are falling apart. It's like they've been sedated, and now the drugs are starting to wear off.'

'That's good then, isn't it?' Peter said. His mouth was dry with nerves, and he swallowed hard before speaking again. 'Problem solved, eh? If they're going to be able to think and control themselves, then they're not going to be a threat to us, are they? They'll see it's not a fair contest and just sit there and rot to pieces.'

'Possibly,' Michael said cautiously, 'but I don't think that them being a threat to us is the issue any more.'

'What are you talking about?'

'I've thought all along that the bodies are driven by instinct: it's like they're being motivated and controlled at the most basic level. Each time there's been a noticeable change in their behaviour, it's as if they've gained another layer of self-awareness.'

'I don't really know what you're on about,' Peter complained.

'Have you seen how they sometimes fight with each other? It always seems to be completely unprovoked, doesn't it? But have you ever stopped and wondered why they do it? What have they got to gain from fighting? There's no class or status or other division among them, is there? They don't eat, they don't want shelter; they're not fighting over food or possessions.'

'So what are you saying?' Brigid asked. 'Why do they do it?'

'I think the only thing they've got left is to fight for is survival. They're fighting just to continue to exist. It's self-preservation, that's what we're seeing here. In a crowd of thousands, they'll take any number of us on. When they're in the minority, they'll hold back.'

'I don't buy any of this,' Peter said. 'Just listen to yourself, will you? Can you hear what you're saying? Can you hear how stupid it sounds?'

'What I'm saying is: the bodies aren't a threat to us, it's more that they're seeing us as a threat to them. And if they really are driven by instinct, then they'll do whatever they have to do to make sure they continue to survive.'

27

Kelly had had enough. She'd been at the airfield for almost a day, and she couldn't take any more. She'd listened to everything the others had said, and she'd tried to understand and see things from their perspective, but it was impossible; she had different priorities. She knew there was no point holding on. No matter what they promised they'd try and do for her and Kilgore, it was never going to happen – they were going to have enough trouble just trying to look after themselves.

It was the waiting that hurt the most.

Kelly had been through her fair share of hard times. She'd cried her way through the first half of basic training like a bloody baby, and she'd been stuck out on the battlefield staring down the barrel of the enemy's gun. She'd dealt with all of that; as hard as it had been, she'd managed to get through it all.

The difference today, she decided, was that everything was out of her control. She knew she couldn't fight her way out of this situation, and she couldn't talk her way out of it either. The end was a foregone conclusion, and all she was doing was putting it off. She couldn't even close her eyes any more without replaying all that had happened in her memory, remembering everything she'd lost.

Things had changed since she'd arrived at Monkton Airfield, and now she felt like she'd reached the end of the road. She'd watched the helicopter leave this afternoon and had realised that events were moving on, while she was an outsider: neither living nor dead. And she couldn't go on like this.

Standing a little way short of the perimeter fence, she stared into the dead faces, which stared back at her. The longer she stood there, the more violent and animated they became. They reached out for her, poked their bony fingers through the fence to get closer to her, ripped and tore at the other corpses getting in their way . . .

but Kelly didn't care. She ripped off her facemask. And for a few precious moments the relief was overpowering.

Cool fresh air flooded her lungs, making her feel stronger and more human than she'd felt in weeks. She could smell the grass again, and the autumn air tasted a thousand times better than she'd remembered. The seconds ticked by, and it began to seem like the impossible might have happened. Was she immune? By some incredible chance, did she share the same physical trait which had allowed the people in the building behind her to survive? She didn't dare believe it at first – what were the odds against her managing to survive like this? In a delirious instant her mind was filled with visions of actually making it to the island, actually *living* again . . .

And then it started. From out of nowhere the pain gripped hold of her like a hand wrapped tightly around her neck. The inside of her throat began to swell. She stayed standing for as long as she could until, with her eyes bulging, she fell back onto the grass and stared deep into the heavy grey sky overhead, seeing nothing.

Thirty seconds later it was over.

28

The fact that he found himself in a warm and comfortable bed for the first time in weeks wasn't helping Michael sleep. Danny Talbot, in comparison, was snoring away in his narrow bunk on the other side of the small, square bedroom. It was almost midnight, and Michael's head was pounding. He wished he could find a way to switch off and disconnect for a while, but it was proving impossible. If he wasn't being distracted by the noise of the others talking downstairs, then he was thinking about the island and how he had finally managed to get there – and when he stopped thinking about the island, he found himself thinking about the changing behaviour of the bodies, and when he stopped thinking about that, he started to think about Emma. And once he'd started, he couldn't stop thinking about her. The distance between them felt immense, almost immeasurable in the circumstances, and it hurt. He knew that she was more than capable of looking after herself (Christ, she'd looked after *him* enough recently), but that didn't make it any easier. He felt responsible for her – more than that, he knew that he loved her. Although he hadn't yet dared to say the words, he was reasonably confident that she loved him too, as much as anyone could love anyone else in this fucked-up world. For the most part, he'd kept his feelings for Emma subdued; it was only now, with this distance between them, that he had realised the true strength of what he felt for her.

Lying on the bed in the dark was pointless: he obviously wasn't going to be able to sleep. He'd not bothered to fully undress; now he just pulled on a jumper, and crept back down the narrow staircase, wincing at the sounds of the creaking floorboards, to where Brigid, Peter, Jim and Gayle were sitting in the kitchen.

'You all right?' Brigid asked.

'I'm okay. Just can't sleep.'

'Coffee?' The kettle was already boiling on a portable gas stove, filling the room with steam and heat.

'Yes please. Where are the others?' he asked, looking around and trying not to yawn.

'Danny, Tony and Richard are upstairs, Harry and Bruce are outside.'

'Outside? What the hell are they doing out there?'

'Keeping watch.'

'Why? Has something happened?'

'No, we're just not taking any chances, that's all.'

'Bloody hell, just being outside would have been taking a chance where I've just come from!'

'It's different here. You'll get used to it.'

Michael stepped over to the window and looked out. It was dark, but he thought he could make out movement, a few yards away – it was too quick and purposeful to be anything other than one of the others.

'Here you go,' Brigid said, handing him a mug of coffee.

'Cheers,' he said, turning back to the window. He could clearly see one of the men now – whichever one of them it was, he was walking back towards the cottage. The door creaked open and Harry Stayt leant inside.

'Okay, Harry?' Gayle asked.

'Bloody cold,' he complained.

'Anything happening out there?'

'Saw a couple of bodies about half an hour ago, that's all.'

'Did they give you any trouble?' Michael wondered. 'I mean, did they go for you, or were they like the others earlier?'

'They went for us.'

'I don't understand,' Jim said. 'Why do some of them still react like that, when others don't?' he asked. He was a young man, though tonight he looked aged beyond his years.

'Who knows?' Michael replied. 'My guess is it depends on what condition their brains and bodies are in. Some of them are more decayed than others, so it follows some will be in a worse mental state than others.'

'Bloody hell, they're all in a bad mental state, aren't they? They're dead!' Harry grinned. 'Look, sorry to spoil the party, but I saw the windows steaming up and guessed you'd put the kettle on.'

Brigid was standing up and spooning coffee granules into two more mugs before he'd even finished speaking. She poured on boiling water, stirred the drinks and then pushed them over towards Harry, who picked them up with one hand. Michael noticed he was carrying a blade of some description in the other hand, and Harry noticed him looking at it.

'Bloody useful this is,' he explained as he lifted the weapon up into the dull light. It was a long, ornately decorated sword. 'I nicked it from a museum a few weeks back. It's the best thing I've found for getting rid of bodies.'

'Put that damn thing down, will you?' Brigid said, scolding him like she was his mother. 'You're like a bloody kid with a new toy. I used to spend half my time locking up idiots who carried things like that – thought it made them big men. Ha!'

Michael looked puzzled.

Harry explained, 'Brigid was a copper,' he said as he turned and walked back out. 'And she still thinks she's on duty!'

'Mind if I come out with you?' Michael asked, surprising Harry.

'You can if you want. If you'd rather spend your first night on the island out in the cold with me and Bruce instead of tucked up here in a warm bed then be my guest!'

'Can't sleep anyway,' Michael grumbled as he zipped up his jacket and followed Harry out into the darkness.

'I don't know why they get so wound up about this sword,' Harry said as they walked away from the cottage. 'I don't know about you, but I'd rather carry a weapon like this than a gun.'

'I've never got on with guns,' Michael agreed. 'They're too bloody noisy, and you have to be a damn good shot to take the bodies out. Miss the head and they'll just keep coming at you.'

'Damn right – and by the time you've got rid of one of them, there'll be another couple of hundred following close behind trying to see what all the noise was about.'

'You stick to your sword, mate.'

'Bruce,' Harry shouted into the darkness, 'oi, Bruce, where are you?'

'Over here,' a disembodied voice replied from the direction of the small hill which overlooked the pyre Michael had seen earlier.

The remains of the fire were still smouldering, and he could see the faintest orange glow in the darkness.

'Two of us coming over,' Harry shouted back. He lowered his

voice again to whisper to Michael, 'Didn't want him thinking you were one of them and trying to take you out!'

Michael managed half a smile. 'Cheers, mate.'

They found Bruce crouched over the embers of the fire, warming his hands. Earlier in the evening they'd stoked up the flames with wood and other general rubbish, but the remains of the fire's original fuel could still clearly be seen, and Michael found it distinctly unnerving, looking at so many charred bones. It looked like the mass graves he'd seen in history books.

'How're you doing, Mike?' Bruce asked cheerfully as they approached.

'I'm good,' he answered, 'just sick of sitting in there and staring at the walls.'

'I know what you mean. Guess we've all done enough of that recently to last a lifetime.'

'That's why we keep volunteering to come out here,' Harry explained. 'I'm not going to be able to relax until I know we've got rid of all the bodies here and the rest of our people are on their way over from the mainland. I just want to get it done now.'

'How were they all doing when you saw them?' Bruce asked. 'Jackie still keeping them in line?'

'Yeah, she seemed to be.'

'Give them a week or so and I reckon they'll all be over here,' Harry said, yawning.

'Why should it take that long?' Michael asked. 'I'm with you two; I'd rather sit around drinking coffee *after* we've got rid of the bodies.'

'We just need to get the village cleared,' Bruce said.

'So we should start tomorrow, shouldn't we? There are enough of us here now, surely.'

Bruce sounded a little less confident now. 'I'm not sure. Maybe we should—'

'Let's be honest,' Michael interrupted, 'we all instinctively make excuses and try to put things off. The sooner we do this and get it done, the sooner we get on with our lives.'

'I know that, but clearing the village is going to be a big job and there's a lot riding on it. We need to make sure we get it right first time.'

'I agree, so we make sure we plan it right. We should get in there quick and strike, then get out again. After that we'll regroup, then go back in and do the same again. And again and again until the job's done.'

'So why are you so keen all of a sudden?' Harry asked.

'Partly because I just want it done, also because of what I heard today,' Michael answered, kicking at the ashes on the ground next to his feet, sending a shower of sparks up into the air. 'I've watched those things steadily changing, almost from day to day. I know there's going to come a time when they've rotted down to nothing, when they won't get in our way any more, but everything I've seen and heard has made me think things might get more difficult before they get any easier. The dead are starting to watch us, to pay attention to what we're doing.'

'What exactly are you getting at?'

'I think that if we don't make a move now, then it might be the bodies hunting us out, not the other way round.'

29

The first light of morning crept across the airfield painfully slowly, almost as if it didn't want to be seen. From the top of the control tower Clare stood and watched the darkness gradually disappear. It looked blustery and cold outside, but the building isolated her from the brunt of the almost wintry conditions. From where she was standing she could see right across to the fence, and the hordes of constantly moving corpses beyond. As the light improved she was able to make out the body of Kelly Harcourt, lying on its back in the overgrown grass, just yards away from the dead.

'You can understand why she did it, can't you?' Emma said, standing just behind her.

'Such a shame, though,' Clare answered quietly, her low voice disconsolate. 'I liked her. She was nice, much nicer than Kilgore.'

'You can't even begin to imagine what the poor girl was going through. You don't know how you'd react if you were in that position, do you?'

'Makes you realise how lucky you are . . .'

'Suppose so.'

'We are lucky, aren't we?'

Emma couldn't answer. On the face of it they had survived where millions had fallen, and that had to make them lucky, didn't it? But every day things seemed to be getting harder, and she couldn't help thinking that in many ways it would have been easier just to have died on the first morning and not known anything.

Feeling guilty for allowing herself to think so negatively, she forced herself to respond positively to Clare: 'Of course we're lucky,' she said. 'We're lucky to be here, and we're lucky to have a chance of getting away from all this.'

Clare was only half-listening. 'So are we just going to leave her there?' she asked, staring at Kelly's body on the ground. 'Shouldn't we move her?'

The sudden arrival of Cooper and Jackie Soames bursting into the room interrupted the conversation. Emma could tell from the expressions on their faces that they were not happy.

'Has anyone seen Keele?' Jackie asked, looking around the room hopefully. Her face looked even redder and more flushed than usual.

'I saw him earlier,' Emma said.

'Do you know where he is now?'

'No, have you tried looking—'

She didn't bother finishing her sentence. Jackie and Cooper were already walking away. Donna, coming the other way, unintentionally blocked their way.

'Any luck?' Cooper asked her.

'Not yet,' she replied. 'He's not in here, then?'

'He's probably hiding in the outbuildings somewhere,' Jackie suggested. 'He's done that before, the cowardly little bastard.'

Jackie and Cooper bustled out of the room, leaving Donna standing alone by the open door.

Emma was confused. 'What the hell's going on?'

'Gary Keele's done a runner,' Donna explained. 'We can't find him.'

'What's he running from?'

'Cooper wants him to try and get the plane moving.'

'And?'

'And that's it. Fucker's had a panic attack. He suffers with his nerves, apparently. Bloody pathetic – I hate blokes like him, I really do. They're all bloody talk and no action. Apparently he's spent the last couple of weeks making noises to some of this lot about how he's going to be the big hero and fly them all to safety, but now the time's come, he's bottled it.'

'But he can't have left the airfield, can he?'

'Not without getting himself ripped apart or letting a couple of thousand bodies in here, he can't.'

'So what happens if they can't get him to fly the plane?' Clare asked.

'Then we'll have to try and get to the island by helicopter, I suppose. Richard will end up making loads more flights, and we'll be limited on the amount of stuff we can take over with us. We'll still get there; it'll just take a lot longer and be a lot more complicated, that's all.'

'But what if—?'

'We'll get there,' Donna assured her.

'What the hell are you doing in here?' Phil Croft asked. Smoking one of his last few precious cigarettes, the doctor had been limping slowly through the shadows between the empty airfield buildings when he'd stumbled across Gary Keele, sitting alone in the corner of a musty waiting room. It was only by chance he'd spotted him moving as he'd walked past a cobweb-covered window.

Keele didn't answer, hoping the doctor would get the message and disappear, but Croft wasn't going anywhere.

'I'm just trying to get some space,' Keele answered eventually, keeping his eyes fixed on the ground in front of him.

'Christ!' Croft laughed, 'the population of this country has been reduced from millions to less than a hundred people and you're trying to get some space? Bloody hell, mate, if you want space there's plenty of it out there. You don't need to hide away in here to be on your own.'

'Just piss off.'

'Fine.'

Croft was about to leave when he glanced out of the window and noticed a number of people moving from building to building. It looked like they were searching for something. He put two and two together and reached the obvious conclusion that they were looking for the man he'd just found. Out of the corner of his eye he noticed that Keele was now watching him anxiously.

'So how long are you planning on hiding in here for?' the doctor asked, still looking out of the window.

'I'm not hiding. I told you, I—'

'Come on, cut the crap. They're looking for you, aren't they?'

Keele didn't want to say anything, but he forced himself to say, 'I'm not hiding!'

'Yes, you are. So I guess what I heard someone saying last night is true, you're too scared to fly the plane.'

'I'm not scared.'

'Oh, right,' Croft said, 'so let me see if I've got this right: you're here sitting in the dark, on your own, in the corner of this dusty shit-hole because you want some space, and you're not hiding from the others, you're just choosing not to let them know where you are, is that it?'

'Piss off,' Keele said again.

'Keele,' Croft continued, turning away from the window to face the man in the corner, 'let me tell you something – and I want to make quite sure you understand what I'm saying, okay? I'm a doctor and I've spent years looking after other people, making sure they get better when they're sick. Things have changed now, and if I'm completely honest, I'm not that bothered about anyone else any more. I'm only really interested in myself. And I tell you now, you will do whatever you have to do to get us out of here, because if you don't, I will break your fucking legs.'

'You don't scare me—'

'Well, I should. You *will* fly the plane to the island, because if you don't, I swear I will kill you,' the doctor said in a calm and emotionless voice. 'I haven't come this far only to have my one chance of survival blown by some stupid, cowardly little fucker like you. Do you understand? Is that clear enough for you?'

Keele didn't respond.

Croft glared at him, then turned and walked out of the building, slamming the door behind him. Smoking the last inch of his cigarette, he began the slow, painful walk back to the control tower. He passed Donna on the way.

'Have you seen—?' she started to ask.

'He's in there,' he replied, pointing back at the building he'd just left.

30

Richard Lawrence took off from Cormansey just after ten o'clock, waved off by the nine survivors, who stood at the end of the runway and watched the helicopter until its bright lights had disappeared into the grey morning gloom. It was supposed to be returning later that day, bringing with it the plane and at least fifteen more people. Michael was hoping that Emma would be one of them.

During the long watch the previous night he had managed to convince Harry and Bruce to listen seriously to his concerns about the changing condition of the bodies. So much remained unpredictable, and it made sense to take action sooner rather than later. Michael had never been the most diplomatic of men, and he had expressed his opinions bluntly and honestly to the rest of them over breakfast. There had been some initial nervous reluctance, but they had been largely receptive.

Then Harry had pointed out the immediate practicalities of their situation, and that proved to be the deciding factor. With the arrival yesterday of Michael, Peter and Danny, there were now too many of them for the single small cottage. Clearing the bodies away now would make their lives immeasurably easier.

Armed with sticks, axes, clubs and blades of varying descriptions, the small group travelled in convoy from the cottage towards the village of Danvers Lye, driving two cars and the pickup truck. This was the first real opportunity Michael, Danny and Peter had had to see anything of the island. Much of it was barren and rocky, covered in patchy grass and bracken. The ocean was always in view on one side or the other, and plumes of cold grey water were constantly shooting into the air as waves pounded the shore. Trees were few and far between, and the wind howled across the weather-beaten landscape. There was a basic network of rudimentary roads connecting the various buildings, most of which were small cottages and houses. Some were old, built of some grey stone; others were more modern in appearance. There was a one-classroom school, and a farm on the southwest end of the island, and a few fishing boats had been abandoned along the shore. Michael struggled to imagine how most of the inhabitants of Cormansey had ever earned a living; life on this harsh, unforgiving land must surely have been difficult at the best of times.

Michael felt increasingly nervous as they reached the village. He stared at the motley collection of unkempt buildings and his unease increased when he realised that this was the first time he'd ever gone out actively looking for bodies to destroy. Until now his time had been spent either hiding from them, or defending himself and Emma against them. Although he knew the corpses would probably offer very little in the way of serious resistance, the trepidation he felt was substantial. And, judging from the expressions around him, he wasn't the only one who felt that way.

Michael had travelled in the Jeep at the front of the convoy with Brigid and Jim. He was hot now – everyone was dressed in boots and gloves and either boiler-suits or strong waterproofs, collected from the empty homes of long-dead fishermen yesterday morning in preparation for this mission. The advanced decay of the bodies had now reached such a stage that their removal and disposal was inevitably going to be a bloody, gruesome and germ-ridden affair, for the rotting shells must be rife with disease. No one was relishing the prospect of close physical contact.

'Stop here,' he said when they were just short of the heart of Danvers Lye. 'I think we're better off leaving the vehicles here. We don't want to go too far in and find we've got ourselves cut off.'

Brigid stopped the Jeep. The other car pulled up behind her and the truck stopped alongside it. The group got out of their vehicles and regrouped in the middle of the road.

'So what now? Do we just go marching in there?' Jim asked.

Michael shook his head. 'No, I don't think so. Maybe we should take it slow, try and clear the buildings one at a time?'

'Sounds sensible.'

'Look,' Gayle Spencer whispered, 'a welcoming party.'

Alerted by the sound of the engines, a number of bodies had

already dragged themselves out into the open and were moving along the street towards the group with obvious intent.

Harry Stayt readied his sword. 'We knew there were going to be a few like this, didn't we?' he said as he anxiously swapped the blade from hand to hand.

'We should try and deal with these first,' suggested Bruce. 'Let's make a bit of noise and flush out all of the bodies that are still reacting like this, get them out into the open.'

'Makes sense,' agreed Brigid. 'What have you got in mind?'

Bruce leaned into the pickup truck, reached across and pressed down on the horn. The unexpected noise echoed across the otherwise quiet island, so loud that for a moment it seemed even to silence the relentless sound of the waves crashing against the greystone walls of the little harbour just a couple of hundred yards away.

'I'll make a start,' Harry said purposefully, and he strode forward to head off the gangly bodies staggering the other way, his sword gripped tightly in his hand and raised ready to strike.

'Does anyone else get the impression he actually enjoys this?' Jim said quietly. 'Sick bastard.'

'At least he's trying,' Gayle snapped. 'We're just standing here looking at him.'

Michael watched as Harry neared the first two bodies. He lifted the blade above his head, and though it was clear he was no expert, he swung it round in a long and surprisingly graceful arc and managed to effortlessly sever the head of the nearest cadaver. The body crumbled to the ground instantly, its decapitated head thumping down onto the tarmac at his feet like a rotten peach. Another flash of the blade and the second corpse was also felled, its head removed with equal speed, if less precision.

'I'm behind you, Harry,' Jim shouted as Harry marched forward with steadily increasing confidence. He jogged down the street after his sword-wielding friend, keeping a safe distance from the razor-sharp blade. Ahead of them were six more figures, and Harry quickly hacked them down while Jim, Michael and Gayle began to collect up the bloody remains of his handiwork which was scattered around the street. Moving quickly, they dragged the remains of the corpses over to an area of scrubland on the other side of the road and began to pile them up.

The emaciated remains of Cormansey's most senior police officer took Harry by surprise, lurching out from behind a high wooden fence and knocking him off-balance momentarily. With one gloved hand he pushed the body away, sending it stumbling backwards, and it tripped over the twitching torso of another dead islander and fell heavily onto its backside. Seizing the opportunity Harry lifted his sword and chopped down at the corpse, slicing the top of its head clean off as the blade followed through and hit the ground. He winced as the vibration of the impact of the sword on the tarmac travelled the length of his aching arms.

Breathless, he moved onto the next body, and then the next and then the next, driven on by a curious combination of adrenalin and revulsion. Bruce and Brigid stood together and watched from a distance, listening as Harry's blade whistled through the cold air.

'That's it, Harry,' Jim shouted at last, 'you can stop now!'

Harry, panting hard with effort, stood still, suddenly aware that the clumsy movement around him had stopped. He looked up and down the road. The previously unremarkable grey village street was now awash with blood and gore, and littered with fallen corpses, but that seemed to be all of them for now. He couldn't see any other moving bodies.

'So where are the rest?' he asked, still looking around. 'This can't be it, surely. There should have been about a hundred of them at least.'

Michael walked over to where he stood staring into the shadowy buildings on either side of the street. 'They're hiding from you and your bloody sword.'

'You've got to be kidding,' Harry laughed. 'They're not hiding!'

Michael pointed into the nearest building, a small, glass-fronted shop. 'Well some of them are,' he said. 'Look.'

Christ, Harry thought, Michael was right. He could see several bodies inside the building, gathered together at the other end from the door. Were they actively trying to keep out of sight? The door was open, so they weren't trapped. What the hell was going on?

'So what do we do?'

'Go in there and flush them out, I—'

Michael was momentarily distracted by a sudden burst of light and noise from the scrubland behind them. Brigid had doused the pile of body parts with fuel and had set light to them and now bright orange flames pierced the grey gloom.

'That might drag a few more of them out into the open,' he said.

Harry walked across the road and pressed his face to the window of a butcher's shop. 'There are only a couple of them in here,' he said. He could see at least two dark figures, shuffling behind a counter which was still piled high with rotting, maggoty meat.

'Let's see what happens then,' Michael said. He pushed the stiff door open and the bodies immediately began to move – but unexpectedly, they were retreating further back into the shadows.

'Are they becoming territorial?' Harry asked.

Michael shook his head. 'I doubt it. Do you think that's what's left of the butcher and his wife?'

'No,' Harry scowled, 'that's not what I meant. I just wonder if they're aware of their surroundings? Are they really just keeping out of our way, or are they standing their ground? Or are they just sheltering in there?'

'I don't think they're sheltering,' he said as he shoved his way through the door. 'Christ, look at them – they're not interested in keeping warm or keeping dry, are they?'

Michael stopped before going any further inside.

'What's the matter?' Harry asked, immediately concerned.

'Look.'

Harry saw that the two bodies had suddenly stopped their clumsy retreat and now they appeared to be standing their ground.

'What the hell's going on?'

'Like I said yesterday, on their own they might not be much of a threat to us any more, but it looks like we're still a threat to them.'

'Come on, let's just get this done.'

'Hold on,' he said, grabbing hold of Harry's arm. 'Take it easy. We've got them cornered. We don't know how they'll react if we just—'

'I've had enough of this,' Harry said, shrugging him off and pushing his way past him and into the shop. The two bodies shuffled forward slightly, then stopped again.

'Careful,' Michael said, just behind him, but Harry wasn't listening.

He marched towards the back of the shop and the nearest of the two bodies immediately launched itself at him. He was taken by surprise, but he managed to impale the creature on his sword and its putrefied innards started dripping out onto the floor from the gash in its gut. Oblivious to the wound, it grabbed hold of Harry's shoulders and pulled itself forward, dragging itself further onto the weapon, forcing the blade out through the small of its back. Harry didn't fully realise what was happening until his right hand and forearm had disappeared into the grotesque cadaver's decaying chest cavity. He began to gag at the stench, which was overpowering.

'Get this fucking thing off me,' he wailed as he pushed the body away with his left hand and struggled to free the right. The creature was flailing its arms around his face, trying to grab hold of him again.

The other rotting figure pushed its way past the first and rushed at Michael. As Harry squirmed free from his attacker and kicked it back across the room and into the window, Michael began to repeatedly punch the face of the corpse now attacking him, and each hard contact made the body's head rock back on weak shoulders before instantly rebounding and drooping forward again. Again and again he struck, and its features gradually became unrecognisable as congealed blood, rotting flesh and brittle bone were ground together. The weak skin split to expose cheek and jaw bones, as Michael prayed the beating would eventually smash what remained of the despicable thing's brain as it rattled round its head.

Harry managed to push the first body to the ground and stamped on its head, crushing its skull, then grabbed the second corpse by the scruff of the neck and pulled it away from Michael.

'I'll sort it,' he said as he lifted the sword and plunged it down through one of its eyes.

As quickly as it had begun, the sudden frenetic activity in the shop had ended. Breathing hard, Harry and Michael stood side by side and looked down at the gruesome pile of remains at their feet.

'Answers a few questions, doesn't it?' Michael panted. 'They're not just going to give up and roll over, are they? Those two went for us with as much force as ever – the difference was, they had more wits about them, if you can call it that. They definitely had more control than usual – they really were keeping out of our way until we took away their options and backed them into a corner. It came down to: attack us, or be attacked.'

31

By mid-afternoon Cormansey was again shrouded in heavy mist. Working their way building by building through the dark streets of Danvers Lye, the nine survivors made good progress with their impromptu cull. The group had naturally divided into threes; two of the trios concentrated on emptying buildings whilst the third, with Brigid in charge, followed behind and cleared the bodies, picking them up from where they'd been unceremoniously dumped and driving them back in the truck to the fire burning at the entrance to the village.

Michael, Harry and Peter had reached one of the larger, more modern buildings, three-quarters of the way along the otherwise quaint High Street. It looked to have been an unusual but practical combination of post office, gift shop, hardware store and supermarket, and had almost certainly been one of the focal points of the island's small community. And on that first morning some eight weeks ago, it had clearly been a busy place.

Michael leaned against the dirty plate-glass window and peered into the building. He could see several corpses lying still on the ground, and others moving nearby.

'Problem?' Peter asked, trying to look over his shoulder.

'There are definitely some of them in there,' Michael replied, his face pressed hard against the window. 'I can see them hovering around the back.'

Harry tried the door. He pushed it open slightly, then it jammed, but even that narrow opening he had forced was enough to allow the fermented stench that had built up inside the building to seep out like a noxious cloud. He turned his head away in disgust at the overpowering smell of death which filled his nostrils.

'Bloody hell,' he complained, screwing up his face. 'It's disgusting!'

'Well, what do you expect?' Michael asked. 'Christ, that door's not been opened in two months, and it's full of bodies in there.'

'The light's fading,' Peter said anxiously, stating the obvious. 'We need to get a move on.'

Michael wouldn't be rushed; he was trying to see what was happening inside the shop. The place was fairly large, and he wanted to get a basic idea of its layout before he risked going inside. 'Pete,' he said, looking over his shoulder, 'do me a favour, will you? Go and bring one of the cars over here.'

Glad to have been given something relatively easy to do, Peter jogged back over to where they'd parked the cars, all with the keys left in the ignition. He climbed into an old but well-maintained silver hatchback and started the engine, and then moved slowly through the misty rain until he was outside the building where Michael and Harry were waiting. Under instruction from Michael, a three-point turn positioned the car at ninety degrees so the headlights were shining full-beam into the shop.

Michael pressed his face against the glass again. Though the dirt meant much of the light was immediately reflected back, there was definitely some improvement.

'Better?' Harry asked, also struggling to see inside.

'A little,' Michael answered. 'I can see at least six bodies moving, but I think there are more. Can't be sure how many.'

'Where?'

'Right at the back. The bloody things are keeping themselves out of sight again.'

As he spoke, a single corpse broke ranks and slammed against the glass, smashing its fists against the window, and shocked, Michael tripped back. He caught his breath, his heart thumping furiously. The sound the creature was making was curious and unexpected: one hand was thumping against the glass like a piece of mouldy fruit, leaving a greasy residue behind every time it connected. The flesh on the other hand had already deteriorated away to nothing, leaving bare bone clattering against the window.

'Come on,' Harry muttered as he watched the pitiful figure, holding his sword ready again, 'let's get this done.'

He shoved the door open and the three of them went inside. They stood just inside the entrance to the shop, illuminated from behind by the car's headlights. The body by the window immediately began to move towards them, tripping through the rubbish on the ground. Grabbing its diseased head in one gloved hand, Michael rammed it up against the nearest wall, managing to wedge it awkwardly between a tall drinks dispenser and a metal magazine rack. He plunged the end of an already bloody crowbar he'd been carrying all afternoon into its left temple, pulled it quickly out again, then watched as the corpse slid to the ground.

'Just look at this, will you?' Peter whispered nervously, pointing straight ahead. Now they were inside, they could hear that the far end of the building was full of constant, shuffling movement, though in the half-light it was impossible to be sure how many bodies they now faced.

'So what do you think?' Harry wondered. 'Should we just go for it or—?'

The movement of the bodies rendered his question unnecessary before he could finish asking it as one of them started towards him and then others followed, spurred on by the actions of the first. The corpses began to stumble towards them *en masse*, moving almost like a pack, filling the building with sudden noise as the clumsy dead collided with fixtures, fittings and each other as they dragged themselves towards the three men.

'Spread out!' Michael yelled, concerned that he might be caught by Harry's sword in the mêlée which was inevitably about to start. 'Spread out and hit the damn things until there's nothing left standing but us!'

He lifted the crowbar again and ran deeper into the building until he reached the first body coming the other way. In one swift movement he swung the crowbar up and forced it into the creature's head, shoving it up through its chin and deep into its decaying brain.

To Michael's right Harry was cutting his way through the crowd with his now-familiar ferocity and style. Behind and to his left, however, Peter was struggling. So far he'd managed to avoid direct confrontation with the bodies, but now there was no escape. He'd chosen a cricket bat, and now he cursed his stupid and inappropriate choice of weapon.

'What do I do?' he screamed as the nearest body lashed out at him with claw-like hands. He didn't really expect an answer, but in the midst of the close-confined chaos and mayhem he got two.

'Hit them, you fucking idiot!' Harry shouted at him.

'And keep hitting them until they stop moving,' Michael added in the middle of dealing with two more bodies. 'Just do it!'

Trembling with nerves, Peter instinctively held the cricket bat as if he were at the crease on a Sunday afternoon. Anticipating the lurching speed of the hideous body which stumbled towards him, he took two steps down an imaginary wicket and swung the bat as if he was trying to hit the ball back over the bowler's head towards the boundary rope. The wood connected with the underside of the creature's jaw, severing the remains of its spinal cord and practically knocking its head off its shoulders. It flew back into an open freezer full of spoiled food and lay still.

More through luck than judgment, Peter eventually managed to dispose of another body, and in the time it took him, Harry had cut down four more and Michael another two. A total of thirteen of the wretched things had been destroyed, and there were still a few more to dispose of.

After dragging more than twenty bodies out of the foul-smelling building Michael, Harry and Peter allowed themselves a short break. The long day's work had been physically and mentally exhausting. Their eyes were now accustomed to the low light indoors, and with the car still providing some illumination, they searched through the building, picking through the wreckage as if they were High Street shoppers looking for bargains on a Saturday afternoon.

Michael leant against a wall and flicked through the faded pages of a lifestyle magazine filled with images of beautiful, immaculately turned out men and women. For a second he was aware of his own scruffy, gore-soaked appearance. 'Look at this,' he mumbled to anyone who would listen, 'just look at this!'

Harry stood nearby drinking a can of beer and eating a bar of chocolate. 'What?' he asked, his mouth full.

'All of this shit,' Michael replied, turning the magazine slightly so that Harry could see what he'd been looking at. It was a double-page spread from some celebrity wedding. He recognised some of the faces in the pictures, but he struggled for a second to remember their names, and what it was they used to do.

'What about it?'

'Just hard to believe, isn't it? Hard to believe that this kind of thing used to matter. Christ, thousands of people used to buy this crap every week; now there's probably not even a thousand people left alive.'

Harry stepped through the rubbish to stand closer to Michael and get a better view of the pictures.

'She was beautiful, wasn't she?' he said quietly, pointing at the face of a television actress he remembered. 'I had a real thing for her!'

'She's probably like that lot now,' Michael half-joked. He gestured at the pile of corpses in the middle of the street that Brigid and her team were busy carting away. 'Hey, remember this?' he asked as he flicked back a few pages to a film review section he'd just passed.

'Bloody hell, yes,' Harry answered, looking at the stills. 'Never got round to seeing that.'

'It wasn't that good,' Michael volunteered. 'I saw it about a week before everything went tits-up. Anyway, you might still get to see it – if we can get the electricity supply working here, then we could fetch a projector from the mainland and show as many films as we can get our hands on. We'll paint the side of one of the buildings white and we'll project against it. It'll be like a drive-in, but without the cars. We'll—'

'No, we won't,' Harry sighed. 'Nice idea, mate, but it's never going to happen, is it? If we're lucky we'll get something set up so that we can watch videos or DVDs if we really want to.' He took another magazine from the rack and began to leaf through its pages. He wiped an unexpected tear away from the corner of his eye. 'Jesus,' he said quietly, 'I'd forgotten about all of this. I hadn't thought about any of it until now.'

Michael continued to look through his magazine as he thought about Harry's words. He understood completely what Harry was saying – he'd spent the last two months either running at breakneck speed or sitting still and hiding in terrified silence. Coming to the island was the first time they'd been able to move around freely. This was the first time any of them had been afforded the luxury of being able to stop and remember, without having to constantly look over their shoulders, in fear of attack from the endless hordes of bodies which plagued them.

Looking back was painful. It hurt more than any of them might have expected it to, but now that they had suddenly been allowed to remember, all three of them found it was impossible to stop. They picked through the musty contents of the shop with mixed feelings of warm nostalgia and heavy, heartbreaking sadness. They finally had a chance to grieve.

On the other side of the room, Peter was sitting on a counter, crying – not just sobbing, or sniffing quietly to himself; he was wailing with pain, almost screaming with the sudden release of previously suppressed emotions.

The noise was so loud that it made Tony Hyde, who was walking past the shop, stop and walk towards the building. Concerned, he leant inside. 'Everything okay in here?' he asked.

'It's okay,' Harry said as Michael walked over to Peter.

'All right, Pete?' he asked pointlessly. Peter looked up with tears pouring down his face. Michael saw that he was holding a small toy; a brightly coloured, die-cast truck which turned into some kind of robot soldier like a cut-price Transformer. Peter was staring at it as if it was suddenly the most important thing in the world.

It was almost an hour later before Peter had composed himself enough to be able to talk to the others. Even now, as he sat next to Michael on the bonnet of the pickup and stared into the mass of burning bodies a short distance away, occasional tears still rolled down his cheeks.

'It's like when you shake a bottle of beer, isn't it?' he said suddenly.

'What is?' Michael asked, confused.

'How it feels today,' he explained. 'I know you feel the same; I can see it in your face. I can see it in everyone's faces.'

'Still don't know what you're talking about, mate.'

'I've been through so much stuff. There are things I can't bring myself to think about because they hurt too much. I've wanted to try and sort them out, but I haven't been able to do it yet.'

'So what's that got to do with a bottle of beer?'

'I feel like everything inside me's been shaken up, but my top's been screwed down tight. So until you take the top off, nothing can get out – but being here today has been like unscrewing the top: a real release. I just wasn't expecting it.'

'So how do you feel now?'

'Half-empty. Flat.' Peter smiled sadly.

Michael nodded thoughtfully as he considered his unusual, but accurate, analogy. He understood completely. 'What was that business with the toy earlier?' he asked. He could tell from the sudden change in Peter's body language that his nerves were still raw.

Peter took the toy from his pocket and stared at it again.

'On the first morning,' he explained, his voice cracking with emotion, 'I was supposed to go and see my lad Joe at school. It was his first class assembly . . .' He stopped talking as the pain threatened to overwhelm him again. Although he'd thought about Joe constantly, he hadn't talked about his son, not once in more than eight weeks.

'What happened?' Michael pressed him, although he thought he already knew.

'I wasn't anywhere near the school when it happened – I was on my way to work. There was a meeting I couldn't get out of, and if I'd missed it I would have . . .'

'Would have what?'

'I would have got the sack.'

'Was it that important?'

'Obviously not, but I thought it was at the time. We'd been working for weeks to close a major deal, and my bonus and an almost guaranteed promotion hinged on getting the papers signed at that meeting. I would have lost a hell of a lot if things hadn't worked out. But looking back now, what did it matter? What good is that bonus now?' Peter shuffled awkwardly. The admission was still not an easy one to make.

'I know now that none of it really mattered – the job, the money, the car, the house – none of it. I should have given up the whole fucking lot months earlier but I thought I was doing the right thing. Saddest thing is I'd probably have done it again too. My priorities were all screwed up. I should have been there when it happened. I should have been there with my wife and my boy when they—'

'We've all got regrets,' Michael broke in. 'I bet every single person here could tell you at least a hundred things they wish they'd done differently. I don't think we'll ever get over it. I just hope these feelings get easier to live with, that's all.'

'I loved Joe, you know. That kid was everything to me, and I wish I'd told him that.'

'You'd only have embarrassed him!' Michael smiled. 'He wouldn't have understood, you know.'

'Oh, I know that – I just wish I'd spent more time with him,' Peter said, correcting himself. 'I just wish I could have been there for him when it happened.'

The two men stared into the fire again, and for a while the cracking and popping of the flames was all that could be heard.

'So what was with the toy?' Michael asked again, remembering that his question hadn't been properly answered.

'Oh, that,' Peter replied. 'It's silly really. Jenny and I went shopping with Joe on the Sunday afternoon before it happened. We'd been walking around town for hours, and Joe was getting tired and fed up, like kids do. I told him that if he behaved himself and if everything worked out at the office over the next few days then I'd get him a present when we next went out, whatever he wanted. I asked him what he'd like, expecting him to go for the biggest and most expensive thing he could think of. Anyway, he dragged his mum and me into this shop and showed us this toy – like the one I found today. It wasn't much and it wasn't expensive, but all his mates were collecting them and I was going to get it for him. That was all he wanted. Christ, Mike, I wish I could see him again. Just once more.'

32

Cooper stood outside the control tower and looked around with satisfaction. Things were moving in the right direction. Richard had returned safely from the island and, perhaps even more importantly, they'd finally got Keele behind the controls of the plane. Okay, so he'd only got as far as moving it out of the hangar and down to the end of the airstrip, but it was a start. Suddenly their chances of getting everyone over to Cormansey in the next few days had dramatically improved.

The day so far had been spent trying to coordinate the evacuation of Monkton Airfield. They'd calculated that Keele would need to make two flights to the island, three at most, and that had been a relief to everyone, not least the pilot himself. He hadn't got as far as thinking about what would happen when they reached the island, but that didn't matter; for now all that was important was getting away from this godforsaken place.

A sudden flurry of noise and activity on the other side of the chain-link fence momentarily distracted him. He peered into the distance, but couldn't see anything unusual.

He kept watching for a second longer, feeling distinctly uneasy. Jack had said something earlier which had been troubling him: he'd been keeping look-out with Phil Croft, and the two of them had decided that the behaviour of the dead was changing again. Croft had been exercising his injured leg, not paying attention to his surroundings, and he'd found himself a little too close to the perimeter fence. Many of the bodies had reacted to him as they normally did, ripping and tearing at each other's flesh in their fever to get close to him, but others had behaved very differently. Some of the dead, Jack had told Cooper, were standing still, almost as if they were watching him and Croft. Richard Lawrence had confirmed that the people over on the island had noticed something similar. He didn't know what it meant, but he didn't like it. Were the bodies about to finally give up and drop, or was this change in their behaviour the first sign of something worse to come?

'You okay?' Emma asked, surprising him as she walked past.

'Fine,' he grunted. He'd been concentrating on the corpses and hadn't noticed her approaching.

'It's too cold to be standing out here,' she said over her shoulder as she disappeared inside. The control tower was dark, but it was a relief to be out of the wind at last. She ran up the stairs and let herself into the main room, where she found Jackie Soames trying unsuccessfully to coordinate the emptying of the building.

'So what's the plan?' Emma asked. Things had stepped up a gear since the helicopter had returned. She could see a few people moving around with apparent purpose, but she could also see many, many more sitting still and staring into space, as they always did. They'd have to make an effort soon or they risked being left behind.

'There is no plan,' Jackie replied dejectedly. 'I just thought it would be sensible to get as much stuff out of here as we could before morning.'

'So what exactly do we need to take? Do you know what's already on the island?'

'Not really.'

'Didn't someone say there used to be about five hundred people living there? So there should be plenty of clothing and beds and the like?'

'Suppose so.'

'So all we really need to take with us from here is any food we've got and any specialist stuff that we know we won't find there. That's not going to be very much.'

'I know,' Jackie admitted. 'You're right, love. I'm just trying to keep myself busy, that's all. I don't know about you, but I can't stand all this bloody waiting around. It's starting to get to me. I just want to get on, get things done and get out of here.'

'We've all done more than enough waiting around,' Emma agreed.

Realising that it was pointless trying to motivate herself – or anyone else, come to that – Jackie slumped heavily in a chair.

Emma sat down next to her. She thought the large, red-faced

woman looked unusually troubled. 'What's on your mind?' she asked quietly.

Jackie pulled a half-smoked cigarette from her box – she had only a couple now – and lit it. 'This just about sums it up,' she said as she blew out the match.

'What does?'

'These bloody cigarettes.'

'I don't understand.'

'I used to run a pub,' Jackie said. She took a deep, tired breath. 'I used to smoke like a bloody chimney. I used to like having a good time first, then worrying about it afterwards. Now I'm down to my last box of cigarettes and I'm hoping there's going to be some on this bloody island when I get there because the last thing I want to do now is give up. Bloody hell, I want to smoke more than ever now.'

'I'm not sure I understand. What point are you making?'

Jackie didn't – or couldn't – give Emma a direct answer.

'And drinking,' she continued, 'I never used to get a hangover because I never stopped drinking. I used to drink every day. But there's hardly a drop of alcohol left here now, and I *need* booze.'

'I still don't understand.'

Jackie laughed sadly to herself and flicked ash from the end of her cigarette. She watched as it fluttered down onto the floor. 'Sometimes,' she said, 'I really have to think hard to remind myself why we're bothering to do all of this. You and Michael have got each other, and you're bloody lucky because that's more than the rest of us have got. From now on we're going to have to fight for everything we want or need. And okay, the bodies might eventually disappear, but we're still going to be out on our own, aren't we? We're going to have to be *self-sufficient*, for Christ's sake! Bloody hell, I've never been self-sufficient in my life! I've never had anything handed to me on a plate, but I've always been able to go out and get what I want, whenever I've wanted it. It's all different now. I'm never again going to be able to nip down to the shops to get myself a packet of cigarettes or a bottle of gin, am I?'

'No.' Emma felt she should say more, but there was nothing else to say. Jackie was right.

'Sorry, Emma,' she mumbled apologetically, 'I didn't mean to go off on one like that.'

'That's okay,' she insisted. 'Really, I understand how you're feeling.'

'Thing is,' Jackie added, 'I know how lucky I am to still be here and to still be in one piece, I really do, but sometimes that's not enough. I can handle this most of the time, but now and then – well, I just want my life back.'

33

Wrapped up in a thick winter coat to protect him from the cold and wearing a baseball cap to keep off the intermittent rain, Michael sat on a low stone wall in the darkness and stared into the distance. He was alone, and at that moment that was just how he wanted it. The only other person he wanted to be with tonight was miles away. He'd left the eight other survivors celebrating their day's work and drinking themselves stupid in the lounge bar of The Fox, Cormansey's only pub.

The sound of the ocean filled the evening air. The constant crashing of the waves on the beach just ahead of him was becoming a welcome, almost relaxing sound. He felt safe, out on his own. Last night he wouldn't have risked being in the open like this, but today the group had worked hard to clear the village and a large number of bodies had been slaughtered and accounted for. From where he was sitting he could still see the bright glow of the huge pyre they'd lit just outside Danvers Lye. If there were any other bodies nearby tonight (and he guessed there probably would be), he knew he'd be able to deal with them easily. His trusty crowbar remained slung at his side in constant readiness.

Michael was keen to escape from the dead village, and had chosen to walk down the twisting coastal road which led back towards the far end of the island. Suddenly feeling the cold, he jumped up from the stone wall where he'd been sitting and ambled down towards the sea, his feet grinding through the shingle. The waves drowned out the sound of his footsteps.

He'd been busy and preoccupied all day, but now that he'd finally stopped working, he was struggling again. The beach, unlike most of the coastline of Cormansey that he'd seen so far, was fairly flat. A wrecked fishing boat had been washed up onto the shore nearby, and as he walked towards it, he thought he had no way of knowing whether it had originally set sail from Cormansey, or whether it had drifted over and crashed into the rocks here by chance. Wherever it had come from, it had ended its working life stranded on this beach, tipped over onto one side like a dead whale. As he got nearer, Michael saw that the captain of the boat (if that was who it had been) was still on board, caught up in the rusted winch machinery. The body was particularly badly deteriorated, almost skeletal in places, no doubt because of its exposure to the harsh ocean conditions. Almost all of the visible flesh had been stripped away, leaving yellow-white bone exposed.

Months ago the discovery of a body like this would have mattered. The lives of many people would have been affected – the family, police, the man's employers . . . the list went on. Today it didn't mean anything to anyone. Michael pitied the poor sod who had died. What would have been headline news in the days before the world had been turned upside down was now little more than an unimportant piece of driftwood. It was getting harder to remember that each of these bodies had once been someone, a person, with a name, a personality, a history, a life. Once he'd forgotten about it, Michael knew this man would be gone for ever.

Today had been difficult, but not for the reasons he'd expected. Like the rest of the group of survivors on the island, he'd been given a sudden opportunity to look back and remember all they'd lost. Now, as he wandered further down the beach, with the driving wind whipping up off the ocean and gusting furiously into his face, he thought back even further, remembering the life he'd lived before this nightmare had begun. He thought about his family and friends, and about his home. He pictured his house in his mind as he'd left it, and then tried to drag that image into the present. He pictured the street where he used to live, now overrun with weeds, the pavements littered with the remains of the people he used to know.

As the shingle gave way to larger, more dangerous rocks, Michael turned his attention to the more immediate past. He remembered finding the farmhouse with Emma and Carl. Christ, they should have done better there. He should have been stronger. But maybe what had happened at the farmhouse had been inevitable? He thought about the military base, and how somewhere so safe, so strong and secure, had been compromised so quickly and disastrously. Would the island be any different? He had to believe it would: in principle the dangers here were less. These days the gulf between predictability and reality was hard to gauge, though.

All he wanted was security and shelter, a quiet, simple life, with his basic needs satisfied. A roof over his head and Emma by his side was all it boiled down to.

34

Just after six the following morning, Gary Keele stood between two of the disused buildings on the airfield, out of sight of the survivors shuffling to and fro between the control tower, the office buildings and the aircraft. He wasn't hiding from them; he just didn't want them to see him. He was literally sick with nerves. He'd already thrown up twice and the sudden mouth-watering and the cramp in his gut indicated that he was about to vomit for a third time. He hadn't eaten anything since late yesterday evening and his stomach was completely empty, but the mere thought of flying that plane instantly made the bile rise again. He retched and threw up a mouthful of acidic bile.

His legs shaking, Keele crouched down and spat into the overgrown weeds at his feet, trying to clear the sour taste of vomit from his mouth. This was stupid, he thought to himself. He had hundreds of flying hours under his belt; why was he so worked up about making this flight now? If anything, flying to the island should be easier than most of his previous flights – apart from the helicopter the skies were otherwise completely empty. Was it the responsibility? The thought of carrying so many passengers, having them rely on him so completely? Was that what was causing his nervousness? In his job as a tug-plane pilot at a gliding centre he'd almost always flown alone; he'd had no one else to worry about once the pilot behind him had released. On the morning it'd happened he'd been up there alone, tugging the fourth of five gliders into the sky, when they'd started falling like stones, dropping out of the air around him.

Get a fucking grip, he thought to himself. Suddenly determined, he took a deep breath and marched to the edge of the building, but he stopped and turned back when he saw the plane. He pushed himself flat against the wall, a cold, nervous sweat prickling his brow again. He *had* to do this. He had to make himself do this. He didn't have any choice – never mind the rest of them; if he didn't get in that bloody plane and fly it, then he was stuck at the airfield too.

'Finally!' Richard Lawrence grinned as Keele marched past him purposefully. 'Here he comes. You feeling all right this morning, Tuggie?'

Keele was concentrating on trying to rise above his fear and focus on the job at hand; he didn't hear Richard's jovial exchange.

Richard looked over at Cooper and raised his eyebrows.

'Don't knock it,' Cooper said, 'at least he's here. As long as he gets that bloody plane up in the air I don't care what state he's in.'

They stood and watched as Keele climbed up into the cockpit of the plane and began to nervously run through his pre-flight checks. In the back of the aircraft, twelve equally nervous survivors sat strapped in their seats, surrounded (as they had been for more than half an hour now) by all the bags and boxes of supplies they'd been able to safely cram inside. Five more people, Donna and Clare included, emerged from the office building. With her arm wrapped around the shoulder of Dean McFarlane, at only eight years old the youngest person left alive, Clare made her way over to the plane.

'You take care when you get there,' Jack shouted to her from where he stood at the edge of the runway.

'I will,' she grinned, hiding her nerves. 'I'll send you a postcard. Let you know what the place is like!'

'Don't bother,' he replied. 'I'll be over there with you before the postcard gets delivered!'

Keele emerged from the cockpit of the plane. He climbed out onto the runway again and looked up and down the length of the aircraft and then up into the sky, obviously psyching himself for the flight.

Richard Lawrence turned and said to Donna, 'Looks like we're ready.' He took hold of her arm and gently ushered her forward. 'Get yourself on board.'

Cooper watched as Donna made her way over to the helicopter to join three other survivors. Richard sensed his concern. 'It'll be fine,' he said. 'I reckon as soon as Keele's off the ground he'll get his nerve back.'

'Either that, or he'll go to pieces. What if he loses it?'

'Then it'll be a short flight, won't it? And I'll end up spending the next week flying backwards and forwards between this hole and the frigging island.'

Keele was walking towards them.

'Ready?' Cooper asked him.

'Suppose,' he replied, his voice sounding less than sure.

'You know where you're going don't you, Keele?' Richard checked for the umpteenth time. Better to be safe than sorry.

'I know.'

'You shouldn't have any trouble finding the place. If the worst comes to the worst, just head for the east coast and then follow it north until you find the island. You'll see the smoke and the people and they'll see you before you can—'

'I know,' Keele interrupted, 'you already told me.'

Cooper and Richard exchanged quick glances, both of them still dubious about the pilot's mental condition and his ability to fly.

'Let's get going,' Cooper urged, and Keele jogged back to the plane.

'We should be back later today,' Richard shouted over his shoulder as he walked away towards the helicopter. He stopped and turned around to face Cooper and Jack. 'I'm aiming for mid-afternoon. Just do me a favour and make sure everyone's ready to go first thing tomorrow. I want to get this done quickly, okay?'

'Okay,' Cooper replied.

He and Jack, suddenly the only two left standing out in the open, moved away from the runway as first Richard and then Keele started their engines. A sudden increase in wind and noise accompanied the take-off of the helicopter, which rose up and then gently circled the airfield, driving the rotting masses beyond the perimeter fence into a frenzy. Keele began to taxi down the runway, and as he increased his speed, Richard hovered high above the ground and watched. Keele cautiously coaxed the plane off the ground and lifted it into the air; there were a few nervous rabbit hops, and then it climbed quickly and powerfully towards the grey clouds.

At the edge of Monkton Airfield, Kelly Harcourt's body began to move. The dead soldier had remained where she'd fallen for almost two days, and now, beginning deep inside the brain of the corpse, and showing itself first at the very tips of numb fingers, the change was starting.

It spread throughout the body quickly, the movement building gradually until dead, clouded eyes flickered slowly open and clumsy arms and legs became animated again. With awkward, uncoordinated movements the body hauled itself onto all fours and then stood up and began to stumble forward. It tripped through the long grass and kept moving until it clattered into the border fence.

In common with the basic reactions of the thousands upon thousands of other bodies which had previously dragged themselves up from the ground and begun to move in this way, the shell that had once been Kelly Harcourt turned and tried to walk away. But it couldn't move. It was trapped, held tightly from behind by the grabbing hands of numerous rotting bodies on the other side of the fence. Already agitated by the noise of the plane and the helicopter flying low overhead just moments earlier, the resurrection of the dead soldier provoked more of the same basic, brutal reactions. The most dexterous of the creatures managed to poke their decaying fingers through the wire mesh and grasped the cadaver's hair and clothing, whatever they could grab onto. The bodies pulled and tugged at the soldier's remains, trying to drag them back through the fence, not understanding that the wire barrier was stopping them. Eventually the numb fingers lost their grip and slipped away, allowing the corpse to stumble off again in the opposite direction.

On the other side of the fence, just to the right of where Kelly's body had been briefly trapped, another body was reacting in a different way. Eight weeks ago this had been an intelligent young clothing store department manager with a bright future ahead of her. Now it was a mud-splattered, half-naked, emaciated collection of brittle bone and rotting flesh. Unlike the majority of the seething crowd, however, this one was beginning to exhibit signs of real control and determination. Unlike those which simply stood there vacantly or those which ripped and tore at the other corpses immediately around them, this body was beginning to think. As it was pressed hard against the fence, surrounded on either side by many thousands of creatures, with a similar number behind, it realised that it needed to move to survive. On the other side of the mesh it could just about make out the dark blur of Kelly's body tripping away, and it decided that was what it needed to do too. It grabbed the wire fence with cold, bony hands and began to shake it. All around it other bodies began to do the same.

35

With Danvers Lye now almost completely cleared and the majority of Cormansey's dead population eradicated, the group on the island set about moving from building to building, uncovering the last remaining corpses, and then beginning to clean and disinfect the houses.

Michael, Danny and Bruce had taken the Jeep down to the southernmost tip of the island, to start with, and were making their way back north. They had cleared one house already, and were getting ready to start on the second. This morning was bright and dry, and warmer than the previous days, and they could see the next building from a fair distance away. Its red-bricked frontage contrasted with the rest of its predominantly green, brown and grey surroundings.

Michael stopped the Jeep outside the house, which had a small front garden surrounded by a low fence. The three men crossed the road and walked up the short garden path to the front door. They paused to assess the situation before barging inside – it didn't matter how many corpses they had previously found and disposed of; each new discovery was different to the last, and was almost always unsettling. Michael found it especially difficult dealing with the bodies he found in their own homes; when he came across a body which had died surrounded by its own belongings, he instinctively tried to piece together the details of its abruptly truncated life. Seeing what these people had once been made it immeasurably more difficult to think of them just as lumps of dead, rotting flesh.

'Listen,' he whispered as they stood at the door. Danny moved a little closer. They could hear something moving inside the house. Bruce peered in through the front windows, first into the kitchen, then the living room. He could see a body lying on the ground next to an armchair, and he could also see shadows and faint signs of movement in the doorway behind it. If there was a corpse moving through the house, then it was in the hallway, no doubt attracted there by their sudden noisy arrival.

'Can't see a lot, Mike,' Bruce said from a short distance away. 'There's only going to be one or two in there, so we might as well just go for it.'

Michael pushed the door and it opened inwards with ease. He instinctively took a step back as the single moving occupant of the house shuffled out of the shadows and lurched towards him. His heart sank. This was one of those occasions when he found it almost impossible to think of the bodies as objects. Sometimes the scale of the tragedy still took him by surprise; sometimes it still hurt. He stood to one side as the emaciated remains of a small child stumbled towards him. The poor kid was half his height; he could only have been five or six when he'd died – that was if it was a boy – the body had deteriorated so much that he wasn't even sure. It continued to move closer with the familiar awkward gait and pointless intent of the dead. It fixed him with its cold, vacant eyes. Funny, he thought, how death had stripped away all individuality from the remains of the population. This thing looked and behaved no differently to those bodies which had been twice its size and many more years older.

Danny Talbot stepped forward and, with a sudden grunt of effort and aggression, chopped down at the body's slender neck with a hand axe. It took five good, hard swipes before the head and spinal cord had been sufficiently damaged to stop the corpse from moving. It fell at Michael's feet and he knelt down next to it.

'Okay?' asked Bruce.

Michael nodded. Holding his breath, trying hard to ignore the suffocating smell of the insect-infested body, he picked it up and carried it out of the garden and over to the roadside. He placed it down on the grass verge, ready to be collected and cremated later on. That was all this poor child had left now, he thought sadly as he stared into what was left of its face. Maggots were crawling under the flesh, making its expression appear to change. This kid would never finish school. He'd never go through adolescence. Never experience his first kiss or leave home or get a job or become a parent. No successes. No failures. Nothing.

By the time Michael had got up again, Bruce and Danny had already gone inside. He followed them indoors.

'Anything else in here?' he asked. The smell in the confined house was typically obnoxious and overpowering.

'Just this one, I think,' answered Bruce. He was pointing at the body on the living room carpet that he'd spotted from outside. He could hear Danny upstairs, checking out the bedrooms. A few seconds later he came crashing back down, his face flushed red with sudden effort.

'Clear,' he gasped.

Bruce grabbed the bony wrists of the corpse in the living room, presumably the mother of the dead child, and dragged it down the hall. Though it had been comparatively well preserved, it still left behind a sticky outline of decomposition on the carpet.

The modest house was quite traditional in style, and the musty smell gave the building an antique, museum-like atmosphere. Michael stood and looked around.

'You sure you're okay?' Bruce asked him as he came back indoors after dumping the body next to the child's corpse. 'You're miles away this morning.'

'Wishing I was,' he replied quickly. He did feel different today, there was no denying it. He felt a strange sense of anti-climax and disappointment. He wondered whether it was because he was gradually becoming aware of the limitations of the island – as safe and protected a place as it would soon be, he could also see the remote location would one day make it restricted and stifling, and the size of the island would inevitably make it difficult for them to expand their small community easily. It was already obvious that Cormansey was never going to be the haven that he and the others had naïvely dreamed it might be. Nothing was going to be easy here. Then again, nothing was going to be easy anywhere, was it? Maybe everything looked worse today because he'd spent too long yesterday thinking about everything he'd lost . . .

Their brief this morning had been simply to clear the bodies from the houses, but looking around this particular unimposing little property, it was obvious that a lot of work would be needed to make each building habitable again. The carpet was ruined where the corpse had lain. In the kitchen, the fridge was filled with rotten food. Everywhere was covered with dust, and one bedroom was showing signs of damp, thanks to an open window which had allowed in two month's worth of rainwater.

Michael realised that what he was looking at was a world slowly being reclaimed. No doubt the arrival on Cormansey of the survivors would prolong the life of this and other buildings, but elsewhere, back on the mainland, the process of decay and deterioration would continue unchecked. The disappearance of man from the face of the planet was inevitably going to cause a massive change to the ecosystem. Crops would no longer be grown or harvested. Vermin would breed, and the decay of millions of bodies would result in a huge increase in the numbers of insects, not to mention germs and disease. The ramifications were endless, too much for him to think about. When he'd arrived on the island he'd felt strong, determined and full of hope. Today, those feelings had started to fade. In comparison to the almost unimaginable scale of the changes the infection had bought to the entire planet, the minor achievements of this small group of survivors meant nothing. Disheartened, Michael dragged himself back out to the Jeep with the other two men.

'Where to next?' he asked.

'Road splits in a while,' Bruce replied. 'We'll keep west. Jim said he was sticking to the east side.'

'Okay.'

Michael sat back in the driver's seat and readied himself for the next building. He stared into the wing mirror and looked at the bodies of the child and its mother for a couple of seconds before turning the key in the ignition, starting the engine and driving away.

'Did that kid get to you?' Danny asked from the back seat with clumsiness but a surprising degree of perception.

'Everything's getting to me today,' he grunted back.

'Decent weather though!' Bruce said cheerfully, doing his best to lighten the increasingly sombre mood. 'Just imagine what this place is going to be like in the summer. Plenty of coastline, good fishing waters . . .'

'Just got to get through the winter first,' Danny reminded him.

'I know, you killjoy, but that doesn't mean—' He stopped speaking, leaned forward and peered up into the sky. 'What's that?'

Michael slowed the Jeep and looked up. He could see the helicopter, crossing the blue sky like a small black spider.

'Bloody brilliant,' Bruce sighed with relief, 'here comes some help! Wonder who he's brought with him? Hope it's someone who's going to pull their weight. The last thing we need here is—'

'The plane,' Danny interrupted. 'I can hear it!'

All eyes switched from staring at the helicopter to scouring the sky, looking for the plane. Bruce spotted it first, and pointed it out: it looked like it was following the exact same course the helicopter had taken.

Suddenly feeling more alive and invigorated than he had done since he'd arrived here, Michael put his foot down and accelerated again.

'Where are you going?' Bruce asked as they sped past the next house and carried on down the narrow road.

'I need to see who's here,' Michael answered, his pulse racing with sudden nervousness and anticipation.

By the time they'd reached the airstrip, both the plane and the helicopter had landed and the passengers were being unloaded. They staggered onto the tarmac strip, looking around in awe as Brigid and Gayle ran towards them. The new arrivals stared at their surroundings like tourists arriving at some long-awaited and much-anticipated holiday destination.

Gary Keele ran in the opposite direction, and stopped when he reached a patch of long grass. He bent over double, put his hands on his knees and threw up. Landing the plane had been even more nerve-wracking than taking off.

Michael stopped the Jeep, jumped out and started to look around hopefully. He could see several faces that he recognised immediately – Donna, Clare and Karen Chase amongst others. But there was no sign of Emma.

36

With the first tranche of people now gone, the control tower had suddenly become an empty place. Emma had become used to seeing loads of people, but now she could see only empty spaces. Several of those who had gone on the plane had done little more than sit silently in the same spot since they'd first arrived at the airfield, and it annoyed her that some of those who had done nothing to help the group had been among the first to get away, but she understood it had to be this way. She wished they had a way of knowing if the plane had reached the island safely.

For an hour or two after they'd left she'd half-expected to look up and see Keele bringing the plane limping home, still full of passengers. She didn't have much faith in him, either as a pilot or a human being . . . but come to think of it, she didn't have much faith in anything any more. If she was honest with herself, the truth was that she wanted the plane back so that she could go. She wanted to get away from this place and the thousands of bodies surrounding it, and she wanted to get away now, not tomorrow.

Well, whatever had happened, they would soon know if the pilots had been successful. The plan had been to drop off the passengers, then get back to the airfield as quickly as they could. They'd hoped to leave the island by three o'clock. It was already almost that time.

Emma had done a head-count earlier: there were just over thirty people left at the airfield, and most of them were waiting in the office building for the aircraft to return. That didn't include Kilgore. He had disappeared several hours ago – she had last seen him heading towards one of the outbuildings close to the control tower. The soldier was exhausted, dehydrated and starving, and he knew that his time would soon be up, but he didn't have the guts to do what Kelly Harcourt had done. Instead he festered inside. The rest of the group kept their distance from him, for their approaches had been met with anger and hostility, or with equally unpalatable outpourings of self-pity and grief. They had quite enough confusion and doubt of their own to deal with; now they did their best to forget about him.

Emma tripped down the control tower staircase and stepped out into the cold but bright afternoon, the sun just beginning to sink towards the horizon. She found Cooper standing outside, scanning the perimeter fence and occasionally the skies with a pair of binoculars.

'See anything yet?' she asked hopefully.

'Nothing,' he answered. Emma watched him as he shifted his attention from the sky to closer to the ground. 'I doubt they'll be back for another hour or so.'

'What are you looking for then?'

'Nothing really,' he replied. 'Just keeping an eye on them.'

Emma shielded her eyes from the low sun and looked towards the fence. Without the benefit of the binoculars she could see little more than a constantly moving and apparently endless mass of dead flesh. The immense crowd didn't look any different today to how it had yesterday or the day before.

'I don't like the look of that,' Cooper said suddenly, focusing his attention on one particular section of fence.

'What?' Emma asked, anxiously.

'Bloody things down there look like they're trying to pull the fence down.'

'What?' she said again, unable to believe what she'd heard. Cooper handed her the binoculars and she lifted them to her eyes. She quickly focused on the fence and then scanned along to her left until she came to the section that Cooper had been watching. 'Bloody hell,' she gasped. He was right. In the distance a tightly packed group of figures had grabbed hold of the wire-mesh and they were pulling it towards them and then pushing it back the other way, working in concert, as if they were trying to work the posts out of the ground. They looked barely uncoordinated, but their intent was clear.

'They won't do it, will they?'

'I don't know if they've got the strength, but . . .'

'But . . . ?'

'But there are thousands of them out there. Give them enough time and who knows what they'll achieve.'

Emma looked deep into the mass of bodies again. The whole crowd was in constant movement, writhing and squirming. 'What do we do about them?'

'Don't think there's anything we can do,' Cooper replied, 'except what we're already doing. The number of bodies still following us around is going to cause us problems whatever happens. We should be out of here by tomorrow, the day after at the latest. We'll just have to ride our luck until then.'

'We've been riding our luck since all of this started.'

'True. So a couple more days shouldn't make much difference. We could go down to that part of the fence, soak the bloody things in fuel and torch the lot of them, but what good's that going to do? It might make us feel a bit better, and it might get rid of a few hundred of them, but will it make us any safer or get us out of here any quicker? And if they really are starting to think logically again, then they might see what we're doing as an act of aggression and try and fight back.'

'You are joking, aren't you?'

'I've seen stranger things happen recently.'

Emma passed him the binoculars back then turned and walked to the control tower, suddenly anxious to get indoors. Cooper continued to look along the fence. There was another small pocket of activity by the main entrance gate, where more bodies were pushing against the barrier. He headed for the office building. He needed to keep people indoors and out of sight, anything to avoid being seen by the bodies and antagonising them unnecessarily. They needed to keep the crowds on the other side of the chain-link fence under control, and the best way of doing that was to keep their distance.

37

Kilgore lay on a dusty sofa in a shadow-filled waiting room. He closed his eyes and tried to ignore the pain. He couldn't remember when he'd last eaten, and he hadn't drunk anything for more than a day and a half. He felt so weak that he couldn't sit upright any more; he could barely lift his arms or his head. He felt leaden. He was lying there staring out of the windows, trying to ignore the relentless physical discomfort; that was hard enough to deal with, but the mental anguish was much, much worse.

Kilgore had come to the conclusion that today (or possibly tomorrow, if he was really unlucky) would be his final day alive. His mouth was dry and he struggled to find enough saliva to lick his chapped lips. His head ached and all that he could hear was the sound of his own laboured breathing echoing around his facemask, and the constant buzz of insects which, in his disorientated state, seemed to swarm around the room like circling vultures, waiting for him to die. The end had to be close now, didn't it?

Lying there waiting for the inevitable was, bizarrely, beginning to get easier in some ways. The first hours he'd spent in this quiet little room had been difficult. He'd shut himself away in here, but he'd still believed that there was some slight ray of hope for him – in his tired mind he'd explored every escape route, every potential outcome. He'd thought about trying to get back to the underground base, and had started to make plans; he'd take one of the trucks and drive back there alone . . . but he didn't know if any of the vehicles had enough fuel, or how he'd get the gate open, or how to get through the bodies . . .

He came up with a multitude of reasons why every plan he considered would be impossible to follow through. He could still have gone with the others to the island, but what would happen to him there? He could have done what Kelly Harcourt had done, and enjoyed one final breath of fresh air, but he knew that he had neither the physical nor the mental strength to take that final step and remove his mask, no matter how desperate he became.

Kilgore was tired. He'd had enough. He wanted it to stop now. He wanted to fall asleep and not wake up again. He'd been hallucinating since early morning and there'd been a sudden, dramatic increase in the strength of the freakish sights which surrounded him. About half an hour ago he thought he'd been visited by his dead mother and father, and one of his teachers from school. In his confused mind the three of them had stood over him and critically discussed his general lack of progress in life. An hour before that, the room had lost all structure and form, the ceiling had dripped down until it had almost touched the floor and the windows on the wall opposite had closed up until they'd disappeared and the room had become dark as night.

The windows were clear again now, but he was having another hallucination: he could see Kelly Harcourt.

Kilgore watched as she came closer. He could tell that it was her, because she was wearing the same kind of protective suit that he still wore. He could see her blonde hair – she didn't have her face-mask on, he realised. Christ, she could breathe! And if she could breathe, he thought, then maybe he could too? Groaning with effort he slowly sat up and lifted his hand to his mask. Then he stopped.

Kelly continued to come closer. She walked awkwardly, with her head listing over to one side. Her arms and legs were inflexible, unresponsive. She must have been hurt. She was dragging her feet, not even able to lift them. And then the sun illuminated her face: a cold and lifeless mask with swollen, bloodstained lips and dark eyes. Her mouth moved constantly as she approached, seeming to form silent words. Despite his lack of energy, Kilgore forced himself to stand up and walk towards her. He hobbled across the room and leant against the window, exhausted. Kelly's body clattered against the other side of the glass and for a split second he stood face to face with her before a sudden noise sent both of them reeling backwards. Swaying unsteadily for a moment, he watched as the corpse turned and began to walk away.

Each step forward took a huge amount of effort, but Kilgore found himself following the cadaver out onto the airfield. He wasn't sure what drove him to do it; was it fear, or curiosity, or nervousness? Was it that he wanted to see properly what he might still become? He waited in the doorway for a moment to catch his breath before leaving the building where he'd presumed he'd die. Just ahead of him Kelly's body continued to stagger away, silhouetted against the afternoon sun. The sky above Kilgore, so clear and blue for much of the day, was beginning to darken as tinges of hints of deep reds and purples began to illuminate the trailing wisps of clouds. Away from the horizon, the moon and the first few bright stars could be seen. He followed Kelly along the runway, past the front of the control tower and out towards the perimeter fence.

Kilgore couldn't keep up. He'd not gone far, but the effort of moving was already too much. He put his hands on his knees and slowly sucked in a mouthful of purified air. Another hallucination was beginning now. This one was more powerful than any of the others he'd had; it seemed to surround and swallow him. It began with a noise, quietly at first, and without direction, but it quickly built to a deafening roar, and it was accompanied by a fierce, angry wind. He managed to lift his head, and saw the helicopter above him beginning its rapid descent. Wrong-footed by the sudden distraction, his weak legs buckled and folded underneath him and he fell onto his backside. Shooting pains ran the entire length of his emaciated body and he winced at the sudden agony. Just over ten yards from the perimeter fence he sat in the long grass and watched as the powerful machine hovered in the air above the heads of thousands of seething bodies. Then another sound came from out of nowhere, and there was a sudden, sweeping movement as the plane glided over him before touching down and bouncing along the runway, finally coming to an undignified, lurching halt at the far end of the strip.

Kilgore watched from his collapsed position at the edge of the airfield as people began to emerge from the control tower. He didn't recognise any of them any more. They were just dark, featureless figures now, as faceless as the thousands of corpses surrounding the airfield.

Too tired to stay sitting up, he lay on his back and stared up into the darkening sky. The relentless noise of the helicopter changed direction and faded away.

*

Once he was sure that the plane had safely touched down, Richard Lawrence began to bring the helicopter in to land. He looked down into the mass of diseased cadavers below as he hovered above the perimeter fence. Bloody hell, he thought, the bodies were more incensed and animated than he'd ever seen them before – some were still slashing at each other, and fighting with those nearest to them, while others were pushing against the fence, no doubt being crushed by the weight of thousands more corpses behind them. But there were now many more who were standing their ground as best they could, looking up at him defiantly with cold, unblinking eyes. Richard forced himself to look away. Concentrating again, he flew towards the control tower and the other buildings.

Cooper was waiting for him. The rotor blades were still spinning as the pilot ducked under them and ran over to the ex-soldier. Together they jogged towards the plane. Keele was sitting in the cockpit trying to recover from the trauma of the second flight. He'd managed to turn the plane around to face back down the runway, but he hadn't yet moved from his seat.

'Everything go all right?' Cooper asked as they stood and waited for Keele to move.

'Like clockwork,' he replied.

'And you're both still okay for fuel? You've got enough to make another flight?'

'Plenty. I should have enough for a good few crossings yet, and I think Keele's got similar.'

'So we'll try and get another load over there first thing tomorrow morning, okay?'

Richard sighed with exhaustion. 'Bloody hell, mate,' he protested, 'give me a chance to get my breath back first, won't you? It's been a bloody long day!'

'Get this lot over there and you can spend the rest of your life relaxing.'

'Everything all right, Richard?' Jackie Soames asked from behind them. She was walking towards them from the office building, and the look of relief on her tired face was clear.

'Everything's fine,' he replied.

Keele had finally composed himself enough to be able to get out of the plane. He walked along the runway towards the others, relieved that his ordeal was over for one day.

'Well done, son,' Richard said when he was close enough to hear him. 'Told you we'd be all right, didn't I?'

Keele nodded. He was still breathing heavily and his shirt was soaked with sweat. His usually neatly coiffured hair was unkempt. The effort of landing had exhausted him.

'You did well,' Jackie said, wrapping her arm around him. 'If I still ran the pub I'd buy you a drink!'

'There's a pub on Cormansey. You can buy me a drink when you get there.'

The four of them stopped outside the office building. Inside, Richard could see many faces staring back at him expectantly. For once they looked positive, happy faces too, all of them sharing a common desire to get away from this unwelcoming, dangerous place. The responsibility he shared with Keele to get these people to safety was humbling. Light from the bright orange sun setting on the horizon reflected off the glass and obscured his view momentarily.

'So they're all okay over there?' Jackie asked.

'What?'

'The people over on the island, are they okay?' she repeated.

'Looks like it,' he replied. 'They've cleared the village and they've managed to get rid of most of the bodies. We left them emptying out the individual houses.'

'So they'll have a place ready for me by the time I get over there?' she joked.

'Shouldn't think so – not yet, at least. I was talking to Brigid earlier. She reckons it's going to take us weeks to get the place cleaned up properly.'

'Doesn't matter,' Cooper said, yawning and stretching his arms up into the cool evening air. 'The one thing we should have plenty of is time. Won't matter if it takes us weeks or months to get everything done, will it? As long as we can get hold of enough food and we're relatively comfortable, then who cares how long it take us to—' He stopped talking.

Emma had appeared from the doorway of the control tower just a short distance away from where they were standing. Breathless from the effort of the sprint downstairs, her face looked ashen with fear. Her unexpected appearance and terrified expression immediately silenced the chatter. In the sudden quiet they became aware of another noise, coming from a different direction. It was coming from the edge of the airfield.

'They've brought the fence down,' she said.

There was a moment of shock and disbelief.

'What?' Jackie demanded.

'The bodies,' she said, shaking, 'they've brought part of the fence down.'

Cooper was the first to react. He turned and sprinted back down the runway, instinctively concentrating his attention on the section of the rotting crowd that had concerned him earlier in the afternoon. The fading light and made it difficult to see clearly, but he could make out the bodies spilling onto the field, falling over a short section of fallen fence, then picking themselves up and moving towards the buildings. The sudden, deafening noise made by the returning helicopter and plane had whipped the dead into a frenzy, he decided, and that hysteria had given them enough impetus to bring down the fence. Cooper could see that one of the metal posts had been pushed over until it was almost lying flat on the ground, and now the combined weight of the surging crowd of bodies was threatening to collapse another section of the barrier.

'Fucking things are going to tear the whole fence down,' Jack Baxter shouted as he ran from the control tower towards the others. 'What the fucking hell are we going to do?'

'Block it off,' someone suggested. 'Get one of the trucks over there and block it off.'

'Where's Steve Armitage?' Emma demanded, but Jack was one step ahead of her. He ran over to the office building and dragged the truck driver outside. Steve pounded over to the truck, already panting and wheezing. He wasted precious seconds staring towards the perimeter of the airfield in disbelief. The fading light made it impossible to make out details, but even from here the scale of what was happening was clear. Weakened by the collapse of the first section, now a second section of fence was falling. They were still several hundred yards away, and they were moving as slowly and awkwardly as ever, but an unstoppable deluge of dead bodies was spilling across the airfield.

'Too late for that,' Cooper screamed to Steve as he sprinted past him, heading back towards the control tower. 'Keele, get that fucking plane back in the air. Get out of here, now, or we'll never get off the ground again.'

The furthest advanced of the bodies were close to reaching the end of the runway. Cooper was right. If the pilot didn't act quickly and get the plane airborne in the next few minutes, the runway would be swarming with corpses and take-off would be impossible. His earlier nerves were suddenly replaced by sheer bloody fear. Keele scrambled back into his still warm seat and restarted the engine. Phil Croft tried to control the flow of people from the office building towards the plane, but he gave up as they surged forward in terrified panic. Word of what had happened had spread quickly. People pushed and jostled each other for position. Cooper tried to head off the crowd, using all his strength to limit the numbers getting onto the plane. Forced to make a decision that was as selfish as it was selfless, Jack came around behind him, pushed his way inside and pulled the door shut, knowing that there were already enough people on board.

'Out of my fucking way!' Jacob Flynn, an obnoxious bully, screamed as the plane door closed in his face. He threw himself at Cooper, almost knocking him to the ground, but the ex-soldier quickly regained his footing and charged at Flynn, pushing him back towards the office building.

'Get back, you stupid bastard,' he pleaded as Flynn began to race forward again. 'The rest of you, get back! It's too late!'

Flynn stopped and looked around. Beyond the terrified faces which surrounded him he could see the dark shapes of the dead, continuing their unstoppable advance. He turned and ran back into the building.

Cooper slammed his hand against the side of the plane and Keele began to taxi forward. 'Get back inside,' he screamed again at the sea of terrified people who still hoped to get onto the plane. 'Stay calm and we'll all still get away from here. Get out of sight, now!'

Croft looked back over his shoulder. Realising how close the first bodies were, he limped back towards the office building as quickly as his damaged body would allow. A short distance away Richard Lawrence was pushing Jackie into the back of the helicopter before grabbing the three nearest survivors and bundling them into the aircraft. He jumped back into his seat, started the engine and took off. Emma watched tearfully from the door of the control tower. She screamed something to Steve Armitage on the other side of the runway, but her words were drowned out by the roar of the plane. She watched helplessly as it powered along the concrete strip and lifted into the air, its wheels missing the heads of the nearest cadavers by little more than a foot.

Cooper pushed the final few survivors through the door of the office building and slammed it shut, then sprinted back to the control tower.

'Upstairs,' he yelled to Emma and Steve as the overweight truck driver dragged himself across the runway, swerving around some of the closest bodies, smashing into others. There were corpses all around them now, some slamming into the sides of the office building, trying to reach the group of terrified people trapped inside, others lurching towards the base of the control tower, where Cooper was scrambling to shut and bar the door. Two lumbering cadavers managed to slip inside, only to find themselves face to face with Steve, who was brandishing a metal chair. He swung it repeatedly at the desperate creatures until they had been reduced to a pile of rotten flesh and smashed bone. He moved out of the way as Cooper dragged tables out from a small ground-floor room to block the entrance.

At the top of the staircase Emma collided heavily with another body. Instinctively she scrambled around in the semi-darkness for something to destroy it with. She grabbed the corpse's leg, to try and prevent it from getting away, and it kicked out at her with surprising strength.

'Don't,' a mousy little woman protested, 'please, don't hurt me!'

Emma relaxed and pulled her to her feet. She recognised her as Juliet Appleby, one of the silent majority who had spent their time here sat hidden in the control tower. As Cooper and Steve rushed past them both she shoved Juliet forward. The terrified, shaking woman stumbled across the room to the window directly opposite and looked down over the airfield. The damaged fence was obscured now by hundreds of bodies, and every moment more of them forced their way through the gap and advanced relentlessly towards the centre of the airfield. An unstoppable tidal wave of dead flesh surged forward, an incalculable number of rotting cadavers, all after one thing.

Monkton Airfield was lost.

*

Kilgore lay on the ground and looked up at the sky.

He was aware of movement all around him, and sometimes on top of him. All of the earlier noise had stopped. The plane had gone again. The helicopter had gone too.

It was getting darker.

Too tired to react, or to fight, or even to take off his facemask, he lay there helplessly as the bodies trampled him into the ground.

38

'So what the hell do we do now, Cooper?' Steve Armitage demanded angrily.

Cooper didn't answer. He walked over to Emma and Juliet, who were staring out at the desperate scene outside.

Tears of fear and frustration were flooding down Emma's face. 'For Christ's sake,' she sobbed, 'this isn't fair. We were so close to getting out of here.'

'We can still get out.'

'How are we going to get past that lot?' she asked, pointing down at the ground.

Cooper peered down himself. From their high vantage point the hopelessness of the situation was painfully apparent. They could see right across the wide expanse of the airfield. In the distance, bodies continued to push their way through the now sizeable gap in the fence, fighting with each other to get through, following each other like an innumerable plague of rats. In the rapidly darkening sky above them the lights of the helicopter and plane could be seen disappearing into the distance.

'Richard will come back,' he said, turning away from the window and massaging his temples. His head was pounding. He couldn't think straight.

'And what's going to happen then?' Steve demanded. 'Do you think those fucking things are going to stand to one side so that he can land and pick us up? For fuck's sake, just admit it Cooper, we've had it.'

Cooper wondered whether he might be right. The bodies below them were congregating around the base of the control tower and other nearby buildings. He moved around so that he had a better view of the small office block where the rest of the group were. By his calculation there were between ten and fifteen people trapped there – Jesus, they were surrounded too.

'How are we going to get them out?' Emma asked. 'We have to

get them out. We can't just leave them there, can we? We have to—'

'Come on, Emma,' Cooper said, 'we're as trapped as they are. There's nothing any of us can do.'

'What do they want?' Juliet Appleby asked. She had gradually moved away from the window and was now standing in the middle of the room, too afraid to look out.

'Haven't you ever seen them like this before?'

'No,' she replied, 'and I've been here for weeks. I've seen the crowds, but never anything like this. I've never been this close to so many of them.'

'Chances are you're going to get a lot closer yet,' Emma interrupted. 'And in answer to your question, I don't know what they want, and neither do they. Those damn things don't know who they were, or what they are now. They don't know who or what we are, or what they want from us. They don't know a fucking thing, and all that I do know is they've probably just taken away our last chance of ever getting away from here.'

'We can still get out,' Cooper shouted instinctively.

'You keep saying that,' she yelled back at him, sobbing again, 'but how?'

Feeling completely demoralised, she sank heavily to the ground, her head in her hands.

Cooper turned away from the window. 'They're crowding around us because we're a distraction,' he said, 'and more to the point, we're the *only* distraction. They're here because we're different, and I don't know if they do it because they want help from us or because they're scared of us or because they want to rip us to fucking pieces or—'

'It doesn't matter why they do it,' Steve said, his voice strained. 'You're right though, the only thing left for them to do is to try and get to us. They won't stop until we're gone.'

'I think,' Cooper continued, 'that all we can do for now is keep out of sight and not make a bloody sound. If they don't know we're up here, then we should be okay for a while. We'll wait for the helicopter to come back.'

'Come on,' Emma protested, 'they already know we're up here. Even if just one of them knows and tries to get inside, then hundreds more will copy and try to do the same. And Richard's not coming back.'

'Yes, he will, and until he does all we can do is shut up, sit tight and wait.'

39

'Just get down, shut your fucking mouth and keep out of sight,' Phil Croft ordered Jacob Flynn. The doctor was crouching behind a desk. Flynn was standing in the middle of the room, in full view of every window. Croft didn't know much about him, other than that he was a volatile, selfish bastard who'd generally kept himself to himself. But he was different now, desperate and frightened, and his fear had forced him into action. He was furious that he'd been left behind, angrier with those who'd got away than with the dead outside; as far as he was concerned, it was every man, woman and child for themselves now, and he was damn sure that he wasn't going to end his time trapped in this fucking building with these stupid fucking people.

'What good is keeping out of sight, you frigging idiot?' he yelled. 'They already know we're in here. The only chance we've got is to open the fucking door and fight our way out.'

'Fight your way out? To where?' Croft asked. 'Can't you see? There's nowhere left to go.'

One of the people cowering in the darkness behind Croft let out a sudden wail of fear. The doctor turned around, but he couldn't see who'd cried out. From his position low on the ground, however, he could see into several of the nearby office rooms, and the angry crowds of rotting bodies which were pressed against every window, trying to force their way inside. Even if Flynn was right and they tried to make a run for it, he thought, the sheer number of cadavers outside would prevent them from getting anywhere. Sensing that his time was running out, he dragged himself back up onto his unsteady feet and walked over to Flynn, who was still standing ranting in the middle of the room.

'Open any of these doors,' he said quietly, his face just inches from Flynn's so that no one else could hear, 'and this place will be full of them in seconds. You won't survive, and I won't survive. Open the door and we're all dead.'

Flynn glared at Croft. He was a good six inches taller than the doctor, a threatening man at the best of times. Now he grabbed hold of Croft by the scruff of his neck and pulled him even closer.

'I want to get out of here,' he hissed, more than a hint of terrified desperation in his voice, 'and you've got to help me get out of here, understand?'

'You can't,' Croft replied, struggling to keep his balance and his nerve. 'All we can do is wait.'

'Wait for what?'

When Croft didn't answer, Flynn shoved him away and he fell back onto a nearby chair. The sudden movement caused searing pain to shoot up the length of his injured leg from ankle to hip. He gasped at the shock, then gathered his wits. 'Listen, we should all get into one room,' he said, his heart racing. 'Let's get everyone together and out of sight. We need to limit what they can see of us.'

Flynn grunted reluctant agreement and looked around the dark building. He pushed open a door to his right, revealing a small bathroom containing a single cubicle and a basin. 'In there,' he said, gesturing. There was only one window in the room, a narrow strip of obscured glass which was well above head height. Flynn made sure he was in first, then another nine people crowded in after him. Apart from the toilet, there wasn't room for any of them to sit or lie down. Phil Croft, the last man in, pulled the door shut behind him.

Someone was crying. He couldn't see who it was, or where they were standing. It might even have been more than one person. Whoever it was, they needed to shut up fast if they were going to have any chance of getting out of here alive.

'Whoever that is, you've got to please be quiet,' he whispered. He winced in pain and leant back against the door. His leg was hurting badly again. He didn't know how long he'd be able to stay standing like this. 'I know it's hard but please, we must be quiet if we're going to survive.'

He could still hear muffled crying, and someone else was sniffing back tears. Wedged tightly up against each other and hardly able to move, the eleven desperate people stood and waited.

40

An hour and twenty minutes later the helicopter appeared in the dark sky over Cormansey.

'What the hell's he doing back here?' Donna asked. She'd been walking down the road which ran through the middle of Danvers Lye with Michael and Karen Chase, trying to get used to the sudden freedom. It felt very strange.

'No idea,' Michael answered, immediately concerned. He stood still and watched the helicopter's blinking lights for a moment.

'Well, either he didn't make it back to the airfield, or they've decided to bring the next lot over here early,' Karen suggested.

'But why would they do that?' Donna asked, trying to make sense of the situation. 'Christ, something must have happened, mustn't it? Something's gone wrong.'

'Come on,' Michael said, turning and running back to the Jeep.

'Let's not jump to conclusions,' Karen said, trying to sound optimistic as she climbed into the back seat. She was trying not to show that she shared Michael's unease. 'They might have just decided to make a move tonight, rather than wait for morning. Let's face it, if it was you flying and you had the energy, then you'd probably want to get the job over and done with too.'

'So where's the plane then?' Michael asked as he started the engine and turned the vehicle round to drive towards the airstrip.

'There,' Donna replied, pointing to the left. She could see the lights on the plane's wings and tail flashing intermittently.

Michael slammed his foot down.

'Take it easy, will you?' Karen complained from the back seat as the car jolted forward, but Michael ignored her. There were any number of plausible reasons why the plane and helicopter might have returned to the island so soon, but until he heard otherwise, he couldn't help but presume the worst.

Driving at such speed, the Jeep arrived at the airstrip before the plane. The helicopter was just touching down as Michael pulled on the brakes. 'What's happened?' he demanded as people began to emerge from the back of the helicopter. He didn't recognise the first woman who appeared, but as she glanced around the airstrip, she looked disorientated and frightened. The noise of the engine and rotor blades made it difficult for her to hear anything – she knew someone was shouting at her, but she couldn't see who or where they were.

'What's happened?' Michael yelled again, grabbing hold of her and spinning her around. He stared desperately into her pale, bewildered face.

'The fence came down,' she gasped. Her breathing was wheezy and asthmatic.

Michael relaxed his grip, realising that he was frightening her.

'The fence came down and they got in,' she repeated, 'hundreds of them!'

Michael turned as Richard climbed down from the cockpit and walked over to him.

'It must have been the noise we made when we landed back there,' he explained. 'The bloody things went wild and managed to pull down part of the fence. It's been brewing for weeks, but all our noise today pushed them over the edge.'

'Did you manage to get everyone away?' Donna asked.

Michael closed his eyes and dropped his head, almost too afraid to listen to the answer. He knew that there wouldn't have been room in the plane for everyone.

'We had to leave some people behind,' he admitted quietly. 'There just wasn't enough space. We'd never have been able to get off the ground if we'd brought any more over with us.'

'We always said we'd need another flight over after this one,' Jackie Soames said tearfully, walking around the helicopter to stand with the others.

'I'll try and get back there tomorrow,' Richard continued. 'Christ knows how I'm going to land – there are thousands of those damn things swarming all over the place . . .'

His voice was drowned out by the deafening noise from the plane as it swooped down behind him. Keele's already fragile nerves had been shattered by the events of the last couple of hours and now he was struggling to keep control. His descent was too steep and too fast, and the plane hit the ground and bounced back up off the runway before crashing down again and finally stopping at an awkward angle in the grass almost twenty yards over the end of the tarmac strip. After a brief pause the door opened and Keele half-jumped, half-fell down and stumbled away to vomit violently as his passengers poured out after him.

'It was a fucking nightmare back there,' Jack Baxter shouted into the whipping wind as he ran back along the runway towards Michael and the others. 'Christ, we didn't have a fucking chance. They were all over us before we knew what had happened.'

Michael wasn't listening. He pushed past Jack to get closer to the plane, fighting his way through the stream of frightened people coming the other way. More still were climbing out onto the runway – Jean Taylor, Stephen Carter, others – but there was no sign of Emma. He stood less than a yard from the door and watched and waited. Still more people – Sheri Newton, Jo Francis – and then the flow of survivors stopped. He ran to the door and peered inside, desperate to see her. She had to be there, didn't she? But the plane was empty. Now beginning to panic he turned around again and began to run back towards the area where the frightened survivors were huddled, further down the runway. Maybe he'd missed her – he must have done. She must have walked straight past him.

Donna noticed Michael approaching and tugged Richard's arm to attract his attention.

'Where the hell is she?' Michael demanded. 'Where's Emma?'

'Sorry, mate,' Richard said, swallowing hard, 'she's still at the airfield. We couldn't get everyone over here—'

'Go back, tonight!'

'I can't – Mike, you don't understand, the whole place is swarming with them.'

'I'll come with you,' Michael said, distraught, not listening to what Richard was saying. 'We'll go now.'

'No, Michael,' Donna said, trying to hold him back, but he pulled away from her. 'You can't go. You have to stay here.'

'I'll come with you,' he said to Richard again, ignoring her. He stared at the pilot with desperate, unblinking eyes.

'Listen, mate, she's right,' Richard said, 'there isn't room. There're at least fifteen, twenty people left back there, and if I get back to them, then I'm going to need as much space as possible to bring them back here. That's if I can get anywhere near—'

'When are you going?'

'Look, I need some time, okay? Before I do anything we need to stop and think about how I'm going to—'

'You have to go back! You can't leave them there—'

'Listen, it's going to take three or four trips minimum.'

'So you make three or four trips.'

'Come on, Mike,' Donna said softly, taking hold of his arm again and trying to lead him away, 'don't—'

He stood his ground, refusing to move.

'Michael,' Richard said, looking straight at him, 'I'm not going anywhere until morning. It's too dangerous.'

Michael stared at him for a few seconds longer, then turned and walked away into the darkness.

Donna watched him disappear into the night. There was no point following. There was nothing she could do to help.

41

It felt like days, but in reality, it had been little more than a couple of hours. The eleven survivors in the office building were wedged into the small bathroom together, hardly able to move, almost too afraid to breathe, listening in terrified silence to the world outside. There was nothing distinct, just a constant soundtrack of shuffling bodies and lumbering footsteps, and occasionally other noises that were most probably single corpses randomly attacking their neighbours.

Their situation was delicately balanced: if they stayed like this, then maybe they could make it through to the morning – but what then? Croft could sense that the people around him were struggling with both physical and mental pressure, which were increasing by the second.

'Need to move,' a frightened female voice said, the first person to have dared speak out loud for hours. She spoke quietly at first, then the woman repeated her words at a louder volume.

'Shut up,' Croft hissed angrily at whoever it was who had dared break the precious silence. The cramped confines were excruciatingly claustrophobic and deeply uncomfortable, and his reaction was disproportionately strong. What he would have given for a seat right now; the pain in his leg was agonising. He didn't know how much longer he'd be able to stay standing. The woman, who was somewhere near to the back of the room, was also close to breaking point.

'I've got to move,' she repeated, sounding close to tears, 'if I don't I'll—'

'Shut up,' he snapped at her again, this time managing to keep his voice low. The last light of the dying day had now disappeared and the small room was swathed in inky darkness. He couldn't see who was speaking, but whoever it was, she had to keep quiet. They'd all done well so far: they'd managed to remain almost completely silent, and somehow they'd stayed safe. At first the bodies had been banging on the walls and windows, but that had died down, leading the doctor to believe they'd lost interest in the office and its occupants. Croft knew that it wouldn't take much to bring them back again, though; even a lone voice could be enough to attract their fatal attention. The entire airfield must surely have been overrun by now.

'I can't—' the woman moaned. Next to Croft another survivor whimpered pathetically, sensing the fragility of their situation. He could see some movement opposite him now. Was it Jacob Flynn again? Whoever it was, they were shuffling backwards, perhaps trying to get to the woman making the noise so they could silence her.

'Get off me!' the woman yelped.

Croft felt his already aching legs weaken with nerves. Fuck, this was all they needed. Just stay calm and don't panic . . .

'Jesus Christ!' he cried out involuntarily as another sudden ripple of movement knocked him off his damaged legs and sent him slamming back into the door with a loud smack that rang through the empty building like a gunshot. His weakest leg buckled underneath him and he crumbled to the ground, knocking others off-balance as he fell. He lay on the cold, tiled floor, unable to move for a moment. This is pointless, he thought, absolutely fucking pointless.

A hand unexpectedly grabbed hold of him and yanked him back up onto his feet.

'Come on, mate,' a tired voice whispered in his ear. 'You all right?'

The doctor nodded, forgetting that the man couldn't see, and was about to thank whoever had helped him when he heard a single loud bang: the unmistakable sound of a dead body slamming a skeletal fist against the outside wall of the building. It was close to where they were hiding. He silently willed the small group of survivors not to respond, but he knew that their reaction was inevitable.

'Oh God,' someone moaned, 'they know we're here – the bloody things know we're in here—'

Before the man had even finished his sentence there was another bang against the outside wall, this time directly behind where Jacob Flynn was standing. He turned round instinctively and tried to back away, but all he succeeded in doing was knocking into more people and pushing them into each other.

There was another bang, then another, then another, then the inevitable sound of countless rotting fists raining down on the outside of the building.

'Let me out,' someone next to Croft demanded, trying to force his way past him. The doctor felt his shoulder being grabbed, then he was pushed out of the way. Another hand pushed on his back, square between his shoulder blades, forced him down again and he hit the ground again. This time his head hit against the corner of a cold metal radiator and for a moment he blacked out. He came too, his head swimming, and tried to get back up. He realised that people were moving past him, leaving the bathroom. *Don't go out there*, he thought. *You stupid, bloody idiots, please don't go out there—*

Cooper, Emma, Juliet and Steve sat in the middle of the room at the top of the control tower. Steve stared at his feet. Cooper looked out at the clear night sky through the wide window opposite. Emma massaged her temples and Juliet stared unblinking straight ahead of her. No one had spoken for almost an hour. Time had often felt like it was dragging in the military base; now it had slowed down to almost a standstill. Each one of the four had silently made their private mental calculations, and each of them had come to the conclusion that if the helicopter was going to come back, it would have returned by now. With each minute that passed, the likelihood that Richard Lawrence was ever returning to Monkton Airfield seemed to reduce.

The sound of shattering glass and splintering wood disturbed the silence.

'What was that?' Emma asked, quickly getting up from her seat and running over to the window. She peered down into the disorienting darkness, but she was having difficulty making out any distinct movement in the relentless confusion outside.

'What's happening?' Cooper whispered, standing over her shoulder.

'Oh, Christ,' Steve moaned from another window a little further down the room.

'What?'

'The office – the fucking things have got inside the office.'

From his position he could see a part of the building which was obscured from Cooper and Emma's view. A window had been shattered three-quarters of the way down the building's longest side and bodies were already half-climbing, half-falling through the broken window. He could see someone was trying to fight their way out.

'We've got to do something,' said Juliet, moving across the room so that she too could see what was happening. 'For God's sake, we have to do something!'

'There's nothing we can do,' Cooper said sadly.

'We have to get the doors open downstairs so that they can get in here.'

'We can't,' he said, 'there'll be a thousand corpses in here before you can take a breath.'

'But we can't just leave them,' she protested.

'We don't have any choice,' Emma said.

'There are people down there—'

'There are people up here.'

As they watched, a lone survivor pushed his way out through the smashed window, the force of his frantic escape sending several dead bodies flying in different directions.

'Who's that?' asked Steve.

Before any of them had time to recognise the man, it was already too late: he had been surrounded immediately and was swallowed up by dead flesh as the bodies crowded around him, blocking every possible escape route like a pack of starved animals closing in on their doomed prey. And all the while, more and more bodies surged towards the office block, drawn there by the movement and noise.

The four of them watched in shaking silence as down below, more survivors forced their way out of the besieged building and were instantly swallowed up by the putrefying hordes. They were stunned by the speed of events and their absolute, inexorable helplessness, but they could do nothing other than stand and watch as the office was overcome.

'So will they come for us next?' Juliet asked, her voice quavering. 'Is that what's going to happen to us?'

'They probably don't even know we're up here yet,' Cooper answered, 'but they will if we give them half a chance.'

'It's just a matter of time,' Steve muttered to himself.

'You're right,' Emma agreed, wiping tears of fear and frustration from her eyes. 'They'll realise we're up here at some point and then—'

'And then what?' Juliet nervously pressed.

'Just look at them. Their physical condition is deteriorating. They can't communicate or reason, so whatever their motives are, they'll only react in one possible way.'

'How?' Juliet asked, her voice barely louder than a whisper. She was shaking so hard Emma could hear her teeth chattering.

'They'll try and tear us to fucking pieces,' she answered. Her blunt delivery and monotonous tone of voice belied the mounting terror she too felt inside.

In the bathroom of the office block, Phil Croft sat on the floor with his back against the locked door, determined to keep the fucking things which now filled the building away from him for as long as he possibly could. But he wasn't stupid; he knew it was only a matter of time.

Reaching into his shirt pocket, he pulled out his last remaining box of cigarettes and opened it up. One and a half smokes left. He lit the first and took a long, beautiful drag on it, filling his lungs with nicotine, tar and smoke. He lit the second, and shoved the glowing stub into a wedge of paper towels, which immediately began to smoulder. On the other side of the door he could hear the screams as the ten people he'd been trapped in here with were torn apart by the dead. He blocked his ears and tried to fill his head with random thoughts to distract him from what was happening outside and his own impending death, but it was impossible. He'd always been able to block out the horror before, but not tonight: tonight the terror and hopeless fear was all he had left.

So this is how it ends, he thought sadly as he watched the flames take hold of the paper towels and then begin to scorch the cubicle's wooden wall. He pushed his back firmly against the door, and now he could feel it being shoved from the other side by the cadavers.

He wedged his feet against the toilet cubicle opposite and smoked his last cigarette. As he waited for the inevitable end, he wondered whether the flames or the bodies would get to him first.

*

At the top of the control tower, high above the ground, Cooper watched the building below him burning. Eleven good people lost. How long before the fire or the dead got to them? He slumped to the ground and covered his face. He didn't want to look outside any longer.

42

It was almost first light.

Richard Lawrence was exhausted, and he had delayed his flight for as long as possible, balancing his own physical fatigue with the need to get back quickly to those people they'd been forced to leave behind. Now, seven hours after he'd left them, he flew the helicopter back over the dead land. Beneath him there was more movement than he'd ever seen, with no sign of the previous uneasy calm. Instead, the entire landscape was crawling with activity. He could see bodies everywhere, staggering relentlessly from place to place, and he wondered whether he was imagining things. Was his nervous mind exaggerating what he could actually see, making things look worse than they actually were? No, there was no way things could things get any worse . . .

This was a dangerous and pointless flight. When he'd left the airfield last night he'd felt beaten: what possible hope could the people left there have against the thousands upon thousands of unstoppable bodies he had last seen heading towards the buildings in the middle of the airfield? He'd considered turning around and heading back to the island several times already – what exactly did he hope to gain from even trying? He couldn't possibly do anything there; the airfield was overrun, that was a fact, and even if there were any survivors left alive, how was he supposed to pick them up? All his return could achieve would be to taunt those left behind, maybe even prolong their agony. What else would he be able to do other than fly around the airfield and watch his friends as they waited to die.

But however bleak the inevitable conclusion of his flight, he knew that he didn't have any choice. He had to try.

In his mind Richard was still picturing the place as he'd left it a few hours earlier: a small collection of buildings, surrounded by empty space and encircled by the wire fence, and beyond that, the many thousands of bodies: circles of light and dark, with the clump of buildings at the centre. He *knew* it would look different now, of course – but he hadn't been prepared for such a complete transformation, and he flew over the airfield without recognising it.

In the gloomy pre-dawn light everything looked the same and it wasn't until he was almost over the centre of Rowley that he realised he'd overshot his target. He turned the helicopter in a wide, graceful arc and flew back the way he'd come, gazing down at the ground below to get his bearings until he eventually spotted the airfield a mile or so ahead, looking like a black scab on the monochrome landscape. As he closed the distance, he realised that just as he'd feared, the airfield had been completely overrun. There were hundreds of thousands of bodies, swarming constantly around the place, filling every square yard of land. Monkton Airfield was lost.

For a moment Richard considered turning tail and heading back to Cormansey. Even if Cooper, Emma, Dr Croft and the others were still there and were still alive, could he do anything to help them now?

43

'What are they doing now?' Steve Armitage asked. Too afraid to look for himself, the burly truck driver leant against the back wall, as far away as he could get from the window without leaving the room. Cooper and Emma remained close to the glass, watching the bodies shuffling below them with mounting unease.

The rear of the nearby office building had been burning for hours now, and more than half of the building had been consumed by flame. The fire had attracted the attention of many of the bodies, but many more continued to surround the other buildings. The physical weight of their immense numbers meant they had been able to force their way into various buildings – the hangar, a waiting room, some of the lounges – where windows and doors had been left open. Those which strayed too close to the burning building had themselves ignited, the remains of their clothing and emaciated flesh quickly becoming engulfed in flame. The bizarre movements of the burning bodies was unsettling; it looked positively surreal. Ignorant of the heat and the flames which were consuming them, the corpses continued to stagger around, colliding with others at random, and setting them alight too.

Cooper was watching the office fire. Although right now it was still confined to the back of the building, it was growing quickly, eating away at the rest of the structure. Any change in wind direction, he thought, and they might have no choice but to escape from the control tower and take their chances with the baying masses outside. He shuddered at the thought.

'They're in at least three buildings now,' Emma said.

'Still reckon we'll be safe here?' Steve snapped angrily, looking at Cooper and demanding an answer.

'I never said we'd be safe,' he replied defensively, 'I just said they don't know we're here yet. Hopefully the fire will keep them occupied.'

'You think so?'

'It might.'

'Assuming it doesn't, how long before they manage to get in here?'

'We blocked the door downstairs. They probably haven't got the strength to get past it.'

'We didn't think they'd have the strength to pull the bloody fence down but they managed that, didn't they?'

Cooper didn't answer. He knew Steve was right.

'Did you block all the doors and windows downstairs?' Juliet Appleby asked from across the room. She had her face pressed against the window and was trying to look straight down the side of the building. Cooper shook his head.

'No, just the main entrance. That was all we had time to do. Why?'

'Because whether they're going to manage it or not, it looks like they're trying to get in here.'

'Where?' Emma asked anxiously.

'I can see a couple of groups of them.'

'Doing what?'

'Nothing much at the moment, just pressing up against the door, I think. It's difficult to see much from up here.'

'Christ, this is fucking stupid,' Steve yelled, getting increasingly frustrated. 'We can't just sit here and wait for them to get in!'

'That's just about all we can do, isn't it?' answered Juliet.

'We could make a run for it?' he suggested. 'Fight our way over to one of the trucks and try and get away?'

'Where would we go?' asked Cooper. 'And anyway, you saw what happened when the others tried to escape from the office . . .'

The truck driver had no answer. The thought of another directionless drive through the decaying countryside was only marginally more appealing than sitting still and doing nothing. It was a last resort, but he knew it might yet turn out to be their only option.

Emma was standing in front of the largest window again, watching what was happening outside. The ground was now completely carpeted in a thick layer of dead flesh, and she could no longer see the ground, not grass, pavement nor runway. The office building was almost completely ablaze, and she knew that there could be no one left alive inside. Elsewhere the creatures were tightly packed around the other buildings, and burning bodies dragged themselves around in an eternal search for who knew what. A thick layer of smoke had settled across the entire scene, and showed no sign of dispersing in the light, directionless breeze.

'What's the roof of this building like?' she asked suddenly.

'What?' Cooper grunted.

'The roof of this building,' she repeated. 'Is it flat?'

'Not sure – I don't think so. You can't really tell from the ground. Why, what are you thinking?'

'I'm thinking that if we are going to get out of here, then we need to be somewhere obvious so that Richard can see us when he comes back.'

'If he comes back,' Steve sneered.

'*When* he comes back,' Cooper corrected him. 'Whether he can do anything for us or not, that's a different matter, but I'm sure he'll be back. We'd do the same if we were in his shoes, wouldn't we? You couldn't just sit there on the island knowing that there still might be people left alive and trapped over here, could you?'

No answer.

'Anyway,' Emma continued, 'as well as being visible, we need to make sure that we end up somewhere the bodies definitely can't get to.'

'Like?'

'Like a flat roof,' she replied.

'I think the roof here is sloped,' Juliet said, still standing at the window but now looking up instead of down. 'And I can't go up there—'

Cooper shuffled around so that he had a better view of the rest of the airfield and, more importantly, the few remaining buildings nearby.

'Not sure about this one, but that one over there's a possibility,' he said, pointing towards a small utility building nestled in the shadows of the hangar where the plane had previously been housed.

'Just a couple of tiny problems as far as I can see,' Steve grumbled from close behind him. 'Getting to it and getting on top of it. Any bright ideas?'

'How desperate are you feeling?' Cooper asked.

'Fucking desperate.'

'Me too, so we'll just have to find a way of doing it, won't we? I don't see that we've got any choice.'

'How then?'

'Try the usual tricks,' he answered, 'because they've worked so far. We'll distract the bodies and make a run for it.'

'Shouldn't the fire already be distracting them?' Emma asked sensibly. She was right: the many bodies crowding around the base of the control tower were completely ignoring the spreading flames.

'She's right. And anyway, that building is at least twenty feet high,' Steve sighed. 'What are we going to do? Jump up, for Christ's sake? Stand on each other's shoulders?'

'We'll find a way.'

'Forget about the buildings,' Emma said, her mind suddenly racing. 'Using the trucks was a better idea. We could do that, couldn't we? Once they see us on top of one of the buildings, we'll have the whole bloody lot of them snapping at our feet. At least with the trucks we'll be able to keep moving.'

'But the trucks are even further away,' whimpered Juliet. 'And how would we drive through a crowd like that?'

'The prison truck's only on the other side of the runway,' Cooper said. 'I can't see the personnel carrier from here.'

'I still don't know how we're supposed to get to it,' Steve said.

'Well, we'd better think of a way pretty bloody quickly,' Emma said suddenly, a new-found urgency in her voice.

'Why?'

'Because the helicopter's back!'

44

Once he was right over the airfield, Richard Lawrence allowed the helicopter to drift slightly lower. He switched on the search-light and guided it around the area. For a while all he could see were the seething bodies and it took him some time to orientate himself and properly identify the outlines of the control tower and other buildings through the smoke. Conscious that the noise and light he had created was again whipping the rancid crowd below into a bloody frenzy, he moved lower still, stopping only when he was level with the top of the control tower.

He could see living people!

The nearby office building had been destroyed and the hangar and other buildings overrun, but he could definitely see people at the top of the control tower, though he had to look twice to be absolutely sure they weren't bodies that had found a way inside. From his elevated position he could see no obvious signs of the entrance to the building having been compromised – and if the dead had forced their way in, he would have expected hundreds of them to have pointlessly crammed themselves inside by now. No, there weren't many people inside, and those he could see were moving with purpose and control. They had to be survivors – but how could he get to them?

Cooper's face appeared at the window, confirming to Richard beyond any doubt that his return to the mainland had been worth-while.

'We have to get out there,' Emma shouted, suddenly having to raise her voice to make herself heard over the welcome noise of the helicopter.

'But there's no way out,' Steve yelled. 'Christ, we've just been through this. We're surrounded. They're out the front and they're round the back and—'

'Emma's right,' Cooper interrupted, 'we have to find a way out, and we have to do it now.'

'Go for the trucks,' Juliet suggested.

'I agree,' Emma said quickly, 'it's the best option. Richard will see us moving. If we can get to one of the trucks we can drive through the bodies until we reach somewhere where there are fewer of them. Then he can land and pick us up.'

'So do we just make a run for it?'

'It's not going to be easy,' Emma replied, looking down at the ground immediately around the base of the building. 'I think we should try and distract them, get them away from whichever door or window we decide to use to get out. Then maybe just one of us could try to get across and bring the truck back over here.'

Cooper stood behind Emma, thinking carefully. He looked outside at the helicopter, which was hovering so close that, despite the drifting smoke, Richard's face could clearly be seen. But the distance was irrelevant: he might as well have been a hundred miles away for all the good it was doing them. Richard looked understandably agitated. Cooper knew he wouldn't wait indefinitely for them to make their move.

'Good God,' mumbled Juliet, 'just look at that!'

She pointed out of the window down at an area of ground which was almost directly beneath the helicopter.

'What the hell are they doing?' Steve asked, crowding forward to try and get a better view. The four of them peered down: Richard had angled the searchlight to one side of the helicopter, and whilst many bodies continued to react just as they always did, now the survivors could see others now were beginning to behave differently. A large number continued to swarm forward, fighting with the corpses closest to them, but many others did not, instead appearing to be visibly agitated and riled by the noise, the light and the downdraught coming from the helicopter hovering above their decaying heads, almost cowering away. It was hard to believe, but it looked like a large group of the bodies was trying to move away from the disturbance above.

'Fucking hell,' said Cooper.

'This is it,' Emma announced, 'this is our chance. It's like you said earlier: they're changing. They're finally beginning to wake up, aren't they? Bloody hell, those things down there are scared!'

'Scared?' Steve said. 'Are you out of your fucking mind?'

'The noise of the helicopter's scaring them. We might not be much of a threat to them, but that thing is.'

'Bullshit.'

'Might be,' she said quickly, 'but look at them. It doesn't matter whatever's causing this, the point is it might give us a chance to get past some of them.'

'How?' asked Juliet.

'We'll use the helicopter as cover, make as much of a disturbance as we can. We'll need to try and get Richard's help. Maybe some of them will disappear, get out of our way.'

'Some of them?'

'The rest will probably still go for us, same as they always do.'

Much as he hated to admit it, Steve knew that Emma was right, but it was better to go out there and face five hundred of the animated corpses than five thousand.

'We should do it,' Juliet announced.

'So we do what, exactly?' Steve asked nervously.

'Shake them up, then go out there and kick their bloody backsides,' Emma answered.

'Because if we don't,' Cooper reminded them, 'then we won't be getting into that helicopter and we'll be stuck here. If we don't go outside and face them now, then we'll be facing them up here when they finally get inside – that's if we haven't all burned to death already. Not much of a choice, is it?'

Richard, dividing his concentration between piloting the helicopter, watching the survivors and looking at the bodies below, noticed that Cooper and the others had shifted their attention from him to what was happening on the ground. He peered down through the observation panels by his feet and saw some of the bodies reacting to his presence. He shifted the helicopter slightly, and realised that as the searchlight moved, so more of the corpses stumbled out of the way. Perhaps if he dropped lower, he thought, he could get more of them to move; then he might be able to land and pick up the survivors. He tried briefly, but the number of corpses standing their ground and continuing to react violently convinced him that landing there was out of the question. But the presence of the helicopter and the fear (that really did seem to be the right word to use) that it was generating amongst the dead was unquestionably important. It might give the survivors a chance, albeit a slim one. He remembered Michael had told him the bodies on the island that had become like these, even though quieter and more hesitant, had still attacked the survivors when they'd been threatened. The bodies wanted to survive; they would fight if they had no other option.

From his position above the airfield, Richard felt completely helpless. He had no way of warning the others, or telling them what he knew.

Emma had stood still and watched and waited for too long. She finally decided it was time to take action. All the talking in the world wasn't going to get them away from Monkton Airfield and, as Cooper had already pointed out, they had nothing to lose and everything to gain from any escape attempt. If they did nothing, then their last chance would have gone. For Emma, the prospect of a relatively safe and secure future with Michael was too great a prize to risk throwing away without a fight. She had to do something.

'Where are you going?' Cooper called after her as she turned and pushed through the doors and began running down the staircase.

'To Cormansey,' she shouted back. 'What about you?'

Suddenly feeling pressured into action, Juliet, Steve and Cooper followed close behind. For all her sudden movement and intent, it was clear that Emma didn't have a plan. They found her at the bottom of the staircase, looking around hopefully for inspiration.

'What now?' Juliet asked.

Through the bitter-tasting smoke which had drifted into the building Steve noticed the light leaking in from under the front door: a mixture of the natural first light of day and the harsh artificial illumination coming from the helicopter. He clambered carefully over the tables and chairs which they'd earlier used to block the entrance and peered cautiously out through a narrow crack between the double doors. There were still a huge number of bodies out there, but in the light from the helicopter he could see there were considerably fewer now. He looked up at the aircraft hanging in the air above them. He couldn't be completely sure, but Richard seemed to deliberately be aiming his light towards the door. He'd obviously seen the same behaviour in the corpses they had, and worked out what was happening.

'We should make a run for it,' Steve suggested, his sudden about-face and positive attitude surprising the others. 'We should do it now.'

'We can't risk just throwing the doors open and going out there,' Emma protested. 'What if we get split up? What happens when we get over to the truck? Do we just stand there and wait for you to open it up?'

'Worse than that,' Juliet added, 'if we open the doors and we all go out there, then that leaves this place wide open and we'll have no back-up if anything goes wrong.'

'We need to get the truck over here,' Cooper said. 'One of us needs to get over to it and get it back here to pick the rest of us up.'

The sound of the helicopter was deafening; it was amplified by the tall, thin shape of the control tower itself. Above the mechanical noise they could hear the sound of bodies slamming against the walls, doors and windows. Although the helicopter seemed to be keeping some of the creatures at bay, its position next to the control tower was also drawing more of them closer.

Steve Armitage could stand it no longer. He was generally a quiet man who was content to sit and wait and watch rather than act, but occasionally, the pressure of a situation proved too much and forced him into action. It had happened before, back in the city, when he'd left the safety of the university complex to help collect transport for the group, and it was happening again now.

'I'll do it,' he said firmly.

'What?' asked Cooper, surprised.

'I said I'll do it,' he repeated before he could talk himself out of volunteering. 'Might as well.'

'You sure?'

'No.' He laughed grimly.

Cooper climbed up the furniture and looked through the narrow gap in the doors as Steve had. His view was limited, but he could clearly see the prison truck on the other side of the runway. It wasn't going to be easy to reach.

'It's got to be a couple of hundred yards away,' he whispered, still looking out through the gap, 'and there are still several hundred bodies in your way. Think you can make it?'

'I can do it,' Steve answered. 'Listen, with enough of those things snapping at my heels, I could run a bloody marathon!'

Cooper looked at him for a moment, then clapped him on the shoulder. He jumped down and started moving the tables and chairs which were blocking the doors.

'When you get out there,' he said as he worked, 'you just put your head down and run, understand? Keep moving until you reach the truck. Don't stop for *anything*.'

'I wasn't planning to.'

'Okay. Ready?' Cooper asked as he dragged the last table away.

Steve turned back towards the door. 'Ready,' he answered, sounding far from it. He took a deep, nervous breath, then threw the doors open and burst out into the cold morning. The light which poured down from the helicopter and saturated the immediate vicinity was momentarily blinding and the unexpected force of the downdraught from the craft above threatened to knock him off his feet. The suffocating smell of burning flesh filled his lungs. For a single disorientated second he stood still and stared at the truck on the other side of the runway. His view was relatively clear, and, for just an instant, the distance he had to cover looked reassuringly short. But then he looked to the left and right and saw that there were bodies all around him, and though some remained cowering in the shadows, others began to quickly converge on him from various directions. The sound of the door being pulled shut behind him, though it was barely audible over the racket from the helicopter above, finally prompted him to move.

'Shit,' he cursed as the nearest body reached out for him. Its bony hands were hard, much of the putrefied flesh rotted away, and as he jogged slowly away from the control tower, Steve grabbed the skeletal figure by the neck and swung it around, sending it flying into a group of four more ragged cadavers and knocking them down like skittles.

He looked ahead again and tried to regain his focus on the truck. When he'd looked out through the crack in the double doors it had looked like he'd have a clear passage, but now a myriad shuffling figures were crisscrossing his path ahead of him. More vicious hands lashed out, and one caught his cheek and tore three long cuts from just under his left eye down to his chin. He needed to pick up his speed if he was going to do this.

Steve forced himself to ignore the bodies all around him and keep moving forward. His mouth was dry and his heart was thumping like it was about to explode, but he had to keep moving. He lowered his shoulder as two more corpses crossed his path and charged through the pair of them, smashing one away in either direction.

Almost halfway there.

Even after two months of this hell Steve was still overweight, and he'd not been fit for years, and now his right knee was beginning to hurt. He knew he had no option, he had to keep running through the pain, but every time his foot hit the ground a grinding pain shot up his leg from his knee to his backside. He started to gasp. The ground under his feet had now given way to the harder tarmac surface of the runway. He was almost there.

The ground was littered with the remains of corpses which had either been burned or brought down and torn apart by other bodies. Steve was focused on the truck, just in front of him, and didn't see the body lying on its back. His boot smashed heavily through the rib cage and sent what remained of its rotting innards flying in every direction. As he frantically tried to pull his foot clear he tripped and fell, and in seconds bodies were swarming all over him like flies over shit.

'Fuck,' Cooper yelled from the control tower, watching through the crack in the door as more and more bodies piled on top of the helpless truck driver, quickly burying him under a mound of constantly moving, decaying flesh.

'Jesus,' Emma wailed, watching through a small window.

Cooper moved to open the door. 'I've got to go out there.'

'Cooper, don't—' Juliet pleaded.

'I can't just leave him.'

'Wait,' Emma said, pressing her face against the window again. She could see movement from the bottom of the pile of bodies: Steve was still fighting, and high above him Richard had moved the helicopter around and dropped lower so that the searchlight was bearing down on him directly. The sudden illumination caused many of the bodies still lurching towards the disturbance to turn and trip away in other directions, looking for cover.

Lying on his back on the cold, hard runway and struggling to breathe through the abhorrent stench, Steve began to kick and punch out at the bodies on top of him. They felt hollow, individually they offered little resistance. He felt their decaying flesh dripping over him, soaking him in the vile discharge of their decay, but the more they fought, he realised, the quicker they deteriorated. He rolled over onto his front and tried to push himself up off the ground. More of them were clinging onto his back – he had no idea how many of the grotesque things were hanging off him, and he didn't care. He managed to scramble onto all fours, and then pushed hard and stood upright and began to smash the bodies away, swatting them like flies. He had knocked half a dozen of them to the ground and at last he found that the only bodies still holding on were those which clung onto his legs. He began to move forward again, and as he moved, he dislodged more of the cadavers until he was completely free and able to run again. He battered more of the corpses out of his path as he reached the side of the truck, and with one last groan of effort he reached up to the handle on the passenger door, yanked it open and hauled himself inside. He pulled it shut (severing a single arm that made a last, misjudged grab for him) and then slid across the cab into the driver's seat.

'He's in,' cried Emma from the control tower window. 'Bloody hell, he's done it!'

Suddenly realising that Steve's last-ditch run for freedom might actually be paying off, Cooper, Emma and Juliet crowded together around the main door and waited for the truck to move. Richard, watching the escape unfold from the relative safety of the helicopter hanging in the air, continued to drench the scene with light, giving Steve what protection he could, however limited.

Inside the truck, Steve was struggling. His eyes stinging from the smoke, he slumped forward over the steering wheel. Dripping with rancid gore and soaked through with sweat, he fought to catch his breath. He needed to keep his mind focused. He reached out to turn the key and start the engine, but stopped. His chest felt tight. He desperately needed oxygen, but the deeper he tried to breathe, the more smoke he inhaled and the worse the pain in his chest became. At first it felt like a stitch, but it quickly became an uncontrollable searing pain which started near his heart then spread out across his whole body. His fingers were numb and tingling, and his feet felt heavy. He struggled to move them onto the pedals.

He didn't have time for this. He tried to breathe slowly and deeply, and did his best to ignore the distraction of the swarming bodies which constantly thumped against the sides of the truck. He took his time now, figuring the slower he moved, the more chance he'd have of getting the truck going. His outstretched fingers eventually made contact with the keys and somehow he managed to turn them. The engine fired up, and he pushed himself back into his seat, feeling a momentary surge of relief and satisfaction as the truck rumbled into life.

His progress was short-lived, however, as another wave of debilitating pain spread quickly across his chest. Groaning with effort he forced himself to concentrate on getting back to the others. He began to move the truck forward, and slowly turned the steering wheel to guide the heavy vehicle back towards the control tower. Still illuminated by the incandescent light from the helicopter, the truck trundled towards the building, mowing down those bodies which foolishly dragged themselves in front of it.

'He's coming,' Cooper said, still watching through the gap between the doors. 'Ready?'

Juliet and Emma nodded. Emma's throat was dry and her legs felt weak: this was make or break time. Never mind the immediate danger they faced outside; what happened in the next few minutes would undoubtedly decide the rest of her life.

'What do we do?' Juliet mumbled anxiously.

'When I open the doors,' Cooper replied, 'you get yourself onto the truck any way you can. Doesn't matter if you get in through the front or the back, or if you're left hanging onto the side, just get over to that bloody truck and hold onto it, okay?'

She was about to ask another question when Cooper threw the doors open. The blood-splattered prison truck ground to a sudden, lurching stop just a few yards ahead of them.

'Move!' he yelled, and he grabbed hold of both women by their arms and dragged them forward, virtually throwing them out of the building.

As bodies began to surge at them from every imaginable direction, Juliet half-ran and half-fell towards the back of the truck, managing somehow to jump up and yank the back door open. She pulled herself inside and then reached out for Emma, who was fighting her way through a dense section of the rabid crowd, struggling to keep moving against the surging tide of rotting flesh which was threatening to swallow her up. It looked like those bodies which had remained on the sidelines had suddenly sensed an increase in the level of their own physical danger and had chosen to move and attack before the survivors' machines attacked them, and what felt like thousands of vicious hands reached out to grab hold of Emma. Unexpectedly, her speed increased as Cooper, running into her at full speed, propelled her towards the truck, then wedged his hands under her arms and threw her up into the air. With her flailing hands stretched out in front of her she managed to grab hold of the back of the vehicle where Juliet was waiting. She caught hold of the scruff of the neck of Emma's jacket and roughly dragged her inside.

The bodies were no match for Cooper's controlled force. The ex-soldier powered through them and jumped up into the back of the truck after the others. Hanging half-out of the open door he smashed his hand repeatedly on the vehicle's metal side. The noise was more definite and controlled than the relentless battering coming from the bodies, and Steve knew it was his signal to move again. Doing everything he could to ignore the constant, agonising pain which still gripped him, he turned the vehicle and accelerated away, driving out towards the gaping hole in the airfield's border fence.

'You okay?' Emma asked Cooper breathlessly. 'Thank you!'

'I will be when we get to this bloody island,' he told her, still standing at the door and holding on tightly as the prison truck lurched its way across the uneven ground. From every direction, bodies turned and stumbled towards the vehicle, ignoring the fact that dozens of them were disappearing beneath the huge wheels to be crushed to splinters.

Cooper looked up through the drifting smoke and with relief tracked the helicopter as it began to follow them away from the buildings.

'What do we do now?' Juliet wondered aloud, but before Cooper could answer the truck began to slow down.

'Steve,' he screamed at the top of his voice, 'keep moving, man! For Christ's sake, don't stop here!'

The truck lurched forward again and accelerated for a few yards more, and was slowing down again when the engine stalled as Steve's foot slipped off the controls and the vehicle jerked to a halt.

The sudden stop almost threw Cooper off the back of the truck and into the silent, frantic crowds.

In the cab, Steve knew that he couldn't drive any further. The pain was unbearable now. He could hardly move.

'What's he doing?' Emma asked pointlessly. She ran deeper inside and began to bang on the inner walls. 'Steve!' she yelled. 'Steve! What's wrong?'

They had stopped just a short distance from the downed section of fence. The crowds were slightly less dense here than they were around the buildings, but within seconds of the truck's abrupt halt, masses of rotting corpses were already battering against its sides. From his high vantage point, Cooper lashed out at any nearby, kicking them away.

'We need to get onto the roof,' he said as he surveyed the desperate scene. Hundreds of cadavers were now surging towards them, looking like an impenetrable grey mist. The helicopter hovered overhead, its noise and light attracting as many bodies as it repelled. Cooper looked down at the sea of swarming faces in front of him and then up at the helicopter again. 'There's no way he's going to be able to pick us up off the ground. We've got to get up.'

Turning around he grabbed hold of Juliet and pulled her closer to the door.

'What—?'

'Roof,' he snapped. He crouched down and cupped his hands for her to use as a foothold. Groaning with effort he lifted her up. With nothing on the roof for her to hold onto she struggled to get a grip. Cooper dug deep into his own reserves of energy and shoved her a little higher. Finally she managed to get a grip. She dug her elbows down and inched slowly forward. He leant out of the truck and watched until her feet had disappeared over the top. Seconds later her head reappeared over the edge.

'Okay?' he asked.

'Okay,' she replied, deliberately looking anywhere but down into the mass of rotting faces which stared up at her.

Emma was next. With the nearest bodies just inches away from him, Cooper lifted her up and supported her relatively slight weight until Juliet had managed to catch hold of her hands from above and had pulled her up onto the roof beside her. Finally Cooper scrambled up himself, using the door at the back of the truck to help him.

The three survivors stood together on top of the truck. Emma looked down at the relentless crowd of decayed creatures below her, and saw how their anger and ferocity increased as Richard lowered the helicopter again.

'Get in,' Cooper shouted, yelling to make himself heard over the deafening noise. They'd all instinctively crouched down and were moving on all fours because of the rotor blades, which now seemed perilously close, and the downdraught which threatened to blow them off the roof of the truck. Obeying Cooper's instruction, Emma and Juliet crawled towards the aircraft. It hovered just inches away, although the distance between the roof of the truck and the helicopter's nearest landing skid looked immense. Taking a deep breath, Emma stepped across the gap and pulled herself up into the back of the aircraft.

While she was doing that, Cooper ran down to the front end of the truck and lay down across the width of the cab. He dragged himself further forward and leant down so he could see into the front and banged on the driver's half-open window. He could see the back of Steve's head. He had fallen face-down across the steering wheel.

'Come on, Steve,' Cooper pleaded, 'we've nearly done it, mate. Let's get you up here.'

Steve slowly lifted his head, every movement taking incredible effort, and turned to look at Cooper. Then he dropped back down again and closed his eyes. 'Can't,' he gasped, his voice hoarse, his breathing shallow and intermittent. 'I can't do it.'

'Come on,' Cooper insisted, although he already knew it was pointless.

Steve's face was ashen, his lips blue. 'Can't, mate.'

For a second Cooper contemplated jumping down and trying to manhandle Steve up onto the roof of the truck, but then he sighed. He knew that it was pointless.

'Go,' Steve wheezed, trying to lift his head again. The light from the helicopter suddenly shifted slightly, illuminating the inside of the cab and Cooper clearly saw the pain in his face. It was clear that he was beyond help.

'Okay, mate,' he said, reaching in through the window and

resting his hand on Steve's shoulder. 'Thanks for the lift,' he smiled. 'You're a good man.' He squeezed gently, and was rewarded with a faint grin.

'Piss off to your island,' Steve said, his voice barely audible, and reluctantly Cooper pulled himself back up onto the roof, where he stood up and ran the length of the truck to get to the helicopter.

Strangely relieved, Steve closed his eyes again and tried to breathe through the increasing pain until it finally stopped.

'What about Steve?' Emma shouted as Cooper scrambled into the helicopter and pulled the door shut behind him. He shook his head. He looked down and watched the truck becoming smaller and smaller as they quickly climbed away.

Below them, Monkton Airfield was a solid mass of crazed dead bodies.

45

More than fifty days since the germ had destroyed almost all of the population of the planet, the final survivors arrived in the air over the island of Cormansey.

Michael had been waiting in the small cottage by the airstrip. Donna and Jack kept him company, although no one had spoken for what felt like hours. Finally the oppressive silence was shattered by the dull thud of whirling rotors. The distant sound increased Michael's nervousness to an almost unbearable level. He was almost too afraid to look, but he had to. He went outside and scanned the skies until he finally spotted the approaching helicopter, and he watched every last foot of its painfully slow descent to the ground.

Then he sprinted the length of the island's short runway.

Cooper was the first to get out, then Juliet. And then, at last, he saw her. Michael ran over to Emma and held her, ignoring everything else that was happening around them – the excited activity, the tears for missing friends, the cars which approached from various directions, the cheers of relief and cries of sadness – he buried her face in his chest and held her tight.

'I thought I'd lost you,' he whispered to her, squeezing her until she could barely breathe.

'No chance,' she whispered back, looking up into his tired, haggard face and smiling through her tears.

After a moment, they loosened their hold and Michael stood silently next to Emma and watched as she looked around her, trying to take in what she could see of the island. He watched her as she tasted the air and soaked up the atmosphere. He watched her as she finally started to relax, and he held her as she wept with relief.

Cormansey was a bleak and unforgiving landscape, but they both knew this was as good as it was going to get.

Epilogue

Michael Collins

I spoke to Jack this morning, for the first time in weeks. He came by the house earlier, and told me he'd been out walking again. I've often seen him in the distance, marching on his own across the horizon. He told me he's started walking circuits of the island to keep himself occupied.

Very few people visit us here. There aren't many houses more isolated than ours. That was deliberate on our part: we both want to be close to the others, but at the same time we want lives of our own too. Most people have chosen to live in or around Danvers Lye. Some people here want to build a close community; they want to live, sleep and eat in each other's pockets. They couldn't survive on their own, they need the closeness of others. We don't.

Christ, we could do with having Phil Croft here now. We've really struggled since Emma fell pregnant. People have tried to support her, of course, but it's been difficult and we miss his expertise, his guidance and his company. It will be hard when the baby's born. At least I'll be able to help more then. At the moment I feel completely useless. The others have been really understanding. They told us about the baby that was born back when they were in the city, and what happened to it, and we know that the same thing could happen to our child. Our medical facilities here are virtually nonexistent, and we didn't have any option but to go through with the pregnancy – not that either of us would have ever done any different. I pray that our baby will be all right. I talked to Donna about its chances. She pointed out that although the mother of the baby in the city had survived, its father had been killed by the germ. She said that maybe the fact that both Emma and I survived will make a difference. I hope that whatever it is that's kept us both alive has been passed down and will protect our child too.

Jack and I had a long conversation about the future today. I've agreed to go back to the mainland with Cooper and some of the others in a few days' time. It'll be only the first time we've been back. Providing the weather stays good, the plan is for Richard to fly us over to the nearest port. We'll salvage whatever supplies we can find, but the important thing is to find a suitable boat and sail it back to Cormansey. There's hardly any fuel left in the helicopter now. We'll try to find more, but even so, we need to look for another way of getting to and from the mainland. We're going to have to keep going back there – we'll always need medicines and food and clothing. No doubt we'll become more self-sufficient as time goes by, but at the moment it makes sense to keep scavenging for what we need.

If I'm honest, we're struggling here, and I can't see that things are ever going to get any easier. Some people are talking about trying to get power to the village. They might manage it, but at what cost? It's going to take an enormous amount of effort for questionable gain. How will they maintain the system? Who will keep it working? It's all going to take time, but that's the one thing we seem to have in abundance.

A few days ago I found one of the dead. I'd forgotten how foul they are. I must have walked past this one countless times and not even known it was there. It was slumped in a ditch at the side of the road, massively decayed, and it just lay there and watched me. It tried to move, but it couldn't. It managed to lift its head slightly and the remains of its cold, black eyes followed me until I put a pick through its skull.

For some reason I've been thinking about that body a lot. I find myself thinking about what happened to turn it from a normal, healthy person into that lump of rotten flesh and bone. I wonder sometimes how aware the bodies were of what was happening to them? Did they feel anything? I wonder whether their brains were more alive than we'd originally given them credit for, and whether it was only the deterioration of their flesh that caused them to react and behave the way they did? Did my friends and family suffer? Did they wander around like that, trying desperately to find comfort or familiarity, a release from their pain? I often wonder whether that last body had been looking at me and remembering what it had once been.

It's getting late. Emma is asleep – she has been all afternoon. No doubt she'll wake up soon and then keep me awake all night talking. She still doesn't like to be on her own at night. No one does.

I'm standing in front of the house looking out over the ocean. It's a bright day, and the water looks deceptively calm and inviting. Everything is quiet, and if I just stand here and listen to the silence then I can almost believe that nothing ever happened. But there's no escaping the fact that our lives have been changed for ever, and no matter how safe or comfortable we try and make this place, the rest of our days are going to be hard. We'll have to fight for everything we need, and if our children survive then they'll spend their lives fighting too.

We won a small victory getting here, but it was a pretty hollow one. Our little achievements are insignificant in the overall scheme of things. There might be other people, other survivors, who have been more successful than us, who are more organised and protected than us. Whoever's left alive and however many of us there are, I think our days are numbered. We are remnants of the past. I sometimes feel like an intruder now, like I shouldn't be here. Jack says that whatever the cause, what happened to the world was supposed to happen, and I think I agree with him. We've been brushed aside. I can't help thinking that everything we're doing is going to come to nothing. We're just kidding ourselves if we believe any different. The balance of our world has been changed for ever. Mankind is being cleansed from the face of the planet. Purification has begun.

All that Emma and I can do is make the most of the time we have left. That's all that any of us can do.

THE END

The story continues in:

AUTUMN: DISINTEGRATION